MURDER
SO TEMPTING

MURDER
SO TEMPTING

A Merry March Mystery

Eileen Curley Hammond

Twody Press

Cover designed by SelfPubBookCovers.com/ RLSather

Eileen Curley Hammond
Visit my website at www.eileencurleyhammond.com

Printed in the United States of America

First Printing: September 2021
Twody Press, West Jefferson OH

ISBN- 978-1-956356-01-4
Library of Congress Control Number: 2021915636

AUTHOR'S NOTE

Thank you, readers. I hope you are enjoying Merry's journey. I am a fortunate author because I have many friends who write and share their expertise. Specifically, I'd like to thank Jenna Grinstead for her support, excellent eye and ideas, and being a great cheerleader for me and my work. I'd also like to thank Eric Henderson for his clear vision, critical feedback, and overall support of my writing journey. In addition, I genuinely appreciate the Buckeye Crime Writers group (especially the Board) for their advice, motivation, and terrific speakers.

A special thank you to Jim Sabin, who arranged for Orman Hall, an Ohio substance abuse expert and Glidden Foundation Visiting Professor at Ohio University, to speak with our writing group. Mr. Hall gave generously of his time and knowledge. I'd also like to thank Jim's son, Chris Sabin, for his help. Any errors in the book are mine and mine alone.

As always, a big thank you to my editor, Lauren Pan, for her gentle nudging, which made the book stronger.

And finally, thank you to my family and husband for their unwavering support.

ALSO BY EILEEN CURLEY HAMMOND

Murder So Sinful
Murder So Festive
Murder So Heartless
Murder So Deadly
Murder So Hot

To Patrick, Caroline and Jim, Mark and Donna, Wanda and Jack, Karen and Pete, Debbie and Paul, and Linda and Jeff. Thank you for being in my life.

FOREWARD

Welcome to the small town of Hopeful. To get a better feel for the town and its inhabitants, I suggest you read earlier books in the Merry March mystery series, starting with *Murder So Sinful*. If you'd like to start with this book, however, some explanation about some of the recurring characters might be in order.

Meredith March (everyone calls her Merry) is a red-haired, curly-headed divorcee who owns a full-service independent insurance agency in town. She has a daughter named **Jenny March** and a boyfriend named **Rob Jenson**.

Jenny March is a tall, blonde-haired active seventeen-year-old who has had some adventures of her own. She is in the process of looking at colleges and is dating **Jacob Winters**.

Drew March is Merry's ex-husband. He served four years in prison for an illegal investment scheme that would have impoverished many people in town had Merry not discovered just enough funds to pay them back. When he was released from prison, he went back to his illegal ways and escaped town as the FBI closed in. Recently extradited from England, he is in jail awaiting trial along with his girlfriend, **Arianna Flores**.

Rob Jenson is a blond-haired, mustached man who is Merry's boyfriend and has assisted Merry in solving some of the murders in town. He bought the local newspaper after retiring from being a "big city" reporter who traveled the globe.

Patty Twilliger has long brown hair and is Merry's sounding board and best friend. She has four children, the oldest of which, **Cindy**, is **Jenny March**'s best friend and has recently restarted her interior design business. She is married to **Patrick Twilliger**.

Andy Perkins and Ed Wall are married and live across the alley behind Merry. They run the antiques and café in town called Tempting Treasures and Tasty Treats. Andy is the antique collector, and Ed is the chef.

Wanda Jenson is Rob's perfectly put together, serially married, demanding mother. She is currently married to number six, **Glen MacNamara** (nickname Mac).

Elizabeth Jenson is a surgeon and is Rob's sister who lives out of town.

Cheryl Porter is Merry's able assistant at work and right-hand person.

Jada and DeShawn Jenkins are Merry's next-door neighbors who have a sixteen-year-old daughter, **Imani**.

CHAPTER 1

There was a loud snort. *That wasn't me, was it?* I looked right and left. The portly man next to the window was still involved with his book. He might have been invading my space, had we not been with the rich people in first class.

I stretched and took a deep breath. *Ow. Ow. Ow.* Flying and having a cracked rib definitely did not mix. My best friend, Patty, was reading across the aisle, and her husband, Patrick, was fast asleep. My gaze lingered on his peaceful face. He'd had such a tough time of it. First, finding Helen, his birth mother, in Phoenix and then losing her a couple of days later.

I rubbed my side and tried to decide if I was in enough pain for a pill. They made me loopy, and I hated not being in control. It was okay, I was people who loved me, and my boyfriend, Rob, was picking us up. I groaned as I remembered the long walk to baggage claim. I pulled the container from my purse, popped a pill, swigged water, then closed my eyes and tried to focus on something else.

Patty spoke softly, "Merry, are you okay? I saw you take a painkiller."

I gave her a wan smile.

"We'll be home soon."

The pilot announced our descent into the airport, and it was an uneventful landing. After we docked at the gate, Patty turned to her husband. "Do you need help?"

"Help Merry—she's the one I fell on."

I shook my head, "We caught the killer. It's just unfortunate you and I were injured in the process. I'm fine. Let's get off the plane."

"To be on the safe side, I think I'll carry Helen." Patty pulled the bag carrying Patrick's mother's urn close to her. "Let's wait for the girls in the terminal."

Given Patrick's recent inheritance from his mother, he had splurged for me, Patty, and him to fly first-class. Since we had taken the last available seats, my daughter, Jenny, and their daughter, Cindy, had been relegated to coach. I slid my book into my purse, and Patty held out her hand. "I'll take that."

"I can carry my purse."

"Maybe. But not with the book in it."

I sighed, handed her the paperback, and she deposited it in her bag.

Patrick put his phone in his pocket. "Rob's here. He'll meet us at baggage claim with a cart for the luggage."

The girls burst through the crowd, and Jenny said, "The woman in front of us took her bag down and must have rearranged everything in it four times. I can't wait to get home!" She nodded to Cindy. "Beat you to baggage claim."

Cindy made a fake move and then ran past Jenny. "Sucker."

Jenny pounded after her.

"For an ounce of that kind of energy again." I sighed.

"We have wisdom." Patty chuckled. "That's far more valuable, I think."

One of the beeping passenger-carrying carts approached, and Patty flagged it down. I climbed aboard. "Never did this before."

Patty and Patrick got in behind me, and Patty murmured, "You're both hurt. We have an excuse." The woman driving built up speed, and soon we passed the girls.

"That's cheating!" Cindy shouted.

Patty waved, a broad smile on her face.

The woman let us off near baggage claim, and Patrick tipped her. I scanned the board. "We're at number four."

Patty pointed down the corridor. "Balloons. Maybe it's somebody's birthday."

"How nice." I paused. "You'd think they'd be blue or red. Strange that they're silver and white. It's near our carousel. Must be someone from our plane." The painkillers had really kicked in, and I almost felt like I was floating. I giggled.

Patty studied me. "Feeling better?"

"Much."

Jenny came up behind us. "Mom, are you okay?" She held out her arm. "You can lean on me."

"I'm fine. Better than fine. Ooh. Look at that woman's shirt. Lots of what's that called? Swirlies? No, that's not it, it's paisley! My clothes are way too plain. I should ask her where she got it."

I turned to follow the woman, and Patty hooked her arm through mine. "We'll find out later. Let's get our luggage first." Patty nodded to Jenny. "Your mom had a pill. We better get her home."

"Balloons! Someone's going to be happy." Cindy scooted ahead.

The crowd milled, waiting for the sweet sound of gears grinding that would signal the carousel beginning its serpentine journey. Patrick moved to the side, and it seemed like Rob magically appeared. He walked toward me with a smile on his face, flowers in one hand, balloons in the other.

Isn't that sweet? Say what you will; that man has me pegged. I love getting flowers. Red roses, purple delphiniums, and green Irish bells. A beautiful bouquet. The balloons are odd. Why would he have brought balloons?

I tried to fight through the fog. *He wasn't going to—no—not here. Not now. Focus, Merry.*

He handed the festive items to Patrick, knelt on one knee, and extended a small box. The glare from the fluorescent lights made everyone look sallow and otherworldly. The crowd hushed.

My breath caught, and my face flushed. I shook my head, trying to clear it. *Not now. This can't be happening now.* I had waited so long and wanted to be able to savor this moment.

Rob reached for my hand. "I love you, Merry, and you would make me the happiest man on earth if you would marry me."

I gasped. *What if the paperwork for my annulment wasn't really final? Could they rescind it if they found out I got engaged?* My hands began to sweat, and I took two steps back, shaking my head. "No, I can't. Not now." I blurted.

Rob's face fell, and he jerked to his feet, placing the box back in his pocket.

Someone in the crowd asked, "What happened?"

A person replied, "She said no."

And then a third opined, "What a shame."

Patty and Patrick looked frozen, mouths agape, and Jenny's eyes started to tear. The carousel clattered, and bags began to flow, mingling and shaking on their way to rejoin their owners.

Rob's face was crimson, and he cleared his throat as he turned his back to me. "Better get the bags. Patrick, can you point them out?"

Patrick looked between the useless balloons and flowers in his hands and Rob's retreating back and extended them to Patty. "Take these." He followed Rob closer to the conveyor belt.

Jenny's eyes were the size of silver dollars. "Mom, what happened? That was so romantic, and you ruined it."

"Father Tom said my annulment came through, but he didn't have the paperwork yet. We have to wait till then." I sank onto one of the chairs. "I'm a bit woozy, and I can't believe that just happened. I can't waltz into Father Tom's office with an engagement ring on before he gives me the official okay."

"You could have accepted." She tossed her blonde ponytail. "No one would know, and you could keep the ring in your sock drawer till then."

"I would know. And my face would give it away." I massaged my temples.

Patty sat next to me with the flowers and balloons. "What about these?"

Rob and Patrick passed us with the loaded cart, faces grim. I shrugged and stood. "Going to be a long ride home."

* * *

Rob, Jenny, and Cindy made short work of loading everything into the back of the van. The girls climbed over the middle seat to the third row, and Patty helped me into the second. Patrick hesitated outside the passenger side door. "Maybe it would be better if you sat here." I shook my head, and he slid onto the seat as Rob started the van.

The balloons danced across the ceiling, and Rob growled, "Would someone please pull those down so I can see?"

Cindy yanked them, so they were below eye level.

I pulled antacids from my purse, popped them in my mouth, and began to chew as I leaned my head against the window and wished I hadn't taken that stupid pain pill. I touched Rob's shoulder. "Rob?"

He barked. "Not now, Merry. We'll talk later."

I tried not to cry. It was his fault for jumping the gun. *He should have waited.*

Patrick started talking to Rob about baseball, but after a few grunted answers, Patrick grew silent. The mile markers added up. Patty looked nervously between Rob and me. She mouthed, "What should I do?'

I shrugged. "Nothing." The silence was driving me crazy, and all I wanted to do was get out of the car.

We finally pulled into the driveway, and Rob leaped out of the car, opened the back of the van, and pulled out our bags. He handed Jenny hers, and as soon as she opened the front door, he placed mine inside. Patty helped me out of the van and escorted me to the door.

Rob pivoted and passed me on the way back to the van.

My mouth sagged. "We need to talk."

"Later."

"I feel bad about leaving you, but the kids—" Patty wrung her hands.

I extended my arm toward the car. "Go. I'll be fine."

Patrick opened his car window. "C'mon, Patty."

She stutter-stepped to the van and gave me a long look. I walked into the house, shut the door, and leaned against it, exhausted from the tension. *What just happened?*

My two cats, Drambuie and Courvoisier, wound their way around my feet, wailing their tale of woe at being abandoned. I sighed and said, "I know. You need some love." My voice caught. "Just like me." I made my way to the laundry room and pulled out their almost empty bag of treats. "Someone gave you way too many of these." I tossed a few on the floor, and they scooted after them.

The stairs rumbled, and Jenny rounded the corner to the kitchen, poured a glass of water, and plopped onto one of the stools. "The suitcases are upstairs." She turned the glass back and forth. "What happens now?"

"What do you mean?"

"Mr. Jenson's been really nice to me. He's come to all my games, and he flew to London for me," her voice wobbled, "I was kind of looking forward to him being my surrogate dad. I'm going to miss him."

I put my arm around her. "Everything's going to work out. Don't worry."

"He looked pretty mad. Are you sure?"

"Positive." I bit the inside of my cheek. "Even if it doesn't, we've been fine all these years on our own, haven't we?"

6

She took a sip of water. "Sure. It was just nice to have him around."

"I agree." I leaned my head against hers. "I should have handled it differently, but he should have known we need to take things in order."

She drained the glass and put it into the sink. "I still think you should have said yes. Jacob's coming by in a few to pick me up. There's a movie he wants to see." She straightened. "I should have told him no. You need me here." She pulled out her phone and started to text.

I touched her hand. "Go with him. I'll be fine. I'm pretty tired anyway."

A horn tooted from the driveway. She stood. "Are you sure you don't need me?"

I nodded.

"Text if you want me to come home." The front door shut.

I filled a mug with water, put it in the microwave, and grabbed a tea bag. My teeth ground. *I hope we work this out. I love Rob. A lot.*

Drambuie jumped on the counter and put her head under my hand. I petted her and said, "You've been learning bad habits while I've been gone." I pointed. "Down!"

She hopped off, and her tail swished as she made her way to the window seat.

There was a quick knock at the back door, and my neighbor, Andy, rushed in. "Well? Where is it? Did people applaud? I can't believe he got down on one knee at the airport. Who knows how often they clean those floors..." His voice trailed off as he lifted my left hand. "Was it the wrong size?"

"I said no."

His mouth dropped. "Why on earth would you do that? You love each other, and the annulment came through. I thought that was what you were waiting for."

"It was, but I haven't gotten the paperwork yet. If he'd told me what he was planning, I could have—I don't know." I plopped the bag in the mug. "Tea?"

"Dinner's almost ready, and you know how snippy Ed gets..." He paused, hand on the doorknob. "Shish kebab tonight—join us. You don't want to be here by yourself—it's too depressing."

"Thanks, but tea and quiet are all I can handle right now."

He left the door and walked closer to me, a frown on his face. "I'll stay. I need all the details, and you need company."

"Go. We'll talk tomorrow." I shooed him with my hand.

"First thing." He shook his forefinger.

"Whatever."

He left.

I sank onto a chair, dunked my tea bag twice, and deposited it onto a plate. *Rob looked so hurt when I said no. Maybe I should have said yes and told everyone to keep it on the down-low until I received the official word. If only I hadn't taken that pill. I could have thought of something.* I took a sip, pulled out my phone, and texted Rob: "Are you coming back? Don't forget, meeting with Father Tom tomorrow morning."

The door opened. Patty walked in, headed for the cupboard, and pulled out another mug.

"What are you doing here?" I shifted in my seat. "I'm surprised the kids let you leave again so soon."

"They're playing a new video game Patrick bought in Phoenix. I doubt they'll even know I left." She lifted the mug. "Teapot?"

"Microwave."

She turned on the tap, filled the mug, and stuck it in the microwave. "I'm worried about you."

"As I told Jenny, Andy, and now you, I'm fine. This is a bump in the road."

"Seemed like more of a crater to me." She plopped a tea bag in hot water and made her way to the table. "I know you like to do things by the book, but I don't think anyone would have faulted you for saying yes. And it would have made Rob far happier."

8

I groaned and put my head in my hands.

"You still want to marry Rob, right? You were talking about children when we were in Phoenix."

"Of course, I do."

Her phone buzzed. "Darn. They noticed I left. Do you need anything before I go?"

I shook my head, and she traipsed out the door. *Should I lock it?* I chuckled and clutched my side. My rib felt like a donkey had kicked it. The doctor had been concerned about me leaving so soon, but I had assured him I would follow up with my GP when I returned. I retrieved an ice pack, carried it into the living room with my tea, and examined my phone—still no answer from Rob. I double-checked to make sure it wasn't on silent mode.

The mystery I'd been reading on the plane was perched on the coffee table. With everything that happened, I was surprised Patty remembered to take it out of her bag. I settled onto a chair, pulled the book close, and tried to concentrate. The insistent ticking of the grandfather's clock didn't help.

What was Rob doing? Was he by himself? *Maybe when he returned Ed's van, they talked him into staying for dinner.* I stood, strode to the kitchen, and parted the mini blinds to peer out. Rob, Ed, and Andy sat at the table on their back deck, wine poured, and they were laughing. I guess Rob wasn't that upset.

My stomach rumbled. Soup. That was comforting. I opened a can, poured it into a bowl, and placed it in the microwave. I started to open the blinds again, but this time turned off the kitchen light. It was getting dark. The sun had just kissed the horizon, and Ed, Andy, and Rob were bathed in the fading hues of twilight, deep in conversation. The microwave beeped, so I flipped the blinds shut and turned on the light. *What would I do if he didn't forgive me?*

CHAPTER 2

I woke from pain several times during the night but finally figured out that two bolster pillows on either side best kept me from moving. The cats hadn't been too happy with the multiple rearrangements and must have left for the greener pastures of Jenny's bed.

My alarm rang, and I staggered into the shower. By exclusively using my right arm, I was able to get fairly clean. Toweling off was a painful adventure, but I powered through. Mostly dry, I struggled into slacks and a blouse. It was odd not to be wearing shorts and a t-shirt. After applying a minimal amount of make-up, I sank back onto the bed, exhausted. Even the tantalizing aroma of coffee wasn't enough to make me move.

The cats were a different story. They must have heard the shower because they sat by my bedroom door and mewed as if to say, "Hurry up with the food." I let them lead me downstairs, petted them, scooped kibble into their bowls, and washed my hands. Then I grabbed a frozen bagel, plopped it in the toaster, and poured a cup of coffee while silently thanking Jenny, who must have set the timer for the pot before she went to bed.

I rechecked my phone—nothing from Rob. I texted my extremely efficient assistant, Cheryl, to let her know I'd be delayed at the church and then spread cream cheese on the bagel. As I took a bite, my phone buzzed with a reply from Cheryl: "Any pictures from last night?"

"Pictures?"

"Rob said he was going to propose."

Was there anyone he hadn't told? I groaned and typed: "Long story. Talk later at the office."

After putting dirty plates in the dishwasher, I grabbed my purse and walked out the door. My new neighbor, Jada Jenkins, wore a lime green shirt that showed her ebony skin to best advantage. She put down the container she was using to water her plants. "I heard you were coming home." Her eyes shifted to my hand and then back. "I still have your basket from when we moved in. I'll bring it by later."

"Whenever you get a chance." I waved and walked toward the church. Had she been looking for a ring? *That man.* I shook my head. As I ambled, various people waved and welcomed me back to town.

I walked into the brown-shingled rectory, and Belinda, the church secretary, motioned to a chair facing her desk. "I heard you had trouble in Phoenix. I'm glad to see you back."

Small towns.

Father Tom opened his office door. "Merry, come in. Coffee? Tea?"

I shook my head. "Had some at home." I sank onto a chair.

"Merry, I'm pleased to tell you I have your official decree of nullity. You are no longer married to Drew in the eyes of the church." He handed me the document.

"Thank you, Father. I appreciate your help with the process. This piece of paper is going to change my life." I smiled.

He nodded. "I was kind of surprised Rob isn't here. Did he have a meeting?"

"I guess he couldn't make it." I flushed.

"I wondered why you weren't wearing a ring." He nodded toward my hand.

"Is there anyone that man didn't tell?"

"What happened? Do you want to talk about it?"

I shook my head. "Nothing that can't be fixed. Thanks again." I stood.

"Don't forget to see Belinda and get signed up for marriage preparation, or Pre-Cana, as you know it."

"I've been through that already. I'm not twenty."

"Important no matter how old you are. Talk to Belinda."

I shook my head as I walked out the door.

Belinda asked, "Do I hear wedding bells?"

"Not yet. And I need to get to work."

✳ ✳ ✳

I opened the door to my business, the Meredith March Insurance Agency. It was a beehive of activity with the client appreciation event coming up. Cheryl was on the phone and waved me toward her as she hung up. "Do you have time to catch up?"

"Absolutely." I walked into my office and tossed my purse in the drawer. "What's first on your list?"

"Saturday. Are you going to be able to make cupcakes with your cracked rib?"

I tapped my lip with the pencil. "If I can enlist Patty and Jenny to help, I should be okay."

"Not your fiancé?" She chuckled.

"He's not my fiancé, at least not yet. And I don't know if he still wants to be."

Cheryl sat back in the chair. "Work can wait."

"It can't. I've been away too long. Jenny can do the mixing for the cupcakes, and Patty can do the finish work. We should be okay."

"Are you sure? Do you want to talk about what happened with Rob?"

"I do not."

She chewed her lip, staring at me, then put a check mark next to cupcakes and focused on the rest of her list. Various associates had volunteered lawn games, and she had placed the final order with the caterer. She stood. "I think this will be our best event yet."

"All due to you. Thanks for shouldering so much of the burden."

Cheryl smiled. "My pleasure. I stuck an ice pack in the freezer. If you need it, let me know."

I pulled out my phone. Still nothing from Rob. I pressed his number and went to voicemail. This was getting ridiculous.

I opened a spreadsheet and tried to concentrate, but I glanced at the phone every two seconds. An hour later, I yanked it toward me and pressed Rob's number.

He answered. "Hello, Merry."

"Rob, I feel so bad about last night. Can we talk? Do you have time for lunch?"

He paused so long that I thought he might have hung up. Then he said, "I guess I need to eat. I'll meet you at noon at the Iron Skillet." Before I had a chance to say okay, he disconnected.

I rubbed my forehead for a moment and then leaped to my feet. I had work to do. I passed Cheryl on the way out. "Have a few errands to run. I'll be back by two at the latest."

I walked past the brick storefronts and ducked into the new chocolatier shop, Extreme Indulgence. The smell made me smile, sweet chocolate and spicy cinnamon. I wanted one of everything, but this stop wasn't about me. I pointed to the dark chocolate-dipped pretzels. "May I have a box of those, and would you wrap it, please?" The clerk complied and added a shiny green bow.

I checked my phone, still about ten minutes before I needed to meet Rob. My next stop was the Party Palace. I chose several balloons emblazoned with "I love you," "I'm sorry," and "I'm yours."

The owner gave me a knowing look. "I hope this works."

I gulped as I exited the shop. The balloons bobbed when I walked, and people stared. My color began to rise as I contemplated what I was about to do. I passed an alley, and my next-door neighbor, DeShawn, was in jeans at the far end talking to someone I hadn't seen before. I raised my hand to wave, but he turned away. I took a deep breath and continued on.

A man opened the door to the Iron Skillet for me and my assorted balloons. I felt a bit ridiculous as they traveled further than I thought and bopped the person at the host stand on the head. I apologized, and he said, "Your guest is already here," and pointed toward the back.

The volume of chatter picked up as I wove through the crowded restaurant, and when I reached Rob's table, died like the sound of songbirds at nightfall. I looped the balloons around the coat hook, placed the wrapped pretzels on the table, and got to one knee. Rob's eyes widened. "What on earth?"

"Rob, you would make me the happiest woman on earth if you married me. Please say yes."

He opened and closed his mouth. Finally, he said, "Are you sure? You didn't seem so keen yesterday."

"Yes, definitely yes."

He stood and lifted me to my feet, "Then I say yes too." He kissed me, and the people in the restaurant cheered.

I waved and slid into the booth, grinning. "Thanks for accepting."

"I was tempted to say no, after last night."

"I'm sorry about that. I had taken a pain pill, and you surprised me. Shocked me, really."

He frowned. "I don't know why it was so surprising. It's not like we hadn't talked about getting married before."

"That part wasn't the surprise. It was the venue—and the timing. I feel awful for turning you down. I've wanted to marry you for quite some time." I lifted the document Father Tom had given me from my purse, "And now I can."

He read it. "It's official. Drew's out of your life."

"Yep." I grinned.

He unwrapped the box on the table and smiled. "My favorites."

"Forgive me?"

"Almost." He took a box from his jacket and pushed it across the table. "Wear my ring?"

I opened it and gasped. It was a one-carat, emerald-cut diamond with two half-carat side diamonds on a platinum band.

"It's beautiful." I slid it on my hand and admired it. "And a perfect fit."

"I may have borrowed one of your rings while you were out of town."

We ate lunch, and several people came by to congratulate us and admire my ring. As we were leaving, I gasped. "Wait. Take a picture of my hand." I gave him my phone.

"What for?" He laughed.

"Jenny. She's going to kill me because she didn't see it before all of these people." I uploaded it to a text and messaged her. My phone binged.

"About time. Is Mr. Jenson taking us to dinner to celebrate?"

I showed Rob the phone. He took it from me and texted, "Fiorella's at seven; bring Jacob."

"Are you sure you don't want to celebrate alone?" I touched his arm.

"We're a family. Once Jenny goes off to school, we'll have plenty of time to be by ourselves."

I hugged him. "I love you, Rob Jenson, and I can't wait to spend the rest of my life with you."

✳ ✳ ✳

It seemed like I floated back to work. When I walked in, Cheryl said, "Everyone's calling to offer their congratulations. Ooh. What a beautiful ring."

"How did they know—" I shrugged as I was surrounded by my associates vying for a closer look. "Enough." I laughed. "Thank you all—let's get back to work."

I walked into my office, shut the door, and opened the spreadsheet I had been trying to work on earlier in the day. The phone rang, and I lifted the handset. "Merry March."

"Merry, it's Elizabeth, Rob's sister. I'm so pleased for both of you. Welcome to the family."

"Thank you. I'm over the moon."

"I also called to warn you."

"About what?" I doodled on a pad.

"Wanda. She called after Rob, and I hung up. She wants to help plan the wedding."

I coughed. "She what?"

"You can't back out now." Elizabeth laughed.

"Rob and I both want something small and intimate. Family and a few friends. It's not my first wedding."

"Wanda said it's Rob's, so it should be a big blow-out. Mac and Wanda have business associates they want to ask. And she'd like Mac's nieces to be in the wedding."

The pencil snapped. "Elizabeth."

"I know. Don't worry, Rob and I will beat her back. I really called to say how thrilled I am. Talk soon." She hung up.

I clutched my chest. *Can stress cause an injury to hurt more?* I pressed the button for Cheryl. "If you wouldn't mind, I'll take that ice pack now."

✳ ✳ ✳

Two minutes after I walked into my house, Patty came through the back door and lifted my hand. "It's a stunner."

"It is that." I smiled.

"You could have saved us a very tense ride home by saying yes, last night."

"Ha, ha." I poured her a glass of wine.

"Who said I was kidding?"

I pulled back the glass.

"Of course, I was kidding."

I handed it to her. "Bad taste."

She sat at the counter. "I miss Helen's house in Phoenix. No cook or maid here. I'll be pining for the help tomorrow when I have to tackle the kids' laundry."

"It was easy to get used to someone else making the bed. I started trying to make mine this morning but decided just to pull the sheet up."

She winced. "How's the rib?"

"Not too bad, as long as I take it easy. That's not why I'm stressing."

Her eyebrow rose.

"Wanda wants to help with the wedding."

Patty's mouth dropped. "That's going to be fun."

"Rob's lucky I love him enough to deal with his mother. Thank goodness Elizabeth gave me a heads-up. What am I going to do?"

"What do you and Rob want?"

"We're thinking small, but we're going to dinner tonight with Jenny and Jacob. Hopefully, we'll get a chance to chat more then. Oh, and Father Tom says we have to go to Pre-Cana."

"Didn't you already go through that with Drew?"

"Different groom means I have to do it again."

She chuckled. "You and a bunch of twenty-year-olds. You'll feel ancient."

"I'm going to see if they have a more mature group. At least that way, we'd have something in common. And now you have to leave. My fiancé will be here soon to take me to dinner."

I ran upstairs and freshened my make-up. The dark circles I had under my eyes this morning were now history. *Amazing what a new ring will do.* I slipped a soft pink dress over my head and sashayed downstairs.

There was a quick rap on the door, and Rob walked in with a beautiful bouquet. He handed it to me. "For my lovely fiancée."

I kissed him on the cheek. "Let me put these in water."

"I spoke with my mother and Elizabeth. They're thrilled."

I nodded as I filled a vase and arranged the flowers.

Jenny rounded the corner into the kitchen. "Jacob will be here in a few minutes." She kissed Rob on the cheek. "Congratulations, Mr. Jenson. I'm happy you're going to be my stepdad."

He hugged her. "We're going to have to figure out something else for you to call me."

"I'm working on it."

Jacob rang the doorbell, and Jenny ran to let him in. Jacob stood a few inches taller than Jenny in heels, topping out at six-two. He wore tan chinos and a light blue shirt. Jacob extended his hand to Rob. "Congratulations, Mr. Jenson and Ms. March." His gaze drifted to Rob's sport coat. "I'm sorry I don't have a jacket, but I outgrew my old one, and my mom says she's not investing in another one till I'm done with this spurt."

"No problem. Why don't I leave mine here too." Rob slipped his off and draped it over the couch. "More comfortable anyway."

Jenny flashed him a smile, and I put my hand through his. "Let's eat."

❋ ❋ ❋

Rob sipped wine. "I'm in total agreement. Small, tasteful wedding, family, friends, and soon."

"Soon might be a bit tough." I broke a piece of bread and dipped it in olive oil. "I understand it's hard to get dates at the church."

"Who's going to walk you down the aisle?" Jenny asked.

"I don't know. Do you want to be my maid of honor? Or do you want to give me away?"

Her brow furrowed. "I'm not 'giving' you to Mr. Jenson. I still want to keep you. You're my mom."

"That's true. The whole giving away smacks of patrimony anyway. Maybe we could rewrite it, so you were inviting Rob to join our family."

"Do I still get to wear a cool dress?"

"Deal, let me talk to Father Tom."

Jacob had been silent during the discussion. He turned to Rob. "Who's your best man going to be?"

"I haven't asked her yet, but my sister, Elizabeth."

"A truly traditional wedding." I laughed.

∗ ∗ ∗

I took Friday off to bake my divine chocolate cupcakes. The secret was a fudgy chocolate cake batter with bits of dark and milk chocolate chunks folded in before baking. They were iced with chocolate, of course, and chocolate sprinkles—a chocoholic's dream.

Jenny chopped the chocolate bars into smaller pieces, and Patty iced the first cooled batch. Rob manned the mixer, and I dropped wrappers into cupcake tins. "This is much easier with help. We're a well-oiled machine."

"How many are we making?" Rob plopped three eggs into the latest batch.

"Hundred and fifty should do it. Cheryl is making a yellow sheet cake, and the caterer is bringing fruit pops." I slid another liner into a tin.

"That's a lot."

Patty laughed. "You'll see. There won't be any left."

"More piping, less chatting. I'll put those in a carrier." I pointed to the ones Patty had finished frosting.

"So demanding." Patty slid them toward me.

The doorbell rang.

"Who on earth can that be? Everyone comes to the back." I strolled to the front door and looked through the side light. *Wanda*. My palms began to sweat, and I patted my pockets for an antacid. I gritted my teeth and opened the door. "Such a surprise. How nice to see you."

She air-kissed a foot from my cheek as she swept into the room, leaving a trail of Eau de Joy behind her as she eyed my jeans and t-shirt. "Is it a casual day? Your assistant told me you were working from home." Wanda wore crisply pleated peach slacks paired with a white shell and a matching light-cotton sweater. Small pearl earrings matched her understated necklace.

"We're making cupcakes for my customer appreciation event tomorrow."

She pointed toward my left cheek. "Chocolate?"

I brushed my face with the back of my hand. It came back smeared. "I must have gotten some—"

"I could tell." She sat on one of the armchairs in the living room. "I came to talk with you about the wedding. Rob tells me you're thinking about a small one. I'm afraid that won't do."

My face grew hot. She hadn't even congratulated me or welcomed me to the family. "Wanda, I've been married before. I'm older. Smaller seems more appropriate."

She sniffed. "I've been married six times, and each one was a large affair. These occasions are to be celebrated. And don't forget, this is Rob's first time."

"Merry, we need more cupcake wrappers." Rob walked into the living room. "Mother, what are you doing here?"

"Are you ashamed of Merry?"

"What? Not at all. What does that have to do with—"

Wanda stood. "How many people are you having at this 'thing' tomorrow? Where you are serving—" she shuddered, "—cupcakes."

I shrugged. "Cheryl has the exact number, but somewhere north of a hundred."

"And how are they going to feel when you slink off to get married like you were embarrassed and wanted to sweep it under the rug?"

I sputtered, "How could you think that—"

Wanda raised her finger to her lips. "Think about it. Let it percolate. I'm sure you'll come to the right decision." She strode out the door and shut it behind her.

"That woman." I brushed past Rob, stormed into the kitchen, took more cupcake liners from the cabinet, and plopped them on the counter.

Rob followed me. "Merry—"

Jenny's eyes were round. "What happened?"

CHAPTER 3

The fete went off without a hitch. It was one of those days where heat shimmered above the pavement, but the park was graced with towering red maples that provided ample shade from the sun. The lake cooled the kids off, and they enjoyed blowing water at their friends through rainbow-colored pool noodles someone had brought. People formed teams for a raucous baseball game at the diamond, and picnic tables covered in red and white checkered cloths fluttered in the breeze weighted down by mason jars brimming with daisies.

As lines began to form at the caterer's tables, I greeted people and thanked them for coming. The only problem was everyone I spoke with mentioned how they couldn't wait to celebrate my wedding. Rob was still playing baseball, so I handled the awkward conversations on my own. *Was Wanda right?*

At the end of the day, parents carried worn-out tykes on their shoulders and gently eased them into car seats. Soon only Rob, Patty, Patrick, Ed, and Andy were left, other than the caterers who were now cleaning up. Patty nodded to the dessert table. "See? No cupcakes left."

"Hard to believe." Rob shook his head.

Andy patted his stomach. "I did my part."

Ed pulled his folding chair closer to me. "Who's going to cater your wedding, hint, hint."

"We haven't talked about it yet, but I guess the answer is you." I laughed.

"I can't wait to make the wedding cake. I'm thinking something tall, multi-tiered, alternating layers. Knowing you, one will have to be chocolate—"

"Whoa. Think small. Think tasteful. Maybe something like a carrot cake with sour cream icing." I licked my lips.

"Small?" Andy leaned forward. "We're invited, aren't we?"

"Of course." I smiled. "Couldn't imagine it without you."

He sat back in his chair.

Rob kissed my hand. "We'll get through this."

"I hope."

* * *

Monday morning was busy because I had reminded several clients on Saturday that we needed to dust off their coverage to make sure it still fit their situations. Midday, Cheryl knocked on my door. "You're going to be fully booked for a while."

I smiled. "Pays the bills."

"Belinda's on the phone. She wants to go over potential dates for Pre-Cana."

"Thanks." I turned to the phone and groaned. I wasn't sure I was ready for this. "Belinda, thanks for calling."

"I have dates for you." She listed them, and I jotted them on a pad. "Oh, and there's one next weekend with younger people, but you wouldn't want that, and it only has two spots left."

"We'll take it."

"Don't you need to check with Rob?"

"I'm sure it will be fine." I circled the date. The sooner we got this over with, the better.

"If you're certain. That one's the full weekend."

"Can I stay at home?"

"It's a group experience, and you'll need to stay at the venue. Need to run. I'll email you the details." She hung up.

I texted Rob to hold the dates.

Within a minute, my phone rang. "The whole weekend?"

"Yep."

"Okay. See you later," Rob groaned.

* * *

We pulled up to the Bishop's Retreat Conference Center the following weekend. The main building had a soaring peaked roof and was clad in chocolate-brown cedar shingles. Two wings extended from the main building, looking like old dormitories. Rob sighed. "I was hoping for a bit more luxury."

"Me too. Let's make the best of it." I exited the car, and Rob grabbed our bags.

Fortyish young people milled about inside the main entry, their raucous voices spilling out the door. Rob stopped in his tracks. "They're so young. I thought you were going to try and get us into a session with people nearer our age."

"We're not that much older than them." I nodded at a couple who looked like they were in their early thirties. "Besides, you didn't want to wait, and this was the soonest." I grabbed his arm and pointed toward the registration desk. We strode toward it, and the older woman at the desk looked up. "Are you the teachers?"

"Attendees." I cleared my throat and pointed to our name tags on the table.

"Glad to have you with us. Here are your workbooks and name badges." She handed a bag to each of us. "Merry, you'll be rooming with a woman named Jane Creedy in the woman's wing, room 204, and Rob, you'll room with her fiancé, Kevin Percher, in the men's wing, room 105.

Since the session is about to begin, you can drop your things in the cloak room."

We walked away from the table, and Rob whispered, "We can't stay together?"

I elbowed him. "Shh."

A man walked from the conference room with a hand-held xylophone. He tapped it with a small birch mallet. Ding dong, ding dong, ding dong. "The session will start in ten minutes; please find a seat."

We entered a large conference room that sat about fifty people in groups of six. A crush of people entered, and the only seats left were directly in front of the lay teachers. I slid into a seat at the round, white cloth-covered table, and Rob sat next to me. We nodded to the two other couples already seated, and then I examined the workbook. The first class was "Marriage as a Sacrament." The woman teacher began to drone, and my mind wandered. *Everything happened so quickly after waiting so long for the decree to come through. Am I ready for this? The other people in the class are so young, so hopeful, so sure their marriages will last forever—what a true leap of faith to pledge yourself to another human being.* I glanced at Rob and smiled. He was the right person for me.

The class was similar to the one I previously attended. There was one big difference, and it was my life experience. At twenty, with no responsibilities, the words washed over me. Now they stuck. *Had I known what "for better or worse" really meant? I certainly hadn't known I was marrying a con man, one who would turn my life upside down. Rob was so different. He cared about other people far more than himself, and he had a solid moral compass. No shortcuts for him. He would be a true partner.* I reached for his hand and held it in mine.

After the class and prayer, they opened the buffet in the adjoining room. Nothing looked particularly appetizing, so I piled my plate with salad that was a tiny bit brown around the edges. Rob whispered, "Let's hope breakfast is better." Plates as full as they were going to get, we wound our way back to the table.

I set my plate down and extended my hand to the woman next to me. "Merry March."

She shook it. "We're roommates. Jane Creedy, and this is my fiancé, Kevin Percher." Jane's stick-straight blonde hair hung like a curtain, covering part of her face when she leaned forward. She looked Jenny's age, about seventeen, but had to have been older. Kevin had apparently foregone shaving that day and wore a rumpled pair of jeans and t-shirt. He didn't look older than twenty.

Rob shook Kevin's hand, and I waved across the table. The other couple introduced themselves as Trudy Jones and Matt Logan. I pegged them as being in their mid-twenties. Trudy wore a buttoned-up white blouse and starched gray slacks. Matt was more casual in chinos and a polo shirt.

Jane gasped. "Your ring is beautiful."

"Thank you." I smiled.

"We could only afford this." She held her hand toward me. The ring was rose gold with a raised diamond chip in the center surrounded by pavé diamonds.

"It's lovely." I smiled. "How long have you been engaged?"

"Two months." Jane placed her hand on Kevin's. "We're getting married next April."

Trudy said, "June for us." She turned toward me. "When are you getting married?"

"We haven't decided yet. It'll be a small wedding."

Jane's eyes widened. "April was the first date we could get when we started looking this past June. I can't believe you don't have a date yet. It's August!"

Trudy preened. "We're having a big wedding. Six bridesmaids, not including my maid of honor." She tapped a pink folder in front of her. "I've been planning this for two years. Checklists and everything."

Matt took a flask from his jeans pocket, held his glass under the table, and poured a dollop into his soda. He nodded to Rob. "Whiskey?"

"I'll pass."

Kevin crooked his finger, and Matt palmed the flask to him.

"Thanks." Kevin poured and slid it back.

Jane frowned. "If you get us kicked out—"

"Don't be such a prude. No one will notice." He sipped and smiled. "Thanks, Matt. Takes the edge off."

Trudy picked up the workbook. "Money Matters is the last class of the evening. I keep telling Matt that once we're married, we need to buckle down. Our next big expense will be a house. And then kids, of course. Isn't that right?"

Matt had a pained look on his face as he nodded.

Kevin extended his glass to Matt. "Better hit me again. This is going to be boring, with a capital B."

The man at the front clapped his hands, and Matt jumped.

"Please clear your tables. The next class will start in five minutes."

Rob stood. "I've got it." He took my plate and his and walked to where the bins were.

"For an older guy, he's pretty cute," Jane said.

"I think so." I smiled.

"You shouldn't be looking at other guys, old or not." Kevin scowled and tipped his glass back.

"I'm not dead yet."

"That could be arranged." He leaned toward her.

I stood. "I'm going to the restroom before they start."

"I'll join you." Jane jumped to her feet. Trudy continued to flip through the workbook, underlining sections, so we walked toward the back of the room.

Several other women had the same idea, which meant a line. I touched Jane's shoulder. "Are you okay?'

"He's gruff around the edges, but he would never hurt me."

When we returned to the table, the class had started. The woman instructor asked us to list all our assets. I groaned. It was clear they were used to a younger crowd who didn't have much. The male instructor followed up by having us list all our debts. They then told us to find a quiet alcove to compare our lists and discuss how we would handle our finances moving forward. Rob and I found two facing wing chairs in the lobby. He pulled them closer, and we sat.

"This is awkward. So much has happened we haven't had the money conversation." My face heated.

"No time like the present." He handed me his lists.

I scanned them. "You're in a good place."

"The news organization paid for all my travel and expenses, so there weren't a lot of places for me to spend the money I made." He held out his hand.

I clutched my pages. "Maybe we should keep our finances separate."

He stared at me.

"It is kind of private."

"What are we going to do if we have kids? What then? Do you want me to sign a prenup?"

"Don't be silly." I sat back. "Though maybe we should. What about Jenny? What if I were to die? You'd get my money, and she'd get nothing. That's not fair to her."

"Do you trust me?"

Other couples chattered around us, voices rising and falling like waves.

"Of course." I caressed his shoulder. "I hadn't thought about this part. After Drew—"

"We don't have to do this tonight. We can wait if you want."

"I'm being silly." I pushed the papers into his hand. "You can look at them." My stomach lurched, and I grew dizzy. I should have saved more, but buying Drew out of both the lake house and my home did a number on my finances. And Jenny would be going to school soon.

Rob looked up. "You're a good financial manager, though I would expect that since you run your own business."

"I know it's nowhere near what you have—"

"I'm impressed with what you've been able to accumulate despite everything that's happened."

I stood. "I think they're starting up again with a final prayer."

"We should talk more about this later. I understand your concerns about Jenny."

✻ ✻ ✻

I decided on an early night, so I was first to my shared utilitarian room. Two single beds were pushed against either side of the twelve-by-ten room, with two narrow nightstands and a small closet. I brushed my teeth down the hall in the dorm-style bathroom and then curled up in bed. The off-white sheets had seen their fair share of bleach and were quite thin, which meant they went perfectly with the flat pillow and threadbare blanket. *Only two nights. I could do this.*

I pulled out Rob's budget sheets and winced. He had been quite the saver. From a monetary standpoint, and otherwise, I was getting the better end of the deal. I put the paperwork back and was soon lost in my book. They were just about to uncover the killer when there was a knock at my door. Disappointed at being interrupted, I muttered under my breath and called out, "Come in."

Jane came through the door.

"It's your room too. No need to knock."

"I didn't want to startle you."

"Bathroom is down the hall." I pointed.

She took some things out of a small night case and left. After a few moments, Jane returned. "You missed the bonfire."

I shrugged and stuck the marker back in my book. "Tell me about it."

"It was fun. They had hay bales for two and played music. The guys were still drinking, and Trudy and I talked wedding stuff." She yawned and slid into bed.

"Will the light bother you if I read for a while?"

Jane shook her head. "My mom says I could sleep through anything."

I had just picked up my book again when my phone almost vibrated off the nightstand. "Sorry. I put it on silent."

"No problem." She turned away from me and pulled up the covers.

The text from Rob read: "Need you now, come to room with pool table second floor. Above where we met today."

"In bed."

"Hurry."

"Sorry, Rob needs me." I put my clothes back on and slipped out the door. I ran down the hall and took a corridor that seemed to be leading me toward the conference room. I saw a small sign for an activities room and figured that had to be where Rob was. I turned the corner. "Better directions would have been—" My mouth dropped. Rob and Matt were ashen and standing over Kevin, who was lying on the floor. "What happened? Is he okay?"

Rob shook his head. "We called nine-one-one and the front desk. But it's not going to be any use. He's dead."

A priest rushed into the room. "I came as soon as I heard."

Rob extended his arm, and the priest knelt by the body. He crossed himself and began to recite the prayers for the dead and uncapped a bottle of holy water. Rob cleared his throat. "Um. Father, I don't think you should touch him until the police arrive."

The priest's eyes widened. "But surely—"

Rob shook his head.

EMTs raced into the room led by one of the staffers. While the first one assessed Kevin, Rob explained to the other what had happened and that he had tried CPR. They gave him some type of shot and then used a defibrillator but were also unsuccessful. We huddled to the side, out of their way.

As they were packing up their equipment, Detective Jay Ziebold, our friend, arrived with a patrolman. By now, there was a small crowd gathered outside of the room. The detective asked the priest, "Do you have a room I can use?"

"The one next to the conference room is free." The priest gave instructions to him.

Detective Ziebold then told the patrolman, "I want this room cleared. Take these people," he gestured to me, Rob, and Matt, "downstairs." He pointed to the priest. "You show him where to go. And shut the door."

We filed out like ducks in a row. The priest leading, followed by the patrolman, then Rob and I, and Matt. The priest showed us into a small room off the conference room we had been in that afternoon. Matt began to shake, and Rob took one of his arms and led him to a chair. I leaned over Matt, "Are you okay?"

He shook his head. "I was talking to him one minute, and the next he was dead. How could that happen? I think I'm going to be sick."

Rob looked at the patrolman. "Okay if he goes to the men's room?"

The patrolman nodded, and Matt stood. He wobbled, so Rob grabbed his arm. "We'll be right back."

I retrieved a glass of water and knocked on the bathroom door. Rob nodded his thanks as he took it. I walked back to the room, and Jay was behind the desk. He asked, "What happened?"

"I have no idea. I was in my room, and Rob texted for me to meet him. When I got there, Kevin was dead."

31

Rob and a very shaky Matt came back. Rob and I helped him into a chair. Matt said, "Better now."

Jay intoned, "Tell me exactly what happened. Don't leave anything out."

Matt turned white again. I asked, "Are you sure you're okay?"

He gulped and gave me a thumbs up. "We were at the bonfire having a drink or two from my flask."

Jay motioned with his hand for Matt to turn over the flask. Matt pulled the silver container from his pocket. "It was my granddad's."

"You'll get it back, continue."

"Our fiancées' were talking wedding stuff, and Kevin said it was boring. He told me there was a pool table and suggested a game. I was up for it. To be honest, I'm getting a bit tired of all these lists, so we had started to play pool, and Kevin was texting with someone between shots. Then he said he'd be back in a few minutes. I thought he had gone to the bathroom, but when he came back, he asked me if I wanted some speed. I said no, and Kevin popped something in his mouth."

Matt gasped, "Two seconds later, he dropped to the floor. Just collapsed, no hands breaking his fall, no nothing. I turned him over, and he wasn't breathing. That's when he," Matt pointed to Rob, "came in. He started CPR right away, and I gave mouth-to-mouth. It didn't work." He gulped water. "He was dead." Matt leaned his head against the wall. "I still can't believe it."

Jay jotted a note and pulled a baggie with a small pill in it from his case. "Was this what he offered you?"

"I never saw what he took."

He put the baggie back and pointed to Rob. "Why were you there?"

"I had gone to my room and realized I left my book at home. I thought maybe they'd have a library here. When I saw the sign for the activities room, I figured that would be my best bet. Kevin was on the ground as I turned the corner, and I jumped into action."

"Where'd you learn CPR?"

"Needed it for all of the reporting I did in various hot spots."

I leaned forward and touched Rob's arm. "How could he have died so quickly?"

"Who knows. Might be a heart condition, shouldn't take speed with that."

"Don't leave the premises till I tell you it's okay. I may have further questions." He frowned and nodded at Rob and Matt.

I rubbed the back of my neck. "Poor Jane. She'll be heartbroken."

Jay's eyebrow raised. "The fiancée? Do you know where she is?"

I nodded.

"Since we're short-staffed, would you get her for me?"

✳ ✳ ✳

"Jane, Jane, wake up." I felt so badly trying to wake her. It'd probably be the last good night's sleep she'd get for quite some time. She muttered something and turned over. I shook her arm again. "Jane, you need to wake up."

She growled, "What?"

"I'm sorry to wake you, but the police are downstairs, and they need to speak with you."

"Why? What happened?" She sat straight up in bed.

"There's been an accident."

"Who? My mom?"

"They just need to speak with you. Get dressed, and I'll show you where they are."

She threw on the clothes she wore the night before. "Is it Kevin? Did he get into trouble? I knew he shouldn't have been drinking." She plopped back on the bed. "They're not kicking us out of Marriage Prep, are they? That would be awful." She slid on sandals.

I couldn't let her go on asking questions. I sat next to her on the bed. "I have bad news. Kevin's dead."

Her mouth opened, and no sound came out. Then she gasped as if coming up for air after a long time under water. "That can't be. He was with me tonight. How could that have happened? Are you sure?"

I nodded. "I'm so sorry."

Tears rolled down her face. "What am I going to do now?"

"Do you want me to call your mom for you?"

She lifted her phone and said, "Call Mom."

I stood and walked to the door. "Do you want me to go?"

She shook her head and spoke into the phone, "Sorry to wake you, but—Kevin's dead," she wailed. "Uh-huh, uh-huh. Okay." She pressed a button, slid the phone in her pocket, and wiped her face with the back of her hand. "She's on her way."

I pulled a packet of Kleenex from my purse and handed them to her.

"Why do the police need to talk to me?" She extricated a tissue and blew her nose.

"They want to talk to everyone he was with tonight."

Jane stood. "Will you come with me? Please?" Her hands shook as she clutched at mine. "I've never talked to the police before. I don't know if I can do this."

"I'm not sure they'll let me stay, but I'll try. I'll show you where the detective is." We walked downstairs, through the conference room, and into the room Jay had commandeered. I rapped on the door and opened it. "I hope you don't mind if I stay, Detective Ziebold, but Jane would like support."

He looked like he was about to say no but sighed. "Fine. Come in. But let her talk." He introduced himself and asked me, "Did you tell her what happened?"

I nodded and hurried in with Jane. She sat, and I took the seat I had been in previously.

Jay opened his pad. "How long had you known the deceased?"

Jane started to cry again.

I rubbed her back and glared at Jay. "Kevin. His name was Kevin."

He cleared his throat. "How long had you known Kevin?"

"Since we were six." She sniffled. "He moved in down the street, and our mothers became best friends. We started dating junior year in high school. I went away to college but didn't date anyone else, and I don't think he did either." She gave a half-smile. "I would have heard about it from his mother. Then two months ago, we got engaged." She began to cry again. "Now, we'll never get married."

"Did Kevin do drugs?"

She shook her head. "Maybe an occasional joint but no hard drugs. His older brother died of an overdose. He said he could never do that to his mother. Oh, God. His mother—who's going to tell her?"

"A policewoman was sent to inform his parents. Tell me what happened last night."

"The class and prayers went till about nine-thirty. Then one of the instructors said there was going to be a bonfire out back. We thought it would be fun, so we went. It was kind of romantic. I guess Merry told you—" She gave me a nervous glance, "Kevin and Matt had been spiking their sodas all night, and Matt must have gone back to his room to refill his flask because they started up again. Matt slipped Trudy and me some too. It was pretty dark on the other side of the fire, so no one saw. They led us in a sing-along, and around eleven, the instructors and most of the attendees left." She coughed. "I'm sorry, but do you have any water?"

"I'll get some. Would you like anything, Detective?" I volunteered.

"Coffee, black."

I walked into the dining room, and apparently, someone had gotten the staff up because there was now a large coffee urn on the table, complete with assorted mugs. I filled a glass of water for Jane and then flipped the nozzle, so black coffee streamed and carried both to the interview room.

"Do you know what time I came back to the dorm?" Jane turned toward me as I pushed the door open with my hip.

"Midnight."

Jay took the mug from me. "Are you sure?"

"I looked at my phone—mom habit—you have kids."

"Speaking of phones, I have Kevin's, but it's password protected." Jay glanced at Jane. "You wouldn't know the password, would you?"

"Our first date. Eleven-five and my name, Jane, with a capital J." She pulled another tissue from the pack I had given her.

Jay wrote it on his pad, then took the bagged phone from his case and typed it in. He pulled up the last text: "Meet you in front in five," and pointed to the number. "Do you recognize this number?"

Jane shook her head. "It's strange he doesn't have the person in his phone book. Who was he meeting?"

The door opened with a bang, and a bottle-blonde woman who seemed to have been poured into a form-fitting loud dress rushed in. "Jane, baby! Oh, my poor little girl." She gathered Jane into a tight hug and glared at Detective Ziebold. "I can't believe the police didn't call me. Don't you need my permission to talk to her?"

"She's an adult; there's no reason for us to call. I'm assuming you're Jane's mother."

"I am. And I'm taking her with me right now. Get up, sweetie."

Jane rose.

"We could always do this down at the station. Seems a shame since I just have a few more questions." He leaned back in his seat.

Jane's mother gave a longing glance at the door.

"Just another minute or two," he said.

"Fine." She plopped down on the empty seat.

Jay stared her down. "I'll send her out when we're done."

I stood. "Since your mom's here, I may as well leave." I turned to the door.

"Who are you?" Her mother asked.

"My roommate from last night," Jane said.

Jane's mother extended her hand. "Tammi Creedy. Thanks for keeping an eye on her for me."

I shook Tammi's hand, then walked out the door and into the dining room. Attendees were milling about, grabbing coffee and food. I pulled out my phone. Eight o'clock? *How was it morning already?*

Rob handed me a cup of coffee. "You were in there a long time."

A priest approached the podium at the front of the room and tapped the microphone. It squealed, and I clapped my hands to my ears. He spoke, "Sorry. As you probably know, we've had an unfortunate incident. The police have instructed us to remain in this room until they have a chance to talk with everyone."

He bowed his head. "Let us pray. All-powerful and merciful God, we commend to you, Kevin, your servant. In your mercy and love, blot out the sins he has committed through human weakness..."

He was so young. How had he died? He seemed fine last night. Could he have had an underlying medical condition?

"Amen."

I jumped as the attendees echoed the priest.

The priest left the podium, and I turned to Rob. "They've already talked to us. Can we leave now? I'm beat."

Rob shook his head. "Jay wants to talk to me again. He thought it was suspicious that I was right on the spot after Kevin took that pill."

"He can't think you had anything to do with this."

"I guess he's being thorough. The good news is that I have a surprise for you."

"I don't know if I can take another one."

He led me through the door as a non-descript sedan pulled up. A young man hopped out with a bag in his hand. "Delivery for Jenson?"

Rob answered, "That's me," and accepted the bag.

"Food?"

"Uh-huh. I'm starving."

"Me too. Let's go to one of the picnic tables in the back." We walked around the building and settled in. I opened the bag, and yeasty goodness wafted toward me. "Bagels? Did you get pumpernickel?"

"With smoked-salmon cream cheese."

"I knew I made the right choice with you."

He handed me a to-go cup.

"Latte?"

He smiled.

I took a bite of the bagel, and he asked. "What happened in there?"

"Jane said Kevin didn't do drugs."

"So?"

"Matt said Kevin took speed, which is a drug in my book. Did that kill him, or was it something else?"

CHAPTER 4

Jenny was lying on the sofa tapping on her phone when I walked in. She sat up. "I thought you weren't coming home until tomorrow."

"Long story." I sat next to Jenny. "Someone died, so they canceled the session."

Her eyes widened. "Who?"

"No one you know. Kevin Percher."

"How old was he?"

"Twenty-two. He was Rob's roommate." I leaned against the sofa back and closed my eyes.

"An accident?" She clutched her phone.

"They're not sure what happened. Detective Ziebold has to wait for the coroner's report."

Jenny elbowed me. "So, are you going to have to do Pre-Cana again?"

"I sure hope not." Courvoisier hopped onto my lap, and I petted her, soothing my jangled nerves.

She shrugged. "What are we going to have for dinner?"

"I was up all night, so the only thing in my immediate future is a shower and a nap. Can you defrost some burgers for later?" I kissed her forehead, walked upstairs to the shower, and turned it on. *They won't make us do it again, will they?*

* * *

After dinner, Jenny left with Jacob, and Rob and I sat in the backyard. The annuals were a tad peaked because it had been so dry, so I used the shower nozzle on the hose to give them a drink.

"I've been thinking about what you said." Rob looked pensive. "What if there was more than speed in the pill he took?"

"The police will know soon enough because they have the other pill—the one Kevin offered Matt. I stretched to reach the hanging baskets and winced.

Rob leaped to his feet. "Let me do that. In fact, I'm going to install a drip system, so you don't have to remember. I'll set it up tomorrow night."

"I'd appreciate it." I handed him the hose.

The back gate opened, and Ed and Andy strolled in, a bottle of champagne in hand. Andy said, "Felicitations. We haven't yet celebrated with you."

Rob turned off the water. "I'll get glasses."

They pulled over chairs, and Ed unwrapped the foil from the cork and popped it. Rob returned, and Ed poured. Andy handed me a glass, then Rob.

Ed raised his. "To the happy couple." We touched glasses and sipped.

"So nice of you." I leaned back in the chair.

"We were talking tonight and realized how little fanfare there's been." Andy leaned toward me. "But we're going to correct it with a party. Next Saturday night."

"You don't have to do that," Rob said.

"I know." Ed grinned. "But we are."

The rest of the evening passed uneventfully. Rob left late, and Sunday dawned far too early. The celebrations were fun, but a sleepless Friday night and a late-night Saturday meant I was operating on a serious sleep deficit. The cats crowded underfoot as I made my way to the can opener. They loved Sundays as it was wet cat food day. Viewing my dwindling supply of cans, I had a sneaking suspicion that, while I had been in Phoenix, they may have coerced their caretakers into a more frequent rotation.

Cats fed, I turned my attention to coffee and a piece of toast spread with butter and apricot jam. As I flipped through my emails, a text came from Rob: "Ten-thirty mass?"

"Yes." I popped the last of the bread into my mouth, grabbed the mug, and headed upstairs.

As I passed Jenny's door, I knocked and opened it. She was face down on the bed, snoring softly. I shook her shoulder. "Jenny?"

She swatted at me. "What?"

"Rob and I are going to Mass. Do you want to come?"

"Noon. I'll go at noon." She pulled the sheet over her head.

I set the alarm on her phone. "Don't hit snooze, or you'll be late."

She mumbled something as I shut the door.

Feeling somewhat more human, I hopped in the shower and then got dressed. The doorbell rang, so I hurried down the steps and peered through the window. Wanda and Mac. Mac's silver hair gleamed in the sun, and Wanda's short blonde bob looked perfect as usual. *What on earth were they doing here?*

I stretched my lips into what I hoped would pass for a smile and opened the door. "Good morning. I'd love to visit, but Rob and I are due at church for mass."

Mac laughed. "He mentioned it to Wanda last night, and we decided to surprise you both by joining you."

"At mass?" Wanda and Mac were more holiday Catholics.

"Of course." Wanda stepped past me, sank onto the sofa, and crossed her legs. "We'll go to brunch afterward. Doesn't that sound nice?"

"Uh-huh."

* * *

I led the way down the church aisle, looking for room for the four of us, and ducked into a pew three from the front. Patty and her crew were in the second row across the aisle. As she turned to shush her youngest, her eyes met mine and then widened as she saw Wanda. She mouthed, "What?"

I shook my head and continued moving into the pew. Wanda sat next to me, Mac next to her, and Rob on the aisle.

Wanda turned to Mac and nodded toward Father Tom. "We'll stop for a moment and talk with him on the way out. I have a few things I want to ask him."

"Few t-t-things?" I sputtered.

"Shush, dear. They're about to start." She faced forward.

At the end of the service, we filed out. Wanda slipped past Rob, who was chatting with Andy, and made a beeline to Father Tom. Her foot tapped as she waited for him to finish speaking with a parishioner. Mac had caught up with her and put his arm around her waist.

I interrupted Rob's conversation, "I think we have a problem." I pointed toward Wanda and Father Tom, who was now leaning toward her and nodding.

Rob and Andy turned, and Andy started to laugh. Rob charged down the aisle, and I followed in his wake. Father Tom waved us toward him. "I'm so pleased you decided on a bigger wedding. You need to get cracking on dates though."

Wanda said, "The first Saturday next June would work best for us. We'll be back from Saint Tropez then, and it will be before we leave for Japan." She checked her phone. "Yes. That date would be splendid. I'll have my social secretary call with all the details."

Father Tom's mouth hung open. "I don't have the calendar in front of me, but I'm fairly certain we're booked on that date. June's our busy season."

"Don't you worry about it. I'll work my magic." She turned to us. "Good. That's settled. Let's go to brunch. Father, you're welcome to join us."

He shook his head as he backed away. "Unfortunately, I have other plans." He looked grateful another parishioner was waiting.

Rob spit, "Mother, we're handling this. We don't need your help."

Her laugh trilled. "Don't be silly. You didn't even have a date." She waltzed out the door with Mac behind her.

Rob groaned. "That woman."

I grabbed his arm. "Not here. Let's go. We'll talk to them at brunch."

During the car ride, I could practically hear Rob's teeth grinding. Mac gave a running commentary on cute new cats that had been dropped off at his veterinarian clinic and how he was trying to get Wanda to let him adopt one.

She placed her hand on his arm. "Mac, we've been through this. They shed, and I'm afraid I may be allergic. You should have heard me cough when I stayed at Merry's this spring, and those were short hairs."

I rubbed my forehead. Wanda hadn't coughed once at my house. She just didn't want pets to interfere with her perfect life and décor.

Wanda continued, "We already have two dogs, horses, and fish in the pond. What do we need cats for?"

"Companionship," I muttered under my breath.

"What was that, dear?" Wanda turned. "You have an awful habit of mumbling. It's strange for someone like yourself who's in business. You may want to work with a speech therapist."

I laughed and then covered it with a cough. "Thanks for your concern."

Mac parked and then came around to open Wanda's door. She swept past us toward the host stand. "Reservation for MacNamara."

Rob put his arm around me and whispered, "I'll handle this."

I nodded and said to Wanda, "I haven't been here before." A wall of glass framed the picture-perfect golf course beyond, and large crystal chandeliers studded the white ceiling, offset by gray, grass-cloth-covered walls with chunky gold sconces. It looked like an advertisement for excess.

"Wait until you see the ballroom. This is understated compared to that."

My stomach churned. "Why would we see the ballroom?"

"That's where your reception will be." She patted my hand. "I have a tour set up for after brunch."

Heat flooded my face.

The host said, "Mr. and Mrs. MacNamara, so good to see you again. Your table is ready." He led us to a four-top near the windows, held out Wanda's chair, and then handed us menus. "Enjoy."

Rob leaned across the table. "Mother, we've had this conversation before. Merry and I are having a small wedding, and it will be well before June."

"No can do," she tutted. "We have a hectic travel schedule."

I lifted the large menu and shrank in my seat.

"No need to go into this now." Mac beckoned the wine steward. "We'll have the Perrier Jouet Belle Epoque."

I stifled a gasp. Patty and I were buying wine in Phoenix, and she had pointed out the pretty, flowered bottle in the locked case. It was the same champagne Mac ordered, and it was nearly four hundred dollars at the store. And with this place's markup... I peered over the menu.

Rob's face was red. "Mac—"

"Let's have champagne, celebrate your upcoming union, and then talk details. I'm sure your mother wants to hear what you have to say."

I slid down again.

"Sit up, Merry. What on earth are you doing?" Wanda asked.

I put down the menu and straightened my spine. "Just looking at the menu. What would you recommend?"

"She'll say any fish broiled plain without butter. Where's the fun in that?" Mac's laugh was low and hearty.

Wanda shot him a look.

He lifted her hand and kissed it. "My beautiful bride."

Her expression softened, and she turned back to me. "Now that you have your wedding coming up, you should pay more attention to what you eat. I suggest a little light protein, no oil or butter, and above all, no carbs."

"Merry's perfect the way she is." Rob put his arm around me. "Mac, what would you suggest?"

Mac put his menu down. "I always have the eggs benedict. The hollandaise is terrific, and they give you asparagus on the side, which makes it a healthy dish." His laugh burbled.

The wine steward poured champagne into Mac's glass. He tasted it and nodded. "Thanks."

She poured champagne into the rest of the flutes.

Mac stood and lifted his glass. "To Rob and Merry, may your life together hold adventure, happiness, and health."

I sipped the wine. It was a riot of fruit, citrus, and bubbles. "This is lovely."

"It is, isn't it?" Mac studied the glass.

"Thank you for the toast and the champagne," Rob said.

The waiter came to the table, and Rob and I ordered the eggs benedict. I handed him my menu and took another sip of champagne.

"I missed out on children, so it's exciting to have both of you in my life. And Jenny, of course. My first grandchild." Mac's eyes misted. "Family's important." He coughed. "I don't want to be indelicate, but are you planning on having more children?"

I almost spit out the champagne.

"Oh, Mac," Wanda chided, "Merry's too old. Aren't you, dear?"

"That's it. Merry, we're leaving." Rob stood.

Mac said, "She didn't mean it, did you, Wanda?"

"It was a question—either she is or isn't." She sipped her champagne.

I got up, looking at the rest of my drink with longing. "Thanks so much for the champagne, Mac."

Rob stalked from the room, and I trailed behind him, finally yanking on his arm. "Slow down."

He stopped. "Sorry. She gets me so riled."

"It wasn't your biological clock she was questioning." I laughed as we walked outside. "Um. I hate to remind you, but Mac drove."

* * *

"She really asked if you were too old to have kids? I can't believe she thought that was normal." Patty kicked off her flip-flops and put her feet on the footstool.

"Nothing about her is normal. And that wasn't the truly tragic part."

Patty's eyebrow arched.

"I left the champagne in my glass."

Patty laughed. "At least you're taking it well."

"She's not my mother. And Mac is darling." Drambuie walked under my foot, hoping to be petted. I obliged and rubbed her back. "What if we can't have kids? Will Rob be disappointed he married me?"

"What did he say?"

"That he'd be over the moon if we did, but that if we weren't able to, he'd be happy sharing Jenny." I picked up the cat and put her on my lap.

"Sounds like you have your answer."

"Maybe. Hard to know how anyone really feels. Isn't that right, Drambuie?" I gave her a thorough rub down.

"Especially men. Speaking of which, I'm bringing spinach dip to Ed and Andy's party on Saturday. What are you taking?"

"I'm one of the guests of honor. They told me I didn't need to bring anything."

"Uh-huh."

"So, I'm bringing a cheesecake topped with blueberries and strawberries."

＊ ＊ ＊

Rob called up the stairs. "Merry, if you take much longer, the party will be over by the time we get there."

Jenny put the curling iron down and yelled, "Two more minutes."

"Thanks for doing my hair." I smiled at her in the mirror.

She picked up another strand and wound it. "No problem. I know how it ends up when you do it." She chuckled.

"How do I look?" I lifted my purse from the bed. I wore a midnight-blue chiffon dress with a fitted bodice I bought because it highlighted my best assets and hid the not-so-perfect ones.

"Old."

"Jenny!"

"Beautiful and nearly as young as me," she laughed.

I kissed her. "I've been thinking about your role in the wedding. I want you to walk me down the aisle, and, instead of giving me away, I want you to welcome Rob to our family. Deal?"

"Deal." She hugged me and then turned toward the door. "I'll go down first. That way, you can make an entrance." She ran down the steps.

I followed at a more sedate pace. Rob met me at the bottom of the stairs. "I'm such a lucky man." He bent to kiss me on the lips.

I pointed to my cheek. "Don't mess the makeup. Jenny, would you get the cheesecake from the fridge?"

She took out the carrier and left with Jacob.

Rob slipped his hand through mine. "Ready?"

We sauntered across the alley and up Ed and Andy's back steps to the deck. Classical music played, and luminaries lit the walk as daisies, hydrangeas, and roses perfumed the air. We strode through the back door.

Ed turned from the stove. "It's about time. The guests are going to be arriving in—" he checked his watch "—five minutes."

Andy took the cheesecake from Jenny. "I'll put this in the garage fridge. There's no more room in this one; people were dropping off dishes all afternoon. Don't let me forget it."

"What can I do?" I asked Ed.

He looked me up and down and whistled. "In that dress? Honey, get into the living room and make yourself a drink—I'm afraid I'll spill something on it."

The party was in full swing when Wanda, Mac, Elizabeth, and two young women I didn't know walked in the front door. Elizabeth's long blonde hair was in a neat chignon, and she wore a navy-blue pantsuit paired with a cream-colored blouse. Andy ran forward to greet them. "I'm happy you were able to make it. Elizabeth, lovely to see you again." He gave her a quick peck on the cheek.

Rob and I made our way across the room. He embraced his sister, and then I hugged her. She said, "Sorry we're late. Plane delays."

Mac cleared his throat. "These are my two nieces, Ann and Amy MacNamara." Ann had blonde hair and wore a short off-pink summer dress, and Amy looked like she had stepped out of an eighty's goth movie. Black hair, black eyeshadow, black attire, all topped with a skull earing.

Rob and I shook their hands.

Wanda stepped forward. "I know you'll get along great. They'll be in your wedding."

My mouth dropped, and Rob's face grew red. I clutched his arm and whispered, "This is our party. Let's enjoy it and our friends. We can deal with them later."

"You're right." His teeth unclenched.

I smiled at the girls. "Thanks for coming to the party."

Andy said, "Let me show you where everything is." The group walked toward the kitchen.

Elizabeth whispered in my ear, "We'll talk later. Remind me to get my suitcase out of their car." She followed them.

Jay was leaning against the wall, chatting with Barbara, his wife. I said, "Let's see if Jay's found out what happened to your roommate."

Jay shook Rob's hand. "Congratulations, you're a lucky man."

"Thanks for coming." I embraced Barbara.

"Wouldn't have missed it. We're so happy for you both."

"Jay, we wondered if you heard anything from the coroner?" Rob asked.

Barbara's eyes widened. "I think I'll check out the dessert table." She wandered in that direction.

Jay said, "Bring me something chocolate." He sighed. "So sad. The kid was young."

"He was." I rubbed my arms.

"Coroner said he had a mix of booze and methamphetamines in his system. But that's not what killed him. That was something else. Fentanyl."

I shuddered. "Don't you have to inject that?"

CHAPTER 5

Elizabeth buttered toast. "You're not going to like this. I had a text from Mom last night. She and Mac are having an impromptu luncheon at their place today to celebrate your engagement. It's at one-thirty."

"That's fine," I said.

Jenny blinked. "What?"

"You don't have to go, sweetie. I'll tell them you had plans you couldn't change."

"I mean, why aren't you upset? Normally you'd have chowed down three antacids by now."

"I prayed last night and decided I was not going to let this get to me. This is Rob's first wedding, and it's not surprising his mother wants to make a fuss. I don't want to cause a rift between them."

Elizabeth chuckled. "She's certainly been to enough of hers. I don't know why she's worried about Rob's."

"If she wants to make this a spectacle, I'm okay with it. It's nice she cares enough to do this for Rob. Speaking of which, did she tell him about lunch?"

"He got the same text I did."

"Good." I swung my foot, and Courvoisier leaned into it.

"Maybe I should go. You need the support." Jenny gulped orange juice.

I waved my hand. "If you want to come, I'm sure Wanda would be thrilled, but it's up to you."

Rob opened the back door. "Coffee? I could trade donuts for a cup." He held out a box.

"Already made. Grab a cup."

Jenny took the box from him and opened it. "French toast crullers. My favorite." She put one on a plate, sat back down, and passed Elizabeth the box. Then she blushed. "I'm sorry, that was rude. I should have let you choose first."

"I don't think that would have been my pick. Besides, I shouldn't have one—" Her hand hovered, and she looked at Rob. "Raspberry filled?"

"Of course."

"My nemesis." She put it on a plate.

I took a plain donut, broke off a piece, and dunked it in my coffee. "Thanks."

"Um—did Elizabeth tell you about lunch?" Rob poured cream in his mug and sat.

"Yep. I'll be there. Jury's still out on Jenny."

"I'm going." Jenny's foot swung as she took another bite.

"Attire?" I asked.

Elizabeth said, "Summer casual. To Mom, that means sun dresses for us, polo shirt and chinos for Rob."

"Uh, Merry, do you have a moment? In the living room?" Rob motioned in that direction with his head.

I popped the last of the donut in my mouth, got to my feet, and grabbed my mug. "Sure."

We sat on the sofa, and he rubbed his neck. "We don't need to go. I know I've been unable to get Mother to shut up about this, but I really will get through to her."

"It's okay. If it means so much to Wanda, we'll let her handle the wedding."

"I want you to have what you want." He kissed my hand.

51

"It's one day. The important thing to me is the rest of our lives. And I want to spend all of mine with you."

He leaned back on the sofa. "The only thing I care about is timing. I'm not waiting until June to marry you. I called Belinda. She said the Friday night before Thanksgiving is open. I booked it. Mother's going to have to work around us."

"A November wedding."

"The longest I'm willing to wait."

I kissed him. "Me too."

* * *

The "small" lunch was held in Mac's barn, where he and Wanda had married in the spring. Fifty people milled about.

"How on earth did she get this many people to come on short notice?" I surveyed the crowd.

Elizabeth shrugged. "Favors, free food, and drinks."

A waiter carried a full tray of champagne glasses, and I snagged one. "May as well enjoy it."

"I'm going to go see the horses." Jenny took a flute of orange juice and walked toward the stables.

Mac waved from across the room and made his way toward us. "The guests of honor. Welcome."

Wanda made a beeline toward us with a small bespectacled man who had come from a side door at the house. She said, "Finally. I almost thought you weren't coming. This is Martin, my new social secretary. He'll be handling most of the details of your wedding." She walked off to greet arriving guests and left him with us.

Even though it was close to eighty-five degrees, Martin wore a navy suit and vest and carried a folio. "Pleasure." He extended a damp hand with fingernails bitten to the quick.

I hesitated for a second and then shook it. "I look forward to working with you."

"Nice to meet you," Elizabeth said, and Rob nodded.

Martin extracted several pages from the folio and handed one to each of us. "Here is the schedule for the afternoon. Right now, everyone is having drinks; we'll send them in to sit at two, where Mac and Elizabeth will make their remarks, introduce you, etc. Then luncheon, and after that gifts, favors for the guests, and we're done." He flipped the folio shut. "Any questions?"

I gulped. "Gifts? Favors?"

"The gifts are for you and Rob, the favors—" He pointed to tables with decorative gold and silver bags tied with matching ribbon. "—I've already taken care of. Anything else?"

Rob shook his head.

"Good." Martin glanced at his watch. "Showtime. Follow me." He carved a path to the front of the barn, and we hurried to keep pace.

"Merry, you're here, Rob, then Elizabeth. And—" He frowned as he consulted his chart. "There's a daughter, isn't there? Jenny?"

"She's by the stables," I said.

"But we're going to start."

"I'll get her."

"We need her here." He sounded like a teapot about to boil.

I took a deep breath and enunciated every word. "I will get her and be right back."

I walked away, practicing deep breathing. *Maybe I should keep walking.* Jenny was petting a deep chestnut horse's nose and talking to one of the stable hands. "Jenny, they're about to start lunch." I paused. "That's a big horse. What kind is it?"

"American Quarter Horse. Nice and docile." She petted the horse one last time. "Need to wash my hands."

We walked back into the barn, and I pointed to the restrooms. "We're in the front."

She nodded.

I walked back to the table. Mac and Wanda chatted with Rob and Elizabeth, and Martin hurried toward me. "Where is she?"

"She'll be here in a moment."

He motioned to the waiters, and they began shepherding the guests to their seats.

I sank into mine and sipped champagne. *I can get through this.* Jenny sat next to me.

Martin shook his head. "Jenny, you're over there, between Elizabeth and Ann."

"Does it matter?" I asked.

"Wanda is next to you, and Mac is next to her."

Jenny stood. "I'll move, no biggie." She sat next to Elizabeth.

Mac tapped his glass with a knife to get everyone's attention. "Who knew we'd be back again so soon to celebrate another joyous occasion, the upcoming marriage of my son-in-law, Rob, and his accomplished fiancée, Merry March." There was polite applause.

"Rob's a good man, and he's part of a noble profession— independent reporting. Although I've only known him a short while, he's brought joy to his mother and me by solving the murder of her previous husband and removing the cloud hanging over our heads. Merry worked hard on that too, and we are thankful." Mac nodded at me. "And now we have a new grandchild, Jenny, who's already showing great interest in one of my happiest pastimes, my horses." He lifted his hand, and Rob, Jenny, and I stood. "Wedding details are still being hammered out, so keep your ears open." He chuckled. "And now, my wonderful bride, Wanda."

Wanda stood, walked into Mac's embrace, and kissed his cheek. "Thanks, Mac. I am pleased that my son is *finally* getting married." She paused for the expected chuckle. "And to a mature woman like Merry.

Although I never thought I'd have a granddaughter as old as Jenny at my age—" She patted her blonde chignon. "—I'm excited to have her join my family. Would you raise your glasses?" The crowd complied. "To Merry, Rob, and Jenny."

Mac boomed, "Here, here."

Everyone drank.

"Enjoy the luncheon."

We sat, and waiters delivered trays to the tables. Plates were placed in front of us, and then cloches removed with practiced hands, revealing crab cakes with a remoulade sauce, new potatoes sprinkled with chives and parsley, and tender stalks of asparagus.

I cut a piece of asparagus. "Thank you for your kind comments, Mac. We appreciate it."

Wanda coughed.

"Oh, and yours, as well, Wanda."

Jenny smirked and then quickly covered her lips with her napkin.

"We haven't had a chance to get to know each other," Rob said to Ann and Amy. "How are you related to Mac?"

"Mac's our father's older brother. There's just the two of them, so they've always been close," Ann answered.

Mac nodded. "He's my best friend. He would have been here today, but he's out of the country."

"What do you do?" Jenny asked Ann.

"I'm a librarian."

"I love to read. Librarians are always helpful in suggesting books I might like," I said.

Elizabeth nodded at Amy. "And you?"

Mac laughed. "Amy's our perennial student. How many times have you changed majors?"

Amy sunk lower in her chair, and her face turned as red as the cherry napkins. "Four. But my father said I couldn't change again. He wants me to graduate next spring."

"You must have a lot of interests." Elizabeth smiled.

"It makes me a better, more knowledgeable person." Amy's jaw jutted.

"I'm sure that's true," I buttered a piece of roll. "What's your major now?"

"Marine biology."

"You must love to swim," Rob said.

"Not especially. But I love to watch everything underwater."

*　*　*

"What are we going to do with all these gifts? Both of us have our places filled with stuff." I surveyed the pile by my front door.

Rob chuckled. "There must have been something you wanted."

I wandered over and picked up a cookbook. "This looks interesting. But I wish Wanda and Mac had told everyone not to bring gifts or had selected a favorite charity for people to contribute to." I turned. "We should do that for the wedding."

Rob patted the seat next to him. "We should."

"Animals. Or people. Maybe that chef's charity—the guy who feeds people in disasters," Elizabeth offered.

"Good suggestions. Maybe we could have a few options." I plopped down on the sofa next to Rob.

"What time does your plane leave tomorrow?" Rob asked Elizabeth.

"Seven. I have surgery at noon. I arranged for a car so no one would have to get up early." Elizabeth examined the pile, picked up a pair of elephant bookends, and raised her eyebrow.

"Cancel it. I'll take you."

"No need."

He stared at her.

"All right." She sat and typed into her phone. "Done."

I laughed. "You gave in pretty easily."

"I know that look."

Rob moved forward on the sofa. "I have an important question for you, Elizabeth. Would you be my best man?"

"Do I have to wear a tux?" Elizabeth said with a cheeky smile.

He laughed. "We'll work that out later."

"I'm so glad you said yes. It will make the ceremony perfect." I smiled. "Now that's settled, do you mind if I ask you a medical question?"

"Go right ahead."

"Fentanyl. How deadly is it?"

Her eyebrow rose. "Personal interest?"

"A young man died from it at our Pre-Cana class."

"That's too bad." Elizabeth frowned. "We see more overdoses every day. Like so many medications, it was created for a good reason: to relieve the severe pain of advanced cancer patients. But now it's also made illegally, and that's the problem."

"How powerful is it?" Rob slid his arm around me.

"According to the Centers for Disease Control, fifty to one hundred times more powerful than morphine."

He whistled.

"Today, on the black market, it's often mixed with cocaine or heroin. It's supposed to increase the 'high.' And it's not as if the dealers disclose it has been incorporated into the customer's drug of choice."

"Why do they add it?" I frowned.

"Cost. Takes a tiny bit to get a bigger high, but it's a lot more opioid than most people's bodies are used to." Elizabeth shuddered.

"Do you have to inject it?" Rob asked.

"It's sold to the dealer in powder form. So, you could inject it, inhale it, drink it, even put it on your skin. It's powerful." Elizabeth rubbed her right foot.

"How quickly would someone die after coming in contact with it?"

"Depends on the strength and how adapted the person's body is to opioids. Could be right away or could take a while."

I leaned back against the sofa. "So, someone might not have known they were taking it."

"Correct."

"Is there a way to save them, an antidote?" Rob asked.

"Naloxone may bring the person back. But with current demand, it's become expensive."

Rob's face paled. "If I had that, I could have saved him."

"I'd be surprised if the EMTs didn't give it to him. But by the time they got there, it was probably too late." Elizabeth picked up the cookbook I had gotten and leafed through it.

I grabbed Rob's arm. "That was probably the shot they gave him."

✳ ✳ ✳

The next day at work, I couldn't get what Rob and Elizabeth had said out of my mind. *Should I have naloxone at work? What if someone here overdosed? And how would I know?* People allergic to bees carry EpiPens. But they usually have enough time to inject themselves. The people who overdose from fentanyl need someone else to do it for them.

And Jenny. What a scary world for her to grow up in. What if someone slipped her something? If I could blanket her in those plastic bubble wrap sheets, I would.

Cheryl rapped at the door and walked in as I was downing an antacid. She frowned. "You seem to be taking quite a lot of those."

"Don't start. I get enough of that from my daughter."

"Your new clients will be here any minute. I wanted to give you a heads up because I know you've been distracted."

"Thanks."

She shut the door after her, and I pulled the clients' file and studied it. *Need to focus.*

A few hours and client meetings later, I turned off my computer and meandered to meet Patty and Jenny at C'est Magnifique, the town clothing boutique run by a sister duo, April and Sandy Poole. They were walking advertisements for their upscale shop. Both striking strawberry blondes, their clothes were always impeccable. April met us at the door in a simple white sheath with a plum rope sash tied around her narrow waist. "The bride! We're so excited you're going to trust us with your wedding dress."

She poured a glass of champagne for Patty and me. Jenny had sparkling apple cider in a flute. I chuckled. "If I had known how much free bubbly I'd get, I would have gotten engaged ages ago."

"Small matter of annulment." Patty nudged me.

"Oh, that. Before we get started, I have an important question to ask. Jenny is going to walk me down the aisle, so the matron of honor position is open. Is that something you'd consider?"

She lifted her glass. "Wouldn't have it any other way."

I hugged her.

April had lined a free-standing clothing rod with selections. "You said you're not looking for a traditional gown."

"Been there, done the lace."

Jenny flicked through the choices. "Definitely not, maybe, a possibility, love it. Ooh." She turned and held out a light peach-colored dress reminiscent of the flapper age but without the fringe. It was a simple, long-sleeved sheath with a waist that sat at the hip.

"Won't that accentuate my problem area?" I caressed the fabric. "So soft."

Jenny moved it and several others to the maybe rack.

Patty combed through Jenny's selections. She picked up one. "Not with her hair, this is nice, I like this brocade—"

I sat in one of the Tiffany-blue armchairs. "It's lovely to let someone else do the work."

"Don't get too comfortable. You'll need to try these on." Patty peered over the rack.

Sandy held up a few more, "We also have these."

Once Jenny and Patty had agreed on several dresses, I stood, moved closer, and whittled the selections to four. April moved them to a new larger changing room, which included a lavender tufted bench. I slid on the first dress. It was the peach number Jenny liked. I twisted right, then left. *Maybe. Though, to be honest, any dress would be better than the poofy monstrosity I wore for my wedding with Drew. These choices were so much more sophisticated.* I opened the door and waltzed out to the three larger mirrors in the back. Jenny and Patty sat in matching chairs, and Jenny said, "I knew that would look good on you."

I turned. "It makes my hips look big. I'm not sure."

"It looks lovely, but I don't want you thinking about your hips on your wedding day. Next." Patty waved her hand, shooing me back to the dressing room.

I put on a more elaborate dress with a fitted bodice of muted pastels, teal, rose, and cream encapsulated by silver thread. The floor-length bottom was cream chiffon. I loved the dress but wasn't sure it spelled wedding. I sashayed from the dressing room, twirled, and giggled.

Patty and Jenny applauded. Jenny stood and said, "That's it. That's the dress."

Patty motioned for me to turn again. "More slowly."

I obliged.

She nodded. "That's the dress. May need to take it in at the waist." She stood and showed Sandy the spot, and Sandy pinned it.

"Are you sure? I have two more to try on."

60

"No need. That's the dress." Patty smiled.

My mouth dropped. I was getting married. Again. I sank onto the chair.

"Wrinkles. Get up," Jenny squealed,

I leaped to my feet. "I'll take it off."

"I'll help you take it off. I don't want you punctured by pins." Sandy went into the dressing room with me and carefully lifted the dress. "I'll have the alterations done later in the week and will text when it's ready."

"Do you think it's the dress?" I asked.

"It is. You looked beautiful in it." She put the dress on a hanger and left the room.

I donned my slacks and shell and took a deep breath. I was ready for this.

✳ ✳ ✳

"What do you mean you selected your wedding dress?" Martin tapped something that sounded like a clipboard. "Wanda wanted you to get your dress from Dreams Realized Boutique in the city. She said they have the best dresses."

I held the phone away from my ear. "I support my local shops. They're starting to get into the wedding business and had lovely selections."

"Nothing to be done now. Send me a picture of the dress, and I'll forward it to the boutique. They can get going on bridesmaid selections. We'll travel there, and Wanda will accompany you." He sighed. "She's not going to be happy with this turn of events."

"I have more bad news. We're going to get the bridesmaid dresses at the same boutique I bought my dress from, C'est Magnifique."

His groan was audible. "I'll let her know." The phone clicked.

I practiced deep breathing, and after a few moments, my shoulders relaxed, and I was able to turn back to work tasks. After making calls to the leads accumulated over the past week, I opened my door and beckoned to Cheryl. "When you have a moment."

She rounded her desk and joined me in the office. We sat.

"Let's go over the next few weeks. They're going to be busy since I'm taking Jenny to visit schools. She has appointments at three this week here. And then another four here." I pointed to the calendar. "So please don't schedule anything important then."

Cheryl jotted a note. "Got it."

"On Thursday, I'll need to leave early. Patrick is having a small service to bury his mother, so don't schedule anything after three."

"Uh-huh."

"I'd also like you to send an email encouraging people to check around their foundations. It's been so dry, and the dirt's gotten cracked. If we get a big rain, we could have issues with flooding."

She nodded. "Anything else?"

"That's it for now."

Cheryl stood and then sat back down. She put her pad on the desk. "Did you hear what happened? Another kid died."

"Accident? Kids drive too fast."

"They're saying it might have been drugs."

"That's terrible. That's what happened to that kid at Pre-Cana." I doodled. "It seems like that's happening more lately. When we were in Phoenix, the coroner was backed up because of the number of fentanyl cases. It's sad."

She stood. "Door open or shut?"

"Shut." I turned back to my computer, pulled up a spreadsheet, and began to work.

Rob texted me at four: "I'll pick up dinner."

I sent him a smiley emoji, packed a few things I needed to work on at home, and headed out.

Cheryl flagged me down to hand me a folder. "Here's the information you wanted on customers with approaching birthdays."

"Thanks." I stuffed it into my briefcase. "I'll get those cards done tonight."

The sun was still high in the sky when I exited. That made it a bit hot, but I was okay with the long evenings.

CHAPTER 6

Andy fell into step with me. "Walk you home? I decided to play hooky since it was so nice out."

"You don't usually close this early."

"I told Ed it was too nice for me to stay inside any longer."

"So, you left him there?" I laughed.

"Every man for himself. I plan on sitting in the shade on the back porch, drinking a tall cold one, and reading my book."

"Sounds like a plan. Rob's bringing an unspecified dinner home. Would you like to join us? We'll eat around six."

"Way to sell it. Yes, I'm up for mystery dinner at six. Ed won't be home till nine."

I texted Rob: "One more for dinner."

We turned into my driveway, and I peeled off through the gate.

"See you at six." Andy continued through to the alley and his house beyond.

I put my briefcase under the stool by the counter, turned the oven on warm, washed my hands, and began to pull things from the refrigerator for a salad.

Jenny walked in the back door, tennis racket in hand. She lifted a banana from the fruit bowl and peeled it. "Starving. What's for dinner?"

"Not sure. Rob's bringing it."

"How do you know we need that?" She pointed to the lettuce I had begun to clean.

"Salads are a great accompaniment to any meal."

"Health freak." She walked past to the living room, eating the banana.

"Dinner is at six."

Some form of mumbling indicated she might have heard me.

Salad made, I tucked the bowl into the refrigerator, put water in a pail, grabbed my clippers, and walked into the backyard. I held the door with my hip, and the cats ran through the opening. Tea roses lined the back fence. I snipped Queen Elizabeth's delicate pink blooms, JFK's clean white, and Ingrid Bergman's daring red. Daisies were next, a few sweet pea, blue balloon flowers, and the mottled fronds from calla lilies to fill in. I hummed as I worked, and when my pail was full, I headed to the house.

I decided on a rectangular vase, filled it, and made short work of the arrangement, giving everything a fresh cut. As I put the last flower into the vessel, Rob walked in the door and lifted the bag in his left hand, which was emblazoned with the Flash Fried Poultry logo. "Dinner." And then the one in his right from Delightful Bites. "Dessert."

I pointed toward the oven. "Stick the stuff that needs to be warm there and dessert in the fridge."

He did and then walked over for a kiss. "Wine?"

"Please."

Rob took a bottle of Chardonnay from the wine refrigerator, opened it, and poured two glasses. "Who's the dinner guest?"

"Andy. He's playing hooky."

"Where's Ed?"

"Working."

Rob laughed. "I'd rather be Andy." He handed me a glass of wine.

"Thanks. Me too."

There was a rap at the back door, and I swung it open. "Right on time."

Detective Ziebold smiled. "I didn't know you were expecting me. I have a few more questions. I hope this isn't a bad time."

Rob lifted his glass. "Wine? Beer?"

"Wouldn't say no to coffee."

I took a pod and inserted it into the machine. While it brewed, I asked, "What's up, Jay?"

"There's been another death. It was Matt Logan."

My eyes widened. "Pre-Cana Matt? The guy at dinner and the one who was hanging out that night with Kevin Percher? He had a flask at the table, but he didn't seem the type to do drugs."

"It was." Jay took the coffee mug from me. "Thanks."

"I can't believe it. He was so young. How weird is it that two people meet at a table at Pre-Cana, and now they're both dead?"

Andy walked through the back door. "Let the eating commence." He pulled up short when he saw our visitor. "Decided to join us for dinner, Detective? Or are you here on official business?"

I poured more wine. "Official. Another guy who was at our table at the Pre-Cana class died, Matt Logan."

"How do you two always get mixed up in these things?" Andy retrieved another glass, held it out, and nodded to Rob. "Come to think of it, maybe you should be nervous. You're the only man from that table who's still alive."

"Don't be silly." A shiver ran down my spine, and I turned to Jay. "We don't have to worry, do we?"

"You're not in the habit of taking drugs, are you, Rob?" Jay asked.

Rob shook his head.

"You don't need to worry, Merry. At least not about that." Jay took a sip of coffee.

"Wait. Did you say Logan?" Andy turned toward me.

I nodded. "Matt."

"I have regulars named Logan. Great taste. I know they have a son." He rubbed the back of his neck. "I sure hope it wasn't their kid." He looked at Jay. "Do you know where they live?"

He nodded. "That big white house with the columns past route 23 near the county line."

"That's them. How horrible." Andy grimaced.

"Didn't mean to upset your dinner plans." Jay crossed his legs. "Rob, are you sure you didn't see anyone else near the room or driving away before you went to the game room?"

"I wasn't near the front of the building. I told you, I was looking for a book and saw the sign for the activities room, so I went upstairs, and that's where I found Matt and poor Kevin."

Jay made a note in his book. "It's more than a little suspicious how quickly you got there. And now the only witness is dead."

I stood. "Are you saying you think Rob killed them?"

"May have been an overdose, plain and simple. But we don't know where they got the tainted drugs. It's a big coincidence. That's all I'm saying." Jay stood and gave Rob a hard stare. "But just in case, until we know what happened, it's best you don't leave town."

✳ ✳ ✳

Patrick's face was pinched as he said farewell to his mother. When she died in Phoenix, Patrick decided to make Helen's final resting place in Hopeful. We had tried to talk him into having a larger service, but he wanted to keep it to his family and mine. Father Tom intoned a prayer as Helen's urn was placed into the small vault. Patty's kids had drawn pictures of birds taking flight, and her youngest gave up one of his prized cars to keep her company. Patty gently laid them next to the urn in the box, and then with a nod from Patrick, the respectful mausoleum worker locked the vault. We gathered around for another prayer and then left for my house.

Rob and Patrick grilled steaks, Cindy and Jenny retrieved tomatoes for salad from the garden, and Patty put a movie in for the younger kids to watch. I worked on mashed potatoes as Patty set the table. She said, "Thanks for having us to dinner."

"We had to do something. Her funeral mass in Phoenix was lovely, but this marks her final resting place." I nodded toward Patrick through the window. "How's he doing?"

"Pretty good, all things considered. It's helped to have the kids around and all their activities. Keeps us hopping. We're going to try and take time at Christmas or New Year's with Patrick's half-brother at the Phoenix house. It'll be the first time we meet his kids." She paused. "How's Rob feeling, now that he's Jay's number one drug-dealing suspect?"

I put aluminum foil over the mashed potatoes and set them on the table. "I still can't believe he's serious."

"But he told Rob not to leave town."

I squirmed. "It's so hard to believe. Jay knows us. We'd never do anything like that."

"Rob's been all over the world and to some unsavory places. He could have contacts."

"You think Rob's a drug dealer?" My mouth dropped.

Patty hugged me. "Don't be silly. I'm just looking at it from Jay's point of view."

"Well, stop that." I sat on the kitchen stool. "Two guys in such quick succession. It makes me wonder."

"Not every death is a murder."

Patrick held the door, and Rob presented a pile of what looked like grilled-to-perfection glistening meat. Patty called, "Dinner," and the next few minutes were dominated by children lining up at the sink to wash their hands. We finally sat, bowed our heads for one last prayer, and then Patrick stood and raised his wine glass. "To Helen."

✳ ✳ ✳

I stretched my neck from side to side, trying to relieve the tension in my shoulders. How had the day gone so fast? Cheryl poked her head in the door. "You need to leave soon to pick out bridesmaid dresses."

I nodded. "Just need to finish one more thing."

She went back to her desk. I sighed and texted Patty: "Can't believe you chose your son's softball playoff game over me. I'm picking something with major ruffles."

Patty sent me a smiley face reply.

I couldn't put it off any longer. I grabbed my briefcase and stood— time to face the music. As I passed the party shop, a car backfired. DeShawn and the man I had seen him with the day I proposed to Rob stood at the end of the alley. DeShawn handed the man something, and he strode away. *Could DeShawn be the drug dealer? He's new to town and has been acting suspiciously.*

I continued my stroll up the street to C'est Magnifique, attention now drawn to the brick storefronts with hanging baskets spilling with ivy and vibrant red geraniums. As I passed Tempting Treasures and Tasty Treats, Andy waved. I struggled to lift my lips into a smile, and he opened the door. "You okay?"

"Bridesmaid dresses today." I pointed to April and Sandy's store. "Can I hide here?"

He laughed.

Wanda's voice interrupted, "There you are, Merry. We've been waiting." She stood in the doorway of C'est Magnifique and tapped her foot.

"Gotta go." I turned and walked toward her. "Sorry. Busy day at work."

"My time is valuable too."

"It is. And I appreciate you wanting to be involved." I gestured for her to go back into the store.

She pursed her lips. "Of course, I do. Rob's my first child to get married. For as long as he and Elizabeth have delayed, you would have thought I hadn't set a good example." She brushed past me toward the back of the store.

April's eyes were wide as she handed me a glass of champagne. "For the bride."

"Thanks."

Jenny looked up as I strode into the back room. "Mom, you're late."

"Sorry. Have you found anything you like?" I sat next to her.

She gritted her teeth as she shook her head.

Wanda said, "Maybe if we saw your dress, it would help."

I nodded to Sandy, and she retrieved an opaque white carrying bag, unzipping it as she walked. She placed the dress on a display hook.

Wanda sniffed, "It's pretty, but it doesn't look like a wedding dress. Although, I suppose since it's not your first time around the square, it will do." She brightened. "And it does give us several colors we could play with. This turquoise, or the rose—"

"Or black. It's on a Friday night, and I've read black is elegant for evening weddings." Amy was dressed in a black tunic, black leggings, and what looked like black combat boots.

"I don't look good in dark colors. I think we should go with something blue that sparkles or chartreuse with frills." Ann wore a pink sheath with a pink bow pinning back her hair.

Jenny paled. What was being described was far from her usual, preppy kind of look.

April wheeled a bar full of dresses into the room. "I've taken the liberty of selecting a few more that might work."

Wanda flipped through the rack. "I do wish we had gone to a 'real' bridal shop. They have a bigger selection."

"These are lovely." I joined Wanda. "I think any of these would look beautiful on you girls."

"But nothing's black." Amy flounced onto a chair.

Ann punched Amy's arm. "Grow up. Everything's not about you."

"Ow, that hurt."

"This I love." Ann selected a pink gauzy dress with enough frills to satisfy a designer gone amok and held it up in the mirror. "I would look great in this."

Jenny shot me a look of pure panic.

"We're going for something more understated." I pulled a sleeveless turquoise dress from the rack with a fitted bodice and two tiers of fabric on the bottom. "This is pretty. Why don't you girls try this one, and Wanda and I will select a few others."

Sandy showed them to the fitting rooms.

Wanda chuckled. "Ann's dress was pretty awful."

My mouth dropped. Had we agreed on something? I smiled. "It was."

She flipped through the other rack. "This, this. And this."

I selected two more. We sat to wait. I struggled to think of something to say. Jenny walked out first and looked lovely. The turquoise highlighted her blue eyes. I leaned forward. "It's beautiful."

"That color is great on you." Wanda agreed.

Jenny grinned and twirled in front of the mirror.

Amy came out, dress on but black leggings still in place. She looked hunched as she walked to the mirror.

Wanda snapped, "Stand up straight, Amy, give the dress a chance."

Her back stiffened.

"This color is so pretty." Ann walked past us to the mirror. "I look great. A little more flounce would be better." She gave Wanda the side-eye, and Wanda shook her head.

They tried on three that didn't work, and then Jenny looked through the dresses we had set to the side. "I still like this." She gestured to the original one she had tried on.

I suggested, "Why doesn't everyone try that one on again?"

After she changed, Ann couldn't tear herself away from her reflection. "I vote for this one too."

Everyone stared at Amy. She looked trapped and then lifted another dress that looked more somber. "What about this—"

Wanda stood and walked toward her. "How did that get in there? Definitely not."

Amy cringed. "I guess this is okay." She ran to the fitting room.

Ann laughed. "She couldn't wait to take it off."

They went into the fitting room to change, and I motioned to April. "Since Jenny's walking me down the aisle, I want her to have something a bit different. Can you have the same brocade from my dress made into a type of belt or sash for her waist?"

April smiled. "Leave it to me."

"What a lovely idea." Wanda patted my arm and sighed. "I know I'm tough on those girls, but someone has to be. Mother in California, and father roaming all over the world. It's tiring, but it means so much to Mac. He's worried about them." She paused. "You've done such a great job with Jenny."

My eyes widened. "Thanks."

* * *

"Two moments. I had two genuine moments with Rob's mother. I feel like I could float. Maybe she's not so bad after all." I sank onto a chair in my backyard.

Patty laughed. "Let's not get too carried away."

"Did you try your dress on? Will it work?"

"Thank you for picking something relatively simple. I'll need to work on my guns though." She flexed her arms.

I petted Drambuie as she passed by my chair. "You look great, and one of the reasons is you still have a child you're hoisting around."

"Kids do make joining a gym optional." Patty stretched. "Want more iced tea?"

"My house, I should get it."

She made a shooing motion with her hand.

"But we're such good friends, why stand on ceremony?"

She got to her feet and lifted our empty glasses. "I live to serve." She returned with full ones with lemon slices clinging to the rims.

"Thank you." I squeezed the fruit into the glass.

Andy's head appeared over the back gate. "Can I join? I have something I want to talk to you about."

"Enter. You'll have to get your own iced tea though. It's serve-yourself day."

He muttered as he walked up the back steps to the kitchen, "Whatever happened to manners?" He came back with a full glass and sat next to Patty. "Tea's good."

"Darjeeling."

He leaned toward me. "I need your help. I told you I knew Matt Logan's parents."

I nodded.

"Ed and I went to see them last night to express our condolences. They were a mess."

"I can't even imagine losing one of my kids." Patty looked up at the cloudless sky.

"They said he was so happy, and he was looking forward to his wedding next year. They are convinced he wasn't doing drugs. They don't have any idea how he might have gotten fentanyl. And they're afraid the police won't investigate; they'll think he was just another drug addict."

"Jane Creedy insisted Kevin didn't do drugs either." I sipped my tea. "Of course, lots of people have secrets."

"That's where you come in."

"Huh?"

"Ed and I mentioned how good you are with puzzles, figuring things out. They want to meet you. I told them I'd bring you by tomorrow night. Talk to them."

I chewed the inside of my lip. Andy stared at me.

"Okay." I pointed toward him. "You owe me."

✳ ✳ ✳

The next evening, I ran out the back door and across to Andy's garage. I slid into his cream-colored Volvo and snapped my seatbelt in place.

We drove two-lane, back-country roads to get there. The summer sun hadn't stopped beating yet, so Andy kept the air-conditioning on. "I know how much you like ABBA." He popped in a CD. "Mamma Mia" blasted, and we both sang.

Soon the house came into view. It was a white-washed, brick Georgian, with round columns flanking the front door, a balustrade around the front terrace topped by a rail, which supported evenly spaced planters filled with grass spikes, fuchsia geraniums, and purple petunia wave. A formal hedge garden led the eye to the beautiful house.

I gasped. "I can't wait to see the inside."

We walked to the front door, and Andy rang the bell. A tall, lithe woman answered. She looked like she was in her mid-to-late forties, with red-rimmed, swollen brown eyes and long brown hair. "Andy. And you must be Merry. I'm Yvonne Logan." She held out her hand.

I shook it. "I'm so sorry for your loss."

"Thanks for coming." She let go and extended her hand toward the inside of the house.

We walked in. The arch above the front door was repeated about twenty feet away, and past that second arch were stairs leading to the upper floors. Yvonne led the way to the second door on the left.

Oak bookshelves lined the walls, which were topped by red and gold two-foot-thick crown molding. The thirteen-foot ceilings were embossed with raised gold octagons and squares, and cream wallpaper lined with subdued green stripes covered the gaps between the crown molding and bookcases. The look was opulent, but the large stone fireplace and comfortable seating gave an overall feeling of coziness.

My mouth dropped. "I've never seen anything so beautiful."

"It is nice, isn't it?" She gave me a half-smile. "It was one of Matt's favorite rooms." Her hand caressed a few of the volumes. "He was always such a reader."

She sat and gestured to the soft green sofa across from her. "Please."

The room was so formal, I perched on the end of the sofa, careful not to touch my hands to the expensive fabric. Andy sat next to me.

"Where's Bill?" Andy asked.

"Business." A slight furrow creased her forehead. "We all have different ways of coping." She studied her hands and then jerked. "Would you like something to drink? Tea, perhaps?"

"Iced tea for me."

Andy said, "Same."

Yvonne tapped into her phone, then put it to the side. "Merry, Andy mentioned you have experience in solving crimes?"

Heat flushed my neck, then spread to my face. "Probably more a matter of being in the right place at the right time."

"Don't be so modest." Andy clapped my back. "Merry's solved many a mystery. She's a regular bloodhound."

The sun beaming through the window felt like an accusing spotlight. Yvonne looked so hopeful, and I was afraid she was going to be disappointed.

CHAPTER 7

A man brought in a silver tray with ice, three glasses, sliced lemon in a bowl, and a large pitcher of iced tea. He poured glasses and handed me one. "I hope everyone likes blackberry tea."

I nodded and took a sip. "This is delicious."

He smiled, handed glasses to Yvonne and Andy, and left.

"Andy said you had an only child. I believe he said her name was Jenny?" Yvonne asked.

I nodded.

Her gaze wandered to the window overlooking the formal garden. "They were supposed to be married next June. Trudy wanted it to be earlier, but he convinced her to delay. He wanted to save money for a house and figured they could move in right after the wedding if they waited. We were contributing, of course, but he was proud, wanted to do it on his own—" She twisted the diamond-studded band on her left hand. "And now there won't be a wedding.

"It's so empty with him gone. I need to find out what happened." Her face flushed. "I owe it to him. For the life he will never live. And you have to help me. Please. Mother-to-mother."

"I don't know anything about drugs or the people involved. I don't want to get your hopes up."

Yvonne stood, walked to the sofa, and sat next to me. "My hope died with my son. This is about justice."

Matt's eyes in the photo on the desk seemed to plead with me, and Yvonne's hauntingly similar ones betrayed a slight twitch as she held her hands tightly clasped.

I suppressed a groan. "I'll do my best."

Yvonne hugged Andy and shook my hand. "I look forward to hearing from you. Andy has my number."

We walked along the gravel path to the car, and I kicked the stones.

"Merry, you have a heart. A big one." Andy opened my door. "At the end, you'll be happy you helped."

"I hope you're right."

The ride home was quiet, and when I walked into the house, Rob was waiting for me. He took one look at my face and said, "I can't believe you agreed to get involved." Rob poured coffee into a mug and sat at the kitchen counter. "This drug and the people who sell it are dangerous. And I don't want to lose you before we get married."

I kissed his shoulder. "You won't get rid of me that easily. And, besides, you're on Jay's short list."

"I don't think he's serious about that. He's just making sure he covers all of his bases."

I sighed. "You should have seen her. So empty. I thought how my life would be if Jenny—" I rapped my knuckles on the wood molding around the back door.

"Promise me you'll be careful."

"I will. Don't worry."

"The last time you ended up with a cracked rib." Rob pulled me closer and whispered in my ear. "Sometimes, you scare me."

"I'll be fine." I pulled a pad from my purse. "I've been working on a list: Talk to Jane and Trudy to see if they've thought of anything. They may be more willing to be open with me than the police. And I want to speak with Jay."

"I know other towns have been especially hard-hit by fentanyl. I could reach out to reporters in those areas to see what they were able to uncover."

"We sound like a team." I kissed his nose. "By the way, did you find out if we have to finish our Pre-Cana session?"

"We do."

"I was afraid of that." My head sank to the counter.

"But Father Tom relented and gave us the option of meeting with him for an hour or so to satisfy the requirement. I told him we wanted to have the entire experience, so I turned him down."

"What? Why on earth would you do that?"

He laughed. "Just kidding. Scheduled an hour and a half with him next Saturday."

* * *

Jane was standing by the door as I walked down the street to Delightful Bites; she wore black shorts with a dark-purple polo shirt. I opened the door for her. "Thanks for meeting me."

As we scanned the chalkboard in front of the kitchen, I said, "Everything is terrific here. You can't go wrong."

"Thanks." She gave me a wan smile.

We ordered, retrieved cups, and chose drinks. I selected a table in the shade. "I hope it's not too hot. Since I work inside, I like to be outdoors every chance I get."

"I love the heat." Jane sat on one of the metal chairs and scooched it closer to the table.

"What do you do?"

"I'm in my last year at school. This summer, I'm working at a restaurant a few towns over. I don't know if you've ever been there, it's called Fiorella's. I'm a sous chef." She placed her napkin on her lap.

"My daughter's favorite, but we've only been once this summer. Are you studying culinary arts in school?"

"I wish. My mother made me study business management." Jane picked up a fry and dipped it in ketchup. "To be honest, it's not that bad. If I want to run my own restaurant one day, I need to know all that stuff."

"What's your favorite dish to make at the restaurant?"

"I don't get to make it often because usually I'm prepping for the chef, but I love making veal osso buco. The layers of flavor you can build over a low and slow cook are intense."

I popped a strawberry in my mouth. "I'll have to try it the next time we go." I paused. "How are you doing?"

She stopped mid-bite and put her hamburger back on the plate. "I try not to think about it. I miss him. We were friends forever, and then, more. It's like a piece of me is gone." She pushed her hair behind her ear. "I keep thinking if I had only left the bonfire with him, nothing would have happened. He'd still be alive."

"You can't blame yourself. He and Matt left together. You had no way of knowing what was going to happen." I hesitated. "Did you know Matt died too?"

She gasped. "You're kidding. How?"

"Same thing."

"Do you think Matt gave Kevin the drug? That detective called and said Kevin offered speed to Matt, but maybe it was the other way around. Maybe Matt was the dealer, and then he made a mistake—"

"There's nothing to suggest Matt was dealing drugs."

Jane lifted another french fry. "But that might make sense. How could Kevin die and then Matt? Who would they know in common? It wasn't like we hung out together. We just met him and Trudy that night."

"From what I've read, this is a fairly widespread problem. They wouldn't have had to know each other."

"Kevin did not do hard drugs." She hesitated, "He only took speed now and again, just to keep him up—that's not the same thing."

I sipped tea. "From what I've heard, dealers have been adding fentanyl to a lot of things. I'm curious, why do you think Kevin may have wanted to take something to keep awake that night?"

Jane made patterns in the ketchup with her french fry. "Whenever he drank, he'd get sleepy. Sometimes, if he were having fun, he'd take a pill."

"Where did he get the speed from?"

"I don't know. A friend. He used to date somebody who had access. Maybe he still got it from her."

"What's her name?" I finished my sandwich.

She shrugged. "I'd rather not say. I don't want to get her in trouble. It was someone he used to date back before we made the leap from friends."

I restrained an eye roll. She was barely twenty-one. How long a time could it have been? "I think you should tell the police her name so they can question her. Kevin's dead, and now Matt, this is serious."

"You said the two might not be connected. I need to talk to her. It's not fair to turn her over to the police. They would ruin her life." She stood. "I'm going to get a to-go container for my burger." Most of it was left on her plate.

I gathered my utensils and deposited them in the appropriate receptacle. Jane bagged her hamburger and turned to me. "Thanks for lunch. I appreciate you trying to find out what happened."

"Please be careful. I wish you would tell the police what you know. It's safer."

Jane smiled. "Don't worry. If you knew this person, you'd know she wouldn't hurt a fly."

＊ ＊ ＊

Rob stopped by on his way home from work as I was pulling weeds in the garden. "Are you sure you've recovered enough to be doing that?"

"Doctor said light work is okay." I stood and brushed mulch from my knees.

"What do you feel like for dinner?"

"You're in luck. I was with someone who had a hamburger at lunch, and now I have a hankering. I asked Jenny to take some out of the freezer."

He smiled. "The ones with green peppers and onions in the patty?"

"You know me so well."

"What time is Jay coming?" He draped his arm over my shoulders.

"Seven-thirty. I told him to come for dessert."

"Good idea. He's always in a better mood when he gets his sugar ration. And maybe that'll mean he'll stop suspecting me."

Rob started the grill. I walked into the house, and Jenny came down the stairs. "I didn't know if you wanted the blueberry pie or the cherry one."

"Cherry." I preheated the oven. "Would you set the table?"

She sat at the counter and pointed. "Already done."

I laughed. "Way ahead of me, as usual. Is everything set for our college visits next week?"

"Affirmative, and I've already taken the virtual tours. We're scheduled for physical tours at all three." Her foot swung back and forth. "Dad called today."

I put the pie in the oven. "What did he have to say?"

"He's worried about Arianna. His lawyer said they wouldn't let her post bail since she's a flight risk. He wants to use me to contact her."

"I'm not comfortable with that." I stopped taking things from the fridge, came around the counter, and sat. "It's fine for you to speak with him. And I know Arianna's keeping in touch with you. But I don't want you to be their conduit. What if they get you into trouble?"

"Dad wouldn't do that."

"London."

"Not his fault." Jenny gripped the counter.

I cupped her cheek. "I love you. When's the next time he's scheduled to call?"

"Friday."

"Come get me. I want to talk with him."

"If I must." She sighed and bit into a celery stick.

I kissed her cheek. "Do you want cheese on your burger?"

"Cheddar."

* * *

Rob eyed the empty pot. "Jay will be here in a few minutes. I better make coffee. I swear that man runs on caffeine."

"Hazard of the job."

There was a quick rap on the back door, and Jay walked in. "Good. Just in time for dessert."

Rob poured him coffee, and I pointed to the two different tubs of ice cream. Jay said, "Vanilla."

I cut pieces for Rob, Jay, and me and adorned them with our frozen flavor choices. Jay took a bite and murmured, "Good."

"Thanks." I sipped coffee.

"I have a funny feeling I'm going to pay for this."

"Whatever gave you that idea?" Rob laughed. "But since you're here—have you been able to tell if Kevin and Matt overdosed on the same product?"

He shook his head. "Strength can vary from pill to pill, even from the same maker, so it's possible they got it from the same person, but we can't test for it."

"I met with Matt's mother the other day."

Jay's eyes widened. "How do you know her?"

I pointed toward the house behind me. "You remember. She's a customer of Andy and Ed's. She asked me to look into what happened."

"You're not a cop. You're not even a private investigator." He stood and threw his napkin onto the table.

"Please sit. I have something else to tell you."

83

He eyed the uneaten portion of his pie and ice cream. "I'm listening. And I'm staying—but just because I haven't finished dessert." He sat and picked up his fork.

"I had lunch with Jane Creedy today, and she may know who could have given Kevin drugs."

"She said he didn't do drugs."

I sighed. "She meant hard drugs. When he wanted to stay up, he took speed. She was going to touch base with the woman who may have given it to him."

He slid the last bite into his mouth. "That's dangerous. I'll talk to her tomorrow."

CHAPTER 8

I looked through my closet before work. What do parents wear for school visits in the heat of the summer? *How have I gotten old enough to have a daughter who's going to school next year?* I sat on the corner of the bed. *Maybe I should do this later.* I texted Patty: "What are you wearing on Cindy's school visits?"

"Hot. Shorts."

"Too casual?"

"Not for the money we're going to be paying."

She had a point. I placed a dressier pair of shorts in the case, dressed for work, and grabbed a power bar. My phone buzzed with a reminder on my to-do list: ask Trudy Jones to meet me. I sent her a quick text and walked out the door.

"Hello, Merry." Jada was watering the flowers on her porch. "Going to be a hot one."

I climbed the steps. "Feels that way. Congratulations on the new job." Jada was going to be a guidance counselor at the high school.

"I'm looking forward to it. Would you like coffee?"

"I'd love some."

She walked inside, and I took a seat on one of the rattan chairs. The cushions were green and brown with an ivy-like pattern. Ferns, spider plants, and fuchsia hung above the porch railings, creating the feeling of an outdoor room. *DeShawn can't be involved in the drug trade. His house looks so normal.* My phone buzzed with a response from Trudy. "Coffee tomorrow after work?" I texted her where to meet.

Jada handed me a mug. "You like a bit of cream, right?"

I nodded. "It's so lush and green, sitting here."

"It's my Zen place." She sat next to me.

"How are you settling in? I'm sorry I haven't been around much. First, there was Phoenix, and now the craziness around the wedding."

"Not to worry. All the neighbors have been very welcoming. I had forgotten what it was like to live in a small town." She sipped coffee.

"This must be very different from Chicago."

Jada laughed. "That's an understatement, but I'm looking forward to starting at the district and having a more manageable case load."

"It seems like this would be harder. Aren't you working across a few schools? How can you keep everyone straight?"

"When I was in Chicago, I had over six hundred students I was responsible for."

"That's a lot."

"Here, I'll have about two hundred. It gives me the chance to get to know the students and make an impact."

"I know Jenny worked with the previous counselor on which schools might be the right fit for her. Is that the kind of thing you'll be doing?" I sipped coffee.

"One of the things. I also work with the kids on self-esteem issues, bullying problems, drugs and alcohol abuse, and grief counseling." She leaned forward. "Kids today have to deal with a lot."

I shook my head. "You don't expect to see a lot of drug and alcohol abuse in Hopeful, do you?"

"Probably less here than in Chicago, but it's everywhere. I'm sure I'll be busy."

I stood. "Big job. And an important one. I'm glad you ended up in our town." I bent to give her a quick hug. "We'll have to have you and DeShawn over for dinner. Sometime next week?"

She checked her calendar. "Just not Tuesday."

"I'll shoot you a few dates when I get to the office." I paused. "When you were in Chicago, did you see any fentanyl problems?"

"That stuff is the worst. Kids try it and die." She shuddered. "And they don't even know they're taking it. I was kind of hoping I left that behind. Why would you ask?"

"It's here. There have been two deaths recently."

✻ ✻ ✻

I pulled into the coffee shop parking lot a few minutes early, hopped out of the car, and walked to the door. A cute black and white striped awning covered the bustling patio, and dogs were sprawled near their owners, who seemed to be far more involved with their phones than their pets. I stepped over an extended paw and opened the door. Trudy was near the front of the line, wearing a black t-shirt and white jeans. She turned after ordering, gave me a quick wave, and pointed to the terrace. I nodded.

I ordered a latte and biscotti and joined her on the patio. "Thanks for meeting with me. I'm sorry for your loss."

She stirred sugar into her coffee. Dark circles under her eyes made her pallor even more apparent. "Thank you. It's been hard. Yvonne told me she asked you to look into Matt's death. I don't know what you think you'll be able to accomplish. I just know that Matt didn't fool around with drugs."

"Are you sure?"

"Of course, I'm sure. He wasn't the type. He'd drink whiskey and beer because he knew what he could expect. But no drugs, he didn't like the idea of losing control." She clutched her t-shirt. "I hope you don't think I'm the kind of girl who would be engaged to a person who took drugs."

"How do you think he came into contact with it then?" I dunked the biscotti and took a bite.

She raised her hands and shrugged. "Who knows. Maybe it was an accident. Maybe he picked up the wrong thing at the grocery store. Maybe it was meant for someone else. It doesn't change anything. He's still gone."

"Did anything unusual happen between the night we met at Pre-Cana and when he died?"

"Unusual?"

"It seems like a big coincidence Matt and Kevin were both there, and one died that weekend, and the other died less than a week later."

Trudy nodded. "It does seem weird. We had a good time that night. The bonfire was blazing, we had a little whiskey, and Jane and I hung out and talked about wedding stuff, dresses, bridesmaids, you know." She rubbed the back of her neck. "Now, all my planning is for naught, and neither one of us is going to walk down the aisle."

"It's so sad, and I am sorry for you both." A Pekingese sniffed at my hand, and I petted him. "Did Matt tell you what happened between him and Kevin that night?"

"Quite a few times. Matt was so freaked he was one of the last people to see Kevin alive. He kept wondering if there was something more he could have done." She sunk lower into her chair as if speaking exhausted her.

"Did he think Kevin met someone from outside that night?"

"Like he told the police, he might have. But maybe Kevin already had the speed and did just go to the bathroom. I told him people are responsible for their own destiny. And look. Now Matt's dead." She shuddered. "I hope he wasn't asking questions where he shouldn't have."

"Do you think he was investigating?" I stirred the leftover foam from my latte into the coffee dregs and took a sip.

Both of her hands gripped either side of the table, so her knuckles showed white. "I don't know. And it's killing me."

* * *

"I felt bad for her. She was so miserable, and she seemed to think he had been investigating on his own. What if that did get him killed?" I took the fish from the refrigerator and laid it on the counter.

Rob uncorked a bottle of Merlot. "From what you said, she wasn't sure. And he could have been doing drugs. But if he was looking into it, and that made him a target, it makes me much more worried for you." He handed me a glass.

"I'm not going to go into a drug den." I put the aluminum-wrapped salmon into the oven.

He took a salad from the refrigerator. "Drug dens are very different these days. Lots of people who look like me and you."

"Not quite like us, I hope."

"You know what I mean."

I shuddered. "Unfortunately, I do. Can you slice the baguette?"

He made even slices with the bread knife and deposited them into a waiting basket. "Ready for your college trips next week?"

"It will be fun to be alone with Jenny for a few days. Our last hurrah before the wedding." I leaned against the counter and sipped wine.

"And then I'll have you all to myself." He hugged me.

"Partially. You and Jenny will have to share me."

He laughed. "And any other little ones who happen along."

"Kittens?"

"Children. You already have two cats." He kissed me.

"Whoa. I thought it was dinner time. Too much of a public display. Way too much." Jenny stood near the table.

"Hilarious, Jenny." I stepped away from Rob. "Did you decide what you're going to wear to the campus tours next week?"

"Shorts. It's going to be hot."

"Maybe dressy ones?" I took the salmon from the oven.

"Mom, I've talked to everyone. No one dresses up. Get past it."

We sat at the table, and I said, "Fine. I give up. I've checked out restaurants in the towns we'll be visiting, and there are good ones."

Rob smiled. "Does your college checklist include a 'best food' column?"

"Of course. That way, Mom will visit me. And there are two separate columns, one for on-campus food and the other for off-campus."

I dished salad onto my plate. "That's something else we'll need to consider. Do you know if your meal plan is mandatory as a freshman?"

"On the spreadsheet." She sat at the table. "Can I borrow the car tomorrow?"

"Where are you going?"

"To the library in Clifton, where your bridesmaid, Ann, works. She said she has a few things I should add to my list of questions for next week and thinks it would be better to talk through it."

"That's fine. Just be back by four. I don't want you driving the highway at rush hour."

* * *

I had finished making small checkmarks on my to-do list when Cheryl walked in. "Sorry to bother you, but there's a Jim MacNamara here to see you."

I frowned, trying to figure out if I knew him or not. "Oh!" I stood. "That must be Mac's brother." I walked out of the office and turned toward the waiting area.

A tall man with piercing blue eyes, thinning hair, and the same ruddy cheeks as Mac was examining one of the miniature car displays Cheryl put together. He turned, and I extended my hand. "You and Mac look so similar."

He clasped my hand and pulled me to him in a tight hug. "We'll be family soon. Hand shaking is for strangers."

I took a step back, a bit stunned at his exuberance. "Your daughters are lovely people, and I'm happy they're going to be in the wedding. Come back to my office." I led the way.

"I'm sorry I missed your engagement party." He sank into one of my office chairs. "I've been missing too many family events lately. First, Mac's wedding and now this."

"It was impromptu, and I understand you were out of town. Water?" I held out a bottle.

"Thanks." He uncapped it and sipped. "You must be wondering what I'm doing here."

"Looking to buy insurance? This is the right place." I smiled.

He laughed. "I've heard so much about you from Wanda that I decided I wasn't going to wait a minute longer to meet you. So after my flight landed, I tossed my bags in the car and drove straight here."

I struggled to keep my mouth from dropping. "Wanda talked about me?"

"She's over the moon you're marrying her son. Speaking of which, he's the next one I need to meet." Jim glanced at his watch. "Say, it's almost lunchtime. Why don't you give that man of yours a call and see if he can meet us for lunch?"

Heat flooded my face as I considered my packed schedule.

"I know it's presumptuous. You're probably too busy for an old geezer like me."

My teeth ground. "Not at all. I'm sure I can shift things around. Excuse me for a moment while I call Rob." I stepped out of my office into the conference room next door and pressed Rob's number.

"What's up, beautiful?"

"Mac's brother wants to have lunch with us."

"Sure, when?"

"Now."

Silence.

"I guess I could tell him we can't today. It's just he got off the plane and came straight here."

Rob sighed. "Give me ten minutes. I'll meet you at the Iron Skillet."

I motioned to Cheryl, and she joined me in the conference room. "What's up?"

"Last minute change, can you clear my calendar till two?"

She groaned.

"I know. And I'm sorry—"

"It's okay. I'll handle it." She trudged back to her desk.

I put a smile on my face and walked back into my office. "All set."

"Do you want to take your car?"

"No need. We have a good place down the block."

We walked out the door, and I acted as the member of the chamber of commerce I was and extolled the virtues of small-town living, especially ours. He said, "It's a beautiful village. The black-iron hanging baskets are a nice touch." Ivies, petunia waves, and geraniums benefited from the watering done by the shopkeepers.

We arrived at the restaurant, and Jim held the door. "After you."

I walked in, and Rob waved from a booth on the far end. I pointed. "That's your new nephew, Rob."

Jim pulled Rob to him in a hug. I couldn't help but smile. "Jim's a hugger."

"I got that," Rob gasped. "Jim, it's nice to meet you."

We sat, and I turned to Jim. "Where did your travels take you this time?"

"This was my southern trip. I started in Peru and made my way north. Last stop was Mexico City." He sipped iced tea. "I'll be glad to be home and see my girls again."

"I guess I should know this, but your wife—" Rob took his silverware out of the napkin.

92

"Divorced. Kind of ugly, but we've gotten to a better place. She lives in California, and the kids are older, so I don't need to deal with her too often." Jim nodded at me. "I heard this is your second wedding?"

I squirmed. "Let's just say the first didn't work out, but my daughter makes it all worthwhile."

"Mac said she's a peach. I can't wait to meet my new grandniece."

The food was served, and we began to eat. Rob asked, "What business are you in, Jim?"

"Import-Export. Antiques, mostly."

"You'll have to meet our neighbor, Andy. He owns the antique store just north of where my business is." I picked up my glass of iced tea.

"I saw it when I drove by. It looked like a nice little shop." He put his fork down. "One of the reasons I stopped by was to talk to you about my daughter, Amy. When the wife and I divorced, she took it hard—she went through a very dark phase. Ann's a trouper, but Amy..." He looked straight into my eyes. "Wanda's been kind enough to step in and provide guidance, but sometimes she can be a bit heavy-handed." He sighed. "I guess what I'm trying to say is thank you for having Amy in your wedding. Even though she may not say it, I know she's looking forward to it. I hate to ask, but maybe you could reach out and spend some time with her before she goes back to school?"

"She's a lovely girl, and other than interesting ideas about bridesmaid dresses, she's been fine. I'm pleased she's in the wedding, and I'd be happy to reach out to her to see if she'd be up to a girl's day out."

"Thank you." He resumed eating. "Rob, heard you're a reporter?"

"Got tired of traveling the globe, so I bought a small paper here in town. It was what I needed, and the bonus was I met this lovely lady." He kissed my hand.

I smiled. "I'm happy you picked our town too."

There was quibbling over the bill. Rob insisted, and Jim let him pick it up. Jim said, "My car's over here." He hugged Rob and me. "Thanks again for lunch. I should be around at least some time between now and the wedding, so let's try to get together again."

Rob nodded and said, "I'll walk you back to the office, Merry."

"What did you think about that?" I held Rob's hand as we walked.

"Strange. Makes me wonder what Amy's dark period entailed."

We stopped in front of my office. "Dinner?"

"See you at six." He gave me a quick kiss and strode toward his office.

CHAPTER 9

Jenny stood in the middle of the quad and twirled. Her blonde hair was pulled into a ponytail, and she wore tailored peach shorts, a crisp polka-dot sleeveless blouse, and comfy walking shoes. She looked more like a sophomore in college than a rising senior in high school. A breath caught in my throat, and tears pricked my eyes. *How on earth has she gotten old enough to be contemplating school, and how am I going to be able to let her go?* The world was turning too fast for me.

Ancient brick buildings shrouded in ivy surrounded us, and concrete paths bisected a lush green lawn that looked perfect for lounging and deep philosophical discussions with close friends. Jenny sighed. "This place looks great, Mom. Just the way a college should."

I cleared my throat. "Looks aren't everything. Don't fall in love till we get some questions answered, like what aid they'll offer." I glanced at my folder. "The tour should start in about twenty minutes. Let's sit over there." I made my way to a bench shaded by a large oak.

She plopped down next to me. "This campus is so much prettier than the last one. It seemed dark." She shivered. "Almost foreboding."

"It was raining yesterday."

"Maybe it was an omen." Jenny's arm extended. "Look at all the light."

The sun glinted off a natural-looking retention pond in the distance, dominated by cattails waving in the slight breeze. A student in dark-green cargo shorts and a light-yellow t-shirt emblazoned with the name of the school approached. She lifted her clipboard. "Are you here for the tour?"

Jenny stood and held out her hand. "Jenny March."

She shook it. "Kandy, with a K, I'm a junior here." She checked off Jenny's name and extended her hand to me. "You must be her mother, Merry March. Glad to have you tour our campus." She glanced down. "I'm expecting a few more—ah, here come people now." She strode to the approaching group and made checkmarks by additional names.

Kandy began her spiel as we walked the campus, the school's history, traditions, and the like.

Once she stopped to take a breath, I broke in with my list. "I was happy to get questions answered during the morning sessions, but I have more, starting with the security on campus. I looked at your Annual Security Report. It says you'll text if there is an emergency on campus within two hours. That seems like a long time."

Kandy's face flushed, and she stuttered, "Sometimes it takes that long to find out what's going on. We don't want to alarm people unnecessarily."

"Do parents get the notifications too?"

"I think so, maybe."

"What kinds of alerts do you send beyond texts? Can you talk about that a little? And I looked at the FBI Uniform Crime report. It seems like areas around campus aren't as secure as other schools."

Jenny elbowed me. "Mom—she doesn't know. Can't you ask someone else?"

"Jenny, I want to make sure you're safe."

"Look at this place. It's beautiful. Of course, it's safe." She rolled her eyes.

"I can call the admissions office, and maybe they could set you up with our Security Division since you have such detailed questions. I'm sure they can set your mind at ease." Kandy smiled.

"I'd appreciate it. Now, I have a few more. I couldn't find some of these online. Graduation rate, percent of students who return after freshman year, how many kids live on campus—"

The kids in our tour group looked bored, and Jenny was turning red. "Is this necessary?"

Kandy shifted from one foot to the next. "That's a lot of information, and I don't think I can help you." She walked a few yards away and lifted her phone. After a few moments, she came back to the group. "Ms. March, if you'll wait here for a few minutes, someone from the office will join you and take you with them to get your answers." Then she said to the rest, "Dorms are next. Jenny, would you like to stay with your—"

"I'll come with you. My mom can text me when she's done."

"But—" I stuttered as my daughter and the rest of the group marched away. *You'd think other parents would be as concerned as me.*

* * *

"The rooms were small, but I loved how people decorated them. This one girl had dyed a sheet dark blue, stretched it across the ceiling, and hung glittery stars from it. It looked like the night sky. I can't wait to decorate my room." Jenny paused for a breath and to munch a french fry.

"I'm glad the décor met your expectations. Don't you want to find out what I learned?"

Her foot swung as she flipped through the song list of the old-time diner. "If I must."

I grabbed her hand. "Jenny, security is important. You're going to be on your own soon, and I need to make sure you'll be going somewhere safe."

She stopped fidgeting. "What did they say?"

"I'd give them a 'B' for security and an 'A' for what I heard from the admissions office."

"That's better than the last place." Jenny smiled.

I frowned. "I'd like both to be 'A's."

Jenny twirled her ponytail. "Guess who I saw when we were touring the dorms?"

"I have no idea. Aren't kids on summer break?"

"Some are taking a summer semester, especially people who are determined to graduate next year. In other words, Amy."

I shrugged.

"Amy, your bridesmaid, Amy."

"Oh. I guess I didn't hear where she was going to school." I bit into my crab cake sandwich. "What did she have to say?"

"I only said two words to her because she was coming out of her room as we were passing by. She said she'd give me a call next week after the semester ends to talk about school. I definitely won't be copying her style, loads of black as you might expect." Jenny's nose wrinkled. "And the smell. I think someone smoked pot in her room."

I sat up. "And how do you know what pot smells like?"

"I'm in high school. People do stupid things. Not me, of course."

"I'll need to tell her father about this."

Jenny turned red. "Why would you do that? She's twenty-one, so she'll be graduating next spring. She won't even be here when I move on campus."

"I know two people who died who may not have known what they were taking." I took both Jenny's hands in mine. "Jenny, you need to promise. No drugs."

"Drugs are stupid." Jenny slid her hands from mine and ate another fry.

* * *

The sun glowed red as it sunk slowly below the horizon, and tea roses perfumed the air. "I can't tell you how happy I am to be home."

Rob kissed my hand. "I'm happy you're back too. Did Jenny pick a school?"

"Waiting to see what they will give us in terms of aid. We have another trip planned at the end of the month, but right now, she's pretty set on the second one we visited. With all the spreadsheets and critical thinking she's put into this, it's coming down to nice weather when we visit and how good the campus looks when the sun is shining."

He laughed. "It should make you feel better she narrowed her choices dramatically before you even went on the trip. At least you know there isn't a bad school in the bunch."

"True." I sipped my wine. "When Jenny toured the dorm rooms, she smelled pot by Amy's room."

"Amy, my step-cousin?" His eyebrow lifted. "Is that what I should call her?"

"Huh?"

"She's my mother's step-niece."

"Look it up, but for now, call her Amy," I huffed. "Should I tell Jim?"

"Isn't she twenty-one?"

"I'd still want someone to tell me about Jenny."

Rob pulled my hand to him. "Jenny's still a child. Amy's an adult making her own choices."

"But people are dying."

"Not from smoking pot."

"You think I shouldn't say anything?"

"It may cause even more family problems than we have already." Rob paused. "I have something to tell you."

"Sounds serious. You don't have a hidden wife somewhere?"

He brought my hand to his lips and kissed it. "Jane Creedy is missing."

I gasped. "What? When?"

"Not sure. She may have decided to go off on her own. Jay said her mother told him she'd been talking about a fresh start recently."

"I spoke with Jane the other day. She didn't say anything about leaving. She had a job and school. It didn't sound like she was thinking about going anywhere any time soon. Were any of her clothes missing?"

"Jay didn't get into all that. He only mentioned it to me because he was wondering if you talked to her after your conversation the other day." Rob frowned.

I shook my head. "Haven't talked to her. But I think I'll give her mom a call tomorrow morning. If only Jane told me who might have given Kevin the drugs."

A large spider captured a grasshopper in its web near the profuse red and yellow lantana blooms by the kitchen window. I shivered.

CHAPTER 10

The next day at work was a slow one. It seemed like everyone realized the dog days of August weren't going to last forever and were determined to play hooky and enjoy them. I asked Cheryl to see if she could find a phone number for Jane's mother, Tammi.

I opened a file and examined the new window display Cheryl had designed for fall. It had a tractor pulling a flatbed with people sitting on hay bales as they wound through a patch dotted with bright orange pumpkins.

Cheryl opened the door and walked in with a slip of paper in hand. "Found her." She laid it down by my left hand and nodded toward my monitor. "What do you think?"

"I love it. It speaks to the fact we sell farm insurance and gives a nostalgic pull for people who pick their own pumpkins. When do you think we should put it up?"

She checked her ever-present calendar. "Just after Labor Day?"

"Perfect, nice job! We're going to have to talk about a raise for you. You're doing a lot more varied work now."

Cheryl made a note in her book. "I'll be sure to remind you." She chuckled as she walked out the door.

I dialed the phone number, and when Tammi answered, I said, "It's Merry March. We met when your daughter was being questioned at Pre-Cana."

"Yes?"

"I wondered if you had time to speak with me today. I saw your daughter last week, and I heard she was missing."

Tammi sighed. "She probably just ran off. It's driving me crazy. She knows I don't do well without her. She should have at least left a note. That girl. I tell you…"

I broke into what seemed like was going to be a long rant. "I could be there by two."

She huffed, "I guess that's fine. Here are directions."

I scribbled them down, even though I was sure either my phone or GPS would get me there. "I'll see you then."

Cheryl was on the phone when I left, so I mouthed, "Call me if you need me."

She nodded as I made my way from the office, turned left, crossed the street, and walked into Delightful Bites. The owner, Gary, was in one of his signature Hawaiian shirts and tan shorts. He waved as I entered. "Late lunch, Merry?"

"Just need something sweet to take to a friend."

He strolled to a rack and pulled out a cinnamon and pecan coffee ring drizzled with white icing. "This do?"

I nodded.

He put it into a white box, tied it with a red and white string, and handed it to me.

"It's still warm."

"Should be. Took it out of the oven twenty minutes ago."

I smiled and handed him a credit card. As I waited for him to ring me up, a seedy-looking guy with tattoos lining his arms wandered in the side door. When he saw me, he blanched and pulled back. Gary handed me my credit card, and I said, "I think someone's waiting for you."

Gary turned toward the door and shrugged. "No one there now. Have a nice day."

The smell of the freshly baked ring made my mouth water as I negotiated the turns out of town. Soon I was on a country road headed west with farms on either side. The corn stalks were on the wane, with browning tips where glistening silk used to stand tall, and sickle mowers had been positioned for the second hay cutting. The sun was high in the sky, and I was happy for air-conditioning.

After about twenty minutes, a subdivision appeared on the horizon. *That must be it.* I flipped the turn signal as insistent directions emanated from my car. Most of the houses were cookie-cutter with one-car garages, peaked roofs, and various shades of beige like the same person had built them. I passed a rickety old farmhouse that seemed to have three times the land of the houses around it. *Must have been the original farm. Were the owners wistful for their way of life gone by, given the sprawl now around them?*

Three doors down was the house I had been looking for. I pulled into the driveway, grabbed the baked good, and exited the car. The house needed a fresh coat of paint, and the roof shingles looked in desperate need of replacement. I put a smile on my face and pressed the doorbell. Nothing happened. *Did it ring, and I didn't hear it?* I waited for a beat or two and then knocked. After another moment or so, Tammi opened the door. It was striking how different she looked. She wore gray sweatpants, a white t-shirt, and a tattered robe, which she pulled tight. Her hair was lank, and she seemed listless. I extended my right hand. "I don't think I introduced myself when last we met. Merry March."

She shook my hand and opened the door wider. "Come in."

I stepped into the foyer and handed her the pastry. "I thought you might want something sweet."

She looked at the box like she didn't know why it was in her hand. She gulped air and said, "I'll make tea."

We went through a clean, yet tired, living room back to an eat-in kitchen. Bright pink and purple polka-dot curtains lined the kitchen windows, which looked out onto a small backyard. I remarked, "Must get deer out here."

"I quit trying to plant flowers in the spring. They acted as if I'd rung the bell for a buffet." She poured water into a kettle and set it on the

103

stove to boil. Then she retrieved a delicate pink and green teapot from a cabinet.

"Is pink your favorite color?"

She gave a smile that seemed to require effort. "How did you know?"

"Just a guess."

"Please sit." She moved magazines off the kitchen table and gestured toward a chair.

"How long has Jane been missing?"

Tammi poured boiling water into the teapot, threaded a few teabags around the top, and sat next to me. "I don't know that she is missing. She ran away once before when she was seventeen. I didn't like the crowd she was hanging around with, so Jane rebelled. She came back after a week. A week where I didn't sleep a wink. And recently, she's been talking about a fresh start."

"I'm concerned about her. The last time I saw her, she said she was going to see an old girlfriend of Kevin's. It's odd she disappeared so soon after. Is it normal for her to go away without saying goodbye?"

She poured tea into mugs, retrieved a sharp knife, and slit the string holding the bakery box shut. She sat again and took a long sip of tea. Then she lifted her head. "Nothing about the last few weeks has been 'normal.'

"When Kevin died, she shut herself in her room for a few days and only ate when I left food outside her door. Then, after his funeral, she had to go back to work and school. It was hard on her, trying to pretend everything was okay when her heart was broken. Then toward the end of last week, she started talking about going away." Tammi rubbed the back of her neck.

"I had lunch with her last week, and she didn't mention leaving."

Tammi seemed to wake up and looked me up and down. "Jane was private. She wouldn't share her troubles with a stranger."

"I wasn't trying to imply—"

She shook her head. "Never mind." She pointed to a lovely bookshelf. "Kevin built that. No college for him when he could do work like this. He was a good'un. Had goals, wanted to work with his hands. I think he was a little afraid that with Jane going to school, she would get uppity and leave him. But there was no chance of that. She doted on that boy.

"His mom, Beth, is my best friend, and she's devastated." Tammi shuddered and rubbed her forehead. "Can't even imagine it. Second child gone. Good thing she's got the other two at home; she has to keep it together for them."

"When was the last time you saw Jane?"

"Thursday. She said she'd be back late. She was going to meet a friend for a drink after her shift."

I leaned forward. "Did she say who she was meeting?"

Tammi shook her head. "Didn't say, and I didn't ask. I was happy she was going out after spending so much time holed up in her room."

I took a bite of the coffee ring. Butter, brown sugar, and toasted pecans with a light and airy cake, delicious. As I chewed, I couldn't help but think Tammi was way too calm for a mother whose daughter had been gone for nearly a week. "Did she take any clothes?"

"Not that I could see. Her backpack was missing, but she usually takes it with her."

"What about a car?"

"Has a beat-up old red chevy pick-up. That's gone too. I already told the police all this when Beth called them."

"Beth called them? I would have thought you'd have contacted—" I traced the pink and blue flowers of the vinyl tablecloth. "I hope you don't mind me saying this, but you seem awfully calm."

She gripped her mug so tightly that I thought it would break. "The last time she did this, I ended up in the hospital. Two weeks involuntary commitment. That was before the divorce; my husband did it. I swore I'd never lose it again." Her teeth ground, and she massaged her jaw.

"I'm going to hold it together. I have my pills, and I'm taking them. She'll be home soon. She'll be fine. She'll be fine." Tammi sank back onto the chair and looked like a toy whose batteries had worn down. "I'm tired. You need to leave now."

"Can I call someone for you? Are you okay to be alone?"

She put her head on the table. "I'll be fine. She'll be home soon. You'll see." Her eyes closed.

I stood. I couldn't leave her like this. Her phone was on the counter, and thank goodness, it wasn't locked. I scrolled through her contacts, and Kevin's mother's name was listed. I pressed dial. "Mrs. Percher? My name is Merry March. I'm so sorry to bother you, but I'm at Tammi Creedy's house. We were talking, and she put her head down—"

"I'll be there in five minutes." Can you stay?"

"Of course."

I sat down and touched Tammi's arm. "Mrs. Percher is coming. She'll be here in a few minutes." No reaction. I chewed my lip as the kitchen clock continued to tick.

The back door flew open, and a short dark-haired woman ran in, knelt by Tammi, and held her hand. "Tammi, it's Beth. You need to wake up." She motioned to me. "Give me a damp towel."

I leaped up, found a drawer with dishtowels, ran one under the faucet, and wrung it. I handed it to Beth.

She lifted Tammi's hair and laid the towel on her neck. "C'mon, Tammi, you need to wake up."

Tammi opened her eyes. "What happened? Beth, what are you doing here?"

"You fell asleep. Can you stand?"

"I think so." She stood and wobbled a little.

Beth looked at me and jerked her head toward Tammi. "Can you take her arm?"

I held one, and Beth lifted the other, and we managed to get her into her bedroom, which looked like a pink elephant exploded. Beth said, "You'll be more comfortable in here. Kick your shoes off and lie down."

She did as Beth asked, and then Beth covered her with a pink and white striped afghan. Tammi said, "I'm so tired," and shut her eyes. We eased from the room.

Beth strode to the kitchen, lifted Tammi's phone, and pressed a number. "I need to speak with the doctor. Her patient, Tammi Creedy, is having another episode." There was a pause. "She'll call me back shortly? Thanks."

Beth sank onto a chair and lifted her eyes to meet mine. "Now, who are you, and what did you say to upset Tammi?"

I gulped. "I didn't mean to upset her. I came to ask about Jane. I'm concerned about her."

"I haven't seen you with Jane before." She cut a piece of the coffee cake and popped it in her mouth.

"We met at Pre-Cana."

Her hand flew to her mouth. "Where Kevin..." She stood, retrieved a cup, and poured tea. The spout of the pot clattered against the lip of the mug, and she sat. "Where Kevin died."

I touched her arm. "I'm so sorry for your loss. He seemed like a nice man."

"Man." She barked a laugh. "He was just a boy. And now Jane's gone too."

"Her mother seems to think she left on her own."

"Tammi's fragile, but I guess you saw that." Beth's brown eyes assessed me. "The police told me another boy at the class died. And now Jane's missing? Too coincidental."

Tammi's phone rang, and Beth answered. "Doctor? Can you hold for a moment?" She covered the receiver and looked at me. "See yourself out."

* * *

"It was awful. That poor woman. She was barely holding it together, and I pushed her over the edge. What kind of person am I?"

Rob hugged me. "It sounds like she wasn't in great shape when you got there."

"I'm leaving this to the police. I can't keep sticking my nose where it's not wanted. I already called Jay and asked him over. He should be here soon." I stepped away from Rob and wiped my eyes. "I caused that woman real pain. Now that Jane's missing, the police have to recognize this is more than kids experimenting with tainted drugs."

There was a rap at the back door, and Jay strolled in. Rob poured him a cup of coffee and handed it to him.

I sagged onto one of the kitchen chairs, and Jay sat opposite me and said, "To what do I owe this pleasure?"

I told him what happened that afternoon. "I'm officially swearing off all investigations from now on."

"Music to my ears. Now, if you'll excuse me, I have a fire to light and s'mores to cook."

"What about the investigation?"

Jay's eyebrow rose. "What about it?"

Rob pulled my hand into his. "Merry, you said you wanted to leave it to the police."

"I still want to know what happens next."

Jay stood, emptied his mug in the sink, and walked toward the door. "We have two drug deaths, like so many others, and a girl who left home of her own volition, according to the person closest to her, her mother. Not a lot of mystery here."

"But her mother's in denial," I objected.

"Who says?"

"Her best friend, Beth Percher."

"She lost her son. She's not thinking clearly." Jay reached for the door handle. "Jane will turn up, safe and sound." He waltzed out the door.

I turned to Rob and spoke the words that had been running on repeat in my brain like an earworm since I'd first heard about Jane. "And if she doesn't?"

CHAPTER 11

My head pounded as I tossed and turned all night, reliving the day before. If the police weren't going to try and find Jane, should I? And how would I start? If she did come back on her own, she'd be embarrassed. But what if she never came back? How would I live with myself? I moved my foot, and Courvoisier swiped at it. "Sorry."

I padded to the bathroom and brushed the stink from my breath. Then I unrolled my yoga mat and began to stretch. A next step would be to go to Fiorella's. Jane might have given notice. And if she did, then it was more likely she left on her own. It wasn't that I was still investigating. I was wrapping up loose ends. I smiled.

After my post-yoga shower, I padded downstairs, poured a cup of coffee, and reviewed my schedule for the day. I penciled in a drive to Fiorella's at four and texted Patty: "In the mood for an early cocktail and an hors d'oeuvre?"

"You bet."

"Pick you up at four-fifteen."

She sent a thumbs-up emoji.

I grabbed my purse and walked out the door. The roses against the fence were looking a bit peaky. I needed to remind myself to give them a drink after I got home. Thank heavens for the drip system Rob installed on my container plants. They were all as perky and full as they were in June, instead of like they'd been baking in the Sahara Desert. Of course, the fertilizer regime I had them on didn't hurt either.

As I strolled to work, my phone buzzed with a text from Yvonne, asking what I had found out about Matt's death. Unsure what to tell her, I dropped my phone back in my purse. Then it rang. I was relieved to see it wasn't Yvonne. "Hello, Belinda. How are you on this fine summer morning?"

"I'm calling to remind you of your appointment with Father Tom on Saturday morning."

"Wouldn't miss it. Have a good day." I grimaced as I hung up. Much as I wanted to marry Rob, I wasn't looking forward to the continuation of our Pre-Cana session.

✳ ✳ ✳

Patty slid into the car. "Where are we going?"

"Fiorella's." I pulled away from the curb.

"Fancy." She tightened her seat belt and turned toward me. "And we are going there, why?"

"I have questions that need answers." I brought her up to speed.

As we pulled into Fiorella's parking lot, Patty said, "So if she gave notice, you think she left on her own?"

I nodded, turned off the car, and slid from my seat. We walked toward the entrance. "Follow my lead."

She extended her hand and went through the door after me. "As always."

We entered the nearly empty bar and climbed onto plush burgundy leather bar stools. I said, "Two chardonnays and an order of pot stickers." I paused. "Oh, and if the chef can spare a few moments."

The bartender poured two glasses of wine. "Be right back."

Patty and I barely had a chance to take a quick sip when a tiny woman in a white chef's coat approached. "You wanted to speak to me?"

"First, my family and I dine here often, and we love your food," I gushed.

"Thank you. We love to hear from satisfied customers." She waited.

"I understand you have a young cook who works for you, Jane Creedy."

"Used to."

"I'm sorry?"

"Hasn't been here since last Thursday night and haven't heard from her either. Good kid and a good cook." She shrugged. "Hazard of the business. Too often, people leave without notice. Wouldn't have thought it of her though. Always on time, willing to work extra shifts, a good kid." She watched a few people being led to tables. "Early birds. Need to get back. Anything else?"

I shook my head as the bartender slid our snack in front of us.

"Enjoy."

Patty slid a pot sticker onto a plate and drizzled sauce over it. "Now what?"

We chewed in silence.

"Flyers." I sipped wine.

"Airplanes?"

"Missing person flyers. That's next. And maybe volunteer searchers." I lifted another cocktail napkin and began writing. Then, I pulled out my phone and typed in Jane's name. Her picture came up on Instagram.

"What about her mother? Shouldn't you give her a heads up?"

My stomach churned. "Probably."

* * *

"Last night, you said you were going to leave this alone. Why are we talking about it again?" Rob uncorked a bottle of Merlot.

"Just half for me, I had a head start."

He handed me a glass.

"Last night, Jay pooh-poohed my concerns. And that girl is still out there." I shivered. "I hope she's still alive. If Jenny were ever missing..."

"There isn't much you can do." Rob and I sat on the sofa, and he put his arm around me.

I lifted a folder and handed it to him. A hundred identical pages were inside. They featured Jane's picture and under that "Missing," and below that "Call" plus my work number.

He pointed to the phone number. "You're going to use people at your office for this?"

"It's slow right now."

"What did her mom say?"

"I haven't told her." I groaned. "I don't want to make her any more upset than she already is."

Rob pulled his arm from the back of the sofa and turned to face me. "It will be far worse if you don't tell her." He sipped wine. "Maybe you could use Beth Percher as a go-between."

"But her son just died." I chewed an antacid.

"All the more reason."

"I'll call her tomorrow before I put these up."

"No time like the present." He handed me his phone.

I gave him my glass. "This is going to take more wine."

I googled Beth and then pressed enter for her number. One of her kids answered and screamed, "Mom, it's for you."

"How many times do I have to tell you to cover the mouthpiece when you yell?" Beth answered, breathless, "Hello." I paused, and she said, "Is anyone there?"

I coughed. "It's Merry March. We met yesterday at Tammi's house."

"Yes?"

"I think we need to let people know Jane is missing." I moved the now full glass, and the living room light shimmered through the burgundy color.

"I agree."

"You do?"

"Of course. I was the one who called the police. Who have done nothing, FYI."

"I put together a missing person flyer. I think someone needs to tell Tammi we're going to do this." I bit my lip.

"And you want that to be me." She paused. My heart raced. "Send it to me. Here's my email address."

The next morning, there was a response from Beth: "Do it." I got out of bed. *Time to get moving.*

As I sipped coffee, I texted Patty: "Put up the flyers." She had agreed to do the area around Fiorella's, and I was going to do Hopeful. Walking to work, I tacked some to telephone poles, and when I got to town, I ducked into shops to obtain permission to tape it to front windows. Finally, I walked into my own business and made quick work of putting one in my window.

Cheryl walked over. "What's this about?"

I crooked my finger, she followed me into my office, and I explained.

By the end of the following day, we had only heard from kooks, conspiracy theorists, and general all-around nuts. My staff was grumpy from the non-productive phone calls, and I was beginning to regret posting the notices. Somehow, I battled through Friday, begged off on an evening with Rob, and ended up in a soothing bubble bath with a book I had been neglecting for far too long.

Drew was scheduled to call at nine. I padded to Jenny's room and rapped on the door. She was lying on the bed, fingers flying on her phone. I asked, "How was the movie?" and motioned for her to scoot over. I sat next to her on the bed.

"It was okay. Animated films are better though." Her phone rang, and she answered. "Hi, Dad. How are you? Uh-huh. Mom wants to talk to you." She handed me the phone.

"You can't use Jenny as your go-between with Arianna."

"Merry, I'm worried about her. Arianna's never been in prison before. I need to know she's okay."

"Have your lawyer talk to her lawyer. Don't involve your daughter."
I rolled my shoulders, trying to release tension.

"No one will know," he wheedled, "you like Arianna. Aren't you worried about her?"

"Not going to work. Seeing my seventeen-year-old daughter being led away by the police in London is permanently seared in my brain. Have a nice life."

I handed the phone back to Jenny and walked out the door, pacing back and forth in my bedroom until Jenny rapped on my door. She dove onto the bed and pulled the covers up. "Dad said to forget about helping him. What should I say when Arianna calls me?"

"How school is going and that you miss her." I climbed in next to her. "She calls you because she wants to hear about you."

"Are you sure?"

"Positive."

* * *

The following day, I felt refreshed and ready to face the world. After I fed the cats, I took my coffee outside, and the sweet perfume of tea roses in bloom welcomed me. I grabbed the hose and swung it back and forth, giving the garden a good drink. Rob waved from over the fence, then frowned. "Going to get black spot that way. You need to water the ground, not the roses."

I turned off the spigot. "If only I knew someone who has experience installing drip systems." I kissed his cheek.

He laughed. "Message received. Ready?"

"As I'm going to be."

"Don't you want to get married?" He pulled me into a hug.

"I do. And I've found the process helpful." I tipped my head for a kiss. "But I still wish we could run away and elope."

He bussed my nose. "If you wanted that, we wouldn't have needed to wait for the annulment."

"Let me grab my purse." I dashed up the stairs, retrieved it and a pad to take notes, and rejoined Rob for the walk to church.

"When I talked to you yesterday, you sounded pretty down." He held my hand.

"I wish we could find Jane. It's so frustrating not knowing if she's alive or dead." We turned up the drive for the rectory. The parishioners had done a marvelous job tending the gardens, so it appeared they were far better at watering than me. Rob held the door, and my phone buzzed. It was another text from Yvonne. I was going to need to get back to her soon.

Father Tom stuck his head out of his office and said, "I thought I heard someone. Belinda's off today. Would you like something to drink?"

I said, "A glass of water would be great."

Rob held up two fingers.

"Join me in the kitchen. We may as well be informal."

He poured us two glasses of water and then joined us at the well-worn table. "My understanding is you got as far as the money conversation."

I felt my cheeks flush. "That was a tough discussion for me."

"It's a sticking point for many couples." Father Tom sat forward and steepled his fingers.

Rob interjected, "Merry was worried about Jenny."

"Jenny, plus I'm still gun-shy after what happened with Drew."

Father Tom nodded.

"I'm going to get an appointment with an attorney to talk about revising our wills so that Jenny gets what Merry wants her to have," Rob said.

"Good. Don't let that slide. It's best to get these things resolved before the wedding." He paused. "One of the other stressors for marriages is children. The church advocates for blessed unions."

I let out a breath and sat back in my chair. "If the good Lord seeks to bless us in that way, we welcome it."

"I can't wait to marry this woman." Rob took my hand and kissed it.

Father Tom led us through a few more sticking points and then said, "I'll be back in a moment."

"That wasn't so bad." Rob put his arm around me.

"One more thing to check off our list."

Father Tom bustled back through the door, certificate in hand. "Here you go. Keep this with your important papers."

Rob took it from him and laughed. "We're official." He lifted me off my feet and spun me around. "Let's celebrate. Father, you're welcome to join us."

He shook his head and turned to leave. "Still working on tomorrow's homily."

"Father, one more thing." I fished a flyer out of my purse. "Could you tack this to the parish bulletin board?"

He studied it. "What a shame. I'd be happy to. I'll see you both tomorrow."

✳ ✳ ✳

Jenny had made cinnamon rolls when she got home Saturday night, so I only had to pop them in the oven on Sunday. When Rob walked in the back door, he smiled. "Why do I smell something good?"

"Thank Jenny."

"I will when she wakes up."

I took them out of the oven and set them on a trivet to cool. "Want one now, or do you want to wait till after church?"

"I had breakfast, but a half wouldn't hurt."

I cut one in two and used a spatula to lift it from the pan as golden strands of buttery-cinnamon goodness dripped onto plates. Rob poured coffee, and we sat to eat. I smiled. "This feels so domestic."

"Can't wait to do this all the time." He cut the roll with the side of his fork, put the bite in his mouth, and groaned. "So good."

"Better eat fast. We'll need to hoof it to get to church on time."

He swirled his last piece in the melted sugar on the plate, placed it in his mouth, and swigged the dregs of his coffee. "Ready."

I grabbed my purse, and we walked out the door. "One thing we haven't discussed is where we're going to live once we're married."

"That's easy. I'll sell my place and move in with you."

"Are you sure? Drew and I bought this house." I stopped.

He lifted my face toward his. "I've only ever thought of it as yours. Plus, this is going to be a big enough change for Jenny. Let's not make it harder."

"You're going to be a terrific father." I glanced at my watch. "And now we're late."

We crept into the back of the church and sat toward the rear. I slid into the pew and said, "It's odd they haven't started."

Five minutes later, after the buzz in the pews had gotten louder due to the unexpected delay, Father Tom rushed in, looking a bit disheveled. "Sorry I'm late. Unavoidable. Let's begin."

The homily touched on the sanctity of life, importance of family, and perils of despair. As we left the church, Father Tom gestured for us to wait. We moved to one side as he greeted the other parishioners. Finally, after everyone had shuffled out, he said, "Let's sit for a moment."

We moved into one of the pews, and Rob asked, "What's up?"

"I'm afraid I have bad news. That flyer you gave me yesterday—" he paused "—a fisherman found her this morning. She was on the riverbank, dead."

I gasped. "No."

Rob put his arm around me. "How did you find out?"

"Their parish priest is recovering from surgery, and they wanted help breaking the news to the poor woman's mother. That's why I was late."

I leaned forward. "How did she take it?"

He paled. "Not well. They had to sedate her."

"How did Jane die?"

"Not sure. The police were still investigating. The fisherman had seen one of your flyers. That's how they identified her."

I wrapped my arms around myself. "First Kevin, then Matt, and now Jane. When will it stop?"

* * *

Rob handed me another cup of tea and wrapped a throw around my shoulders. I couldn't get my teeth to stop chattering, even though the air temperature was warm. Jenny bounded down the stairs and came around the corner into the kitchen. Her eyes widened as she saw me. "What's wrong, Mom?"

Rob looked up. "They found Jane Creedy. She was dead."

"That's awful. Are you okay?"

I waved my hand, not trusting my voice.

She sank next to me on the window seat. "There was nothing you could do. Her own mother didn't report her missing."

"I should have gotten a search party together."

"You did the flyers. Got the word out."

"That's how the fisherman knew." Rob nodded.

I pushed my hair back from my face and shoved the afghan from my shoulders. "Her poor mother."

The back door opened, and Jay walked in. "Coffee? I need a cup. Badly."

Rob retrieved a mug, poured, and handed it to him.

Jay eyed me. "Looks like news travels fast."

"I hope I don't look that bad." I stood and walked to the counter. "Cinnamon roll? Jenny made them."

"Love one. Didn't get breakfast, out since dawn."

I placed two on a plate and set it in front of him with a fork and knife. "What happened?"

"She was on the riverbank. A mirror was next to her along with a rolled-up dollar bill."

I shrugged. "What does that mean?"

"Cocaine?" Rob guessed.

"Huh?" I looked at him.

"Won't have the results back from the lab for a bit, so can't tell. Also, it rained, so any residue that might have been on the mirror is long gone. The dollar bill will tell the story." Jay bit into the cinnamon roll. "Good."

Jenny said, "Thanks."

"What are you talking about? Mirror, dollar bills, what does that have to do with cocaine?" I raised my voice.

"Haven't you seen any movies from the eighties?" Jay sipped coffee. "People place lines of cocaine on a mirror and use the rolled-up dollar bill to snort them."

"She was a pretty driven young woman. It's hard to believe she was doing drugs."

"You'd be surprised at the people who get high." Jay wiped his lips with a napkin. "Got to get back. Thanks for breakfast."

CHAPTER 12

J enny joined me as I pulled down the "missing" flyers. Since it was Sunday, many of the shops were closed, so we had to leave those. I told her, "Thanks for your help. I couldn't face seeing these reminders on my way to work tomorrow."

"It's so sad. She wasn't much older than me."

I put my arm around Jenny. "You need to be very careful. There's something bad going on, and I'm not exactly sure what it is."

"Can I borrow the car again later? I want to go back out to the library to thank Ann for her help with my college visits."

"A drive in the country sounds good. Mind if I come with you?"

"As long as I get to drive."

I took down the last poster. We walked back to the house, and I tossed Jenny the keys. "I get to choose the music."

"Deal."

Jenny pushed the memory button for the driver's seat, it moved back several inches, and then she slid into the car. "You have stubby legs."

"Do you want to drive?" I frowned at her.

"Just kidding." She smiled and started the car. "Not."

As she drove, I played with the radio, finally landing on a country station I liked. She whined a bit, but I noticed her tapping her fingers in time with the music on the steering wheel. I asked, "Have you thought about what extracurricular activities you're going to sign up for in school this year?"

Her head tilted. "Definitely basketball. I'd like to try Drama Club, but it conflicts with the B-Ball schedule, so probably not. And swim team. I'm cutting back a bit because I want my last year to be easier."

"Sounds like you're still doing a lot."

She shook her head. "I've decided to give up dance, so that frees up time."

"Whatever makes you happy."

Jenny pulled into the library parking lot. "Do you want to wait in the car? I shouldn't be long."

"I'll come in."

We walked to the low-slung brick building. It was far smaller than ours, but the summer decorations in the windows were homey. There were cut-outs of beach balls, swimming pools, and kids reading books by a lazy river, which made it look welcoming. Ann was helping an older gentleman with one of the computers. She wore a bright pink short-sleeve sweater with shimmery turquoise slacks. I blinked. *That's a loud combination.* I pointed to the mystery sign on the stacks. "I'll be over there when you're done."

She walked toward Ann as I ducked into one of the aisles. They had a good selection of Agatha Christies, as well as other well-known authors. A display toward the end showcased local authors, so I made my way there. As I exited the aisle, I almost ran into Yvonne Logan.

"Merry. You haven't returned any of my texts."

"I'm sorry. It's been hectic. How are you?" I was concerned. She appeared to have lost weight, and the black bags under her eyes had gotten deeper.

"I'd be better if I knew what was going on." She held up a book. "Escaping helps."

My face flushed. I didn't know what to say.

"The police aren't doing anything."

"They're trying. It's hard. There are so many more people affected every day."

"But those are true drug addicts. My son wasn't." She took a step toward me.

"I'm sorry for you. But all the people who've been lost were someone else's sons and daughters. It's such a scourge."

"I didn't mean to imply—" Her hand went to her mouth.

"I know." My heart ached for her. "It's so difficult for you, Beth, and Tammi." I touched her arm.

"Beth's the mother of the other boy from Pre-Cana who died, Kevin? But who is Tammi?"

"Tammi Creedy. Her daughter, who was Kevin's fiancé, just died."

Yvonne's face flamed red. "Three of them? All dead? All from the same session? This has to be related. The police are going to hear from me." She stormed from the building.

Ann ran after her, "Ma'am, you need to check out that book." A few minutes later, Ann returned, book in hand. She held it up. "Success. But that poor woman looked so upset I almost let her leave with it."

"She just lost her son."

"That's sad. Was he ill?" Ann moved closer.

Jenny shook her head. "Drugs."

"People who do drugs are idiots." She turned, walked back to the circulation desk, and placed the book on it, making a pencil that had been part of a regiment go off-kilter. She pursed her lips and moved it back in line. "I'm getting so excited for your wedding. They said the dresses should be ready for our fitting soon."

I stared at her. It seemed a bit heartless to move from someone's death to anticipation about a new dress. I chalked it up to her being young. "When they call, I'll arrange a time when we can all be there. Are you ready, Jenny?"

"Thanks again, Ann. I appreciate your help." Jenny twirled the car keys as she walked out the door.

I slid into the passenger seat, and Jenny started the car. She said, "Ann's the best. She has her whole life figured out."

"Oh?"

"She's going to work her way to head librarian and then get married and have three kids."

"Is she dating anyone?" I fiddled with the radio station.

"Not yet, but she's looking. Apparently, she had her eyes on someone a few years ago, but he didn't have long-term potential, so she dropped him." Jenny flipped the turn signal. "Maybe I should be thinking that way. Do you think Jacob is 'the one?'"

I coughed and grabbed my water bottle. "You're seventeen. You have your whole life ahead of you. Go to school, figure out who you are, and then find the right guy."

"You're just worried I'm going to end up like you."

"Some parts of my life are great. I own a company, have a super daughter, a fabulous fiancé—" Jenny was driving way too close to the car in front. As it started to break, I slammed my foot on the floorboard.

Jenny backed off. "Mom, I know how to drive. One of these days, you're going to put your foot right through."

I sighed.

"Anyway, I don't want to get married as early as you did, so you don't need to worry."

"Let's get home in one piece, please."

She rolled her eyes and turned the volume higher.

✳ ✳ ✳

Patty stirred macaroni and cheese while I browned beef and onions. She handed me the bowl and said, "I still don't know why I have to go."

"Phoenix. You still owe me."

She sighed. "You're never going to let me forget, are you?"

"Nope." I poured tomatoes and the beef mixture on top of the macaroni, stirred it, and slid the whole thing into an aluminum pan. "Food is comforting. Her daughter died. It's the right thing to do."

"But I don't even know this woman. And you hardly do." She sprinkled cheese on top, taped instructions for cooking to the lid, and walked out to the car. "Let's get this over with."

I beeped the trunk. Patty placed the casserole, slid the car jack and a sack of books against it so it wouldn't move, and slammed the lid closed.

I hopped in the driver's seat, she joined me in the car, and I pulled out of the driveway. "I'm not sure Jenny looks up to me anymore."

Patty stared at me.

"Why on earth would you think that? You have one of the best relationships I've seen."

I shrugged. "She was extolling Ann's virtues."

"Ann seems like a nice girl and has a good job. Nothing wrong with someone who encourages reading."

"I know." I sighed. "I don't want Jenny to grow up. I want her to stay my daughter forever."

Patty pushed my shoulder. "You can't help the first, and you have nothing to worry about when it comes to the second."

"Cindy's going to school after next year too. How are you so calm?"

"I'm not. She's such a help with the boys. It'll be tough without her. Actually, it'll be tough without her, full stop. Thanks for reminding me."

Both lost in our thoughts, the miles ticked by. Finally, I turned into Tammi's subdivision and parked in her driveway. Patty and I got out of the car, and I retrieved the casserole. Patty beat me to the door, and I said, "Doorbell's broken. Need to knock."

She rapped three times, and after a minute or so, Beth Percher answered instead of Tammi. "Oh, it's you. May as well come in." She walked toward the kitchen, and Patty and I followed. Covered dishes lined the island. Beth pointed to a bare spot. "Stick it there, please."

I complied and introduced Patty. Beth nodded as she sank onto a seat at the table and, after a moment, gestured for us to do the same. I asked, "Where's Tammi? Is she napping?"

She shook her head. "No." Her hand trembled as she lifted a half cup of tea to her lips.

We waited.

"She tried to overdose on pain pills she had from when she broke an ankle a few years ago. I hadn't heard from her and called. No answer. I came over, and she was in her bedroom, the pill jar on the floor." Beth shuddered. "I'm not sure she's going to make it."

I gasped, "That's awful."

"All these—" she swept her hand toward the counter "—were here when I came. I guess people dropped by all morning, and after a while, she couldn't take the reminder."

"What can we do?" Patty grabbed a kettle on the counter and put it on the stove.

"Don't even know where to start. If she doesn't come back..." Beth shook her head.

"Is there someone we could call for you?"

Tears dripped from her face. "How could this happen? How could she give up hope?"

"Would you like me to see if I can find room in the refrigerator for these?" Patty asked Beth.

"Please."

The kettle whistled, and Patty brought it to the table, put more hot water in Beth's mug, and dropped in a new tea bag. Then she began loading the casseroles into Tammi's refrigerator and freezer.

I wanted to help Patty but didn't want to leave Beth alone at the table, so I sat there, becoming increasingly uncomfortable.

Eventually, she broke the silence, "I can't believe it's come to this. A few short weeks ago, Tammi and I were shopping for dresses for our kids' weddings. Jane was so pretty, and her gown was amazing. They had found the nicest place for the reception. Fuchsia azaleas ringed a pond with a bridge leading to a bright-white gazebo in the middle. The pictures would have been beautiful."

She wiped her eyes with a napkin. "They knew each other a long time. When they were little, Tammi and I joked they'd get married eventually, and finally, when they were high school juniors, the flame was lit." She took the teabag from her mug and sipped. "It made me happy. Especially after that one girl he dated. There was something off about her."

I sat up straight. "Who was she?"

Beth glanced at the clock and leaped to her feet. "Is that the time? The kids are home. I need to go."

Patty wiped her hands on her slacks. "I got all of them in but ours." She pointed toward it. "For dinner tonight. Instructions are on the top."

Beth said, "Thanks," and walked with us to the front door.

I handed her one of my cards. "Please keep me updated on Tammi. I'm so sorry."

I got in the car like someone who was eighty and sat there staring at the house as my stomach churned.

Patty said, "Earth to Merry."

"So much sadness. So much death."

"Time to get away."

"What?" I turned toward her.

"Last dregs of summer. I say we escape to the lake."

"The two of us?" I started the car.

"Everyone. It'll be like old times."

I backed out of the drive. "When?"

"This weekend. You need it."

* * *

Rob and Patrick unloaded the cars, and I gave instructions. "Patty, me, Cindy, and Jenny will be in my bedroom, you and Patrick will be in Jenny's room in the twin beds, and the other kids will be on blow-up mattresses in the office."

Patrick grumbled as he hauled yet another suitcase, "Why does it seem like we packed for a month when we're only going to be here for a long weekend?"

"Nine people, assorted pillows and air mattresses, and food." Patty laughed.

Rob lifted a box of wine. "Don't forget the drinks."

The boys ran for the dock, and Patty yelled. "Don't go in yet! Wait for us."

As I put the groceries away, Jenny and Cindy ran down the stairs and out the door. I turned toward the picture window as Jenny passed the boys and dove in. Shawn objected, "No fair. We were here first." Within minutes, the kids were in the lake, and Jenny and Cindy had swum out to the raft.

Patty yelled from upstairs, "Cindy, please keep an eye on them."

Cindy gave her mom a thumbs up. A few minutes later, Patty joined me in the kitchen. "Sheets on the beds, reporting for duty down here."

I laughed. "Good call on coming. I needed this."

Rob and Patrick joined us, wearing their swim trunks. Patrick asked Rob, "Beer first or swim?"

"Swim." Rob ran out the door, down the path, and cannonballed one of the kids. Patrick was on his heels.

Patty said, "Why don't you go get changed? I'll put snacks in a bowl for the kids, and then we'll join them."

I ran upstairs, changed into my suit, and slathered sunscreen on anything that remained exposed. I stopped as I walked by the window. Jenny and Cindy were lying on the raft, Rob and Patrick were blowing through green and blue pool noodles to soak the other kids, and Patty was relaxing on one of the Adirondack chairs. I smiled, and my shoulders relaxed. It seemed like it had been an eternity since I had any fun. I ran down the stairs and out the door.

✷ ✷ ✷

Long after the obligatory s'mores, exhausted kids were tucked into various make-shift beds. Patty, Patrick, Rob, and I chatted around the dying fire as embers sporadically glowed red in the inky dark. Patty asked, "Have you decided where your honeymoon will be?"

Rob lifted my hand to his lips. "Maybe it will be a surprise."

"You're welcome to the Phoenix place." Patrick offered.

"A cook, a maid, and a beautiful hacienda sounds like heaven to me." I sipped wine.

"A lot of people." Rob shook his head. "I was thinking something smaller. Like you and me."

"We should probably decide soon, or places will be booked." The stars seemed much brighter, and then one streaked across the sky.

"Make a wish!" Patty said.

Rob closed his eyes.

I asked him, "What did you wish for?"

"You." He smiled.

CHAPTER 13

The weekend had been just what I needed. Good friends, kids getting lots of fresh air versus screen time, and Rob. I snuggled deeper into the lilac-scented sheets. *I can't wait to marry that man.* The thought of him becoming my husband would get me through the fitting tonight. At least Patty would be there. She'd provide a buffer. And who knows, maybe Wanda and I would connect again. *Miracles can happen.*

My alarm rang, and I made quick work of showering and getting dressed. I was hoping for another slow day, although my bank account would probably prefer one with more action. I fed the cats, gave each one a perfunctory pat on the head, and walked out the door. As I strolled toward the gate, plaintive cries followed. I turned and said, "I'll let you out later."

Andy smirked from the other side of the gate. "Talking to cats? They don't understand English."

"Sure they do. They know what out, food, and treats mean."

"Uh-huh." He gave me a doubtful look. "Have a good weekend?"

"The best. Went to the lake with Patty and her clan. Lots of fun." I fell into stride with him as we walked to work.

"We haven't gotten an invite since last year," he sniffed. "Not that I'm angling. You've hardly been here this summer."

I laughed. "We'll have to have you and Ed again. I want to get out there more often."

"I hate to ask, but have you found out anything more about Matt's death? Yvonne stopped by the store on Saturday, and she was so hot I thought she'd set the drapes on fire. She said you've been ducking her, and she had been to see Jay and felt he still wasn't giving the investigation the attention it deserves."

I snapped my fingers. "Darn it. I knew there was something I needed to do before I left. I forgot to give Jay a heads-up she'd be stopping by."

"You told Yvonne you'd try to figure out what happened." Andy stopped.

"I have been looking into things. It's tougher than I thought. The girl who just died, Jane, her mother tried to kill herself last week."

Andy said, "That's awful, Merry. But what does it have to do with Yvonne and her son?"

I sighed. "It's all tied together somehow. And I'm tired of people dying."

We reached my business, and Andy hugged me.

I walked through the door and almost into Cheryl. She stepped back. "I thought you'd be looking far more relaxed. Maybe you need to take more time."

"Maybe I need to drive to work," I muttered as I rounded the corner to my office. Just before shutting the door, I turned. "Cheryl, would you please see if Detective Ziebold has time for lunch today? My treat."

I started on my call list and arranged a few appointments with new clients. It seemed like more people were home enjoying their last days together before the kids needed to go back to school. Feeling accomplished, I turned to my next task.

Cheryl popped in the door. "You're meeting Detective Ziebold at noon at Delightful Bites. He only has a half-hour."

"Meaning I should get a move on."

"Your words, not mine." She smiled and walked back to her desk.

I grabbed my purse and hurried out the door. Jay was waiting in front of the shop. "Wasn't sure if you wanted to sit inside or out."

"Out, if we can find shade."

He nodded and joined the short line inside. After a minute or two, he ordered. "Roast beef on rye with horseradish mayo and fries. Coffee."

I followed. "Salad with salmon, medium please, and dressing on the side. Oh, and iced tea."

The woman finished writing the order and turned to place it in the kitchen window as Jay and I got our drinks and walked outside. A couple got up from a table with an umbrella, and I nudged Jay. "Over there."

He claimed the table, and I sat next to him and said, "Nice breeze."

He nodded. "What's this about, Merry? You only call when you need something."

"You make me sound terrible."

"Single-minded." Jay crossed his arms over his chest.

The waiter brought Jay's sandwich and my salad. Jay took a large bite and chewed. I drizzled dressing on the salad. "I was wondering where you were on the investigation of all the kids who died."

Jay swallowed and said, "Last year, over four thousand people in our state alone died from unintentional drug overdoses, and of those deaths, seventy-six percent involved fentanyl. And that number is climbing. We can't investigate all the deaths. We don't have the manpower." He dipped a french fry in ketchup and ate it.

"That many?" My mouth dropped.

He nodded as he took another bite of his sandwich.

I cut a piece of salmon with the side of my fork. "But how many of those people knew each other and died so close together?"

He sighed as he put his sandwich back on his plate. "Last week, a couple in the next town was driving with small children in the back seat and took drugs in front of them. They both passed out. Luckily, the car was going slowly and came to a rest near a tree." He shuddered. "Their kids were in the car! Who does that? People are crazy."

"Did they make it?" I put my fork down.

"We had naloxone; we always carry it now, but we didn't get to them in time. Those kids are now going to be raised by their grandparents." He looked at the rest of his sandwich and fries. "Going to get this to-go."

I stood. "I'll get boxes." I went into the restaurant and picked up two near the cash register. *Such a horrible story.* I felt light-headed as I made my way back to the table and handed a box to Jay.

"You look a little pale. Should you sit down?"

"I'm okay." I shook my head.

He opened one of the boxes and slid his leftovers into it. "I'm sorry if I upset you, but that's what we are dealing with nearly every day now. And it's worse out in the country. You wouldn't think so, but it is. I wish we could find out who's bringing this stuff in and shut off the supply."

"I hear what you're saying, but I sat with those people—at the same table." I wrung my hands. "I talked to them about their plans for the future. Their hopes for their weddings. And now, three of them are dead. They were good kids. I have to get to the bottom of it."

Jay lifted his now full container. "Save yourself the heartache. They got a bad batch. Nothing more than that. Thanks for lunch." He walked away.

I sank back onto the chair. *Am I tilting at windmills?*

* * *

Somehow, I got through the rest of the day at work and trudged to C'est Magnifique for the bridesmaid's dress fittings. I walked through the door, and an explosion of sound greeted me. Jenny, Ann, and Amy had their dresses on and were dancing to music playing from someone's phone. Sandy was in the process of trying to pin Jenny's dress. Sandy said, "Please stop moving. I'm afraid I'll stick you."

Wanda walked into the shop behind me and yelled, "Silence. What's that racket?"

133

Amy turned off the music and placed the phone in her purse.

"Now, let's get this done. I need to meet Mac for dinner." Wanda perched on a chair as if it were her throne. "Ann, that dress is sagging in front." Wanda snapped her fingers at Sandy and pointed. "Fix it."

"Let me finish with Jenny." She put in a few more pins and said, "Turn to the right, please. That's better."

I said, "It looks lovely. Thank you, Sandy."

April walked in with champagne and tried to hand a glass to Wanda. She waved her away. "Not tonight."

I took one. "Thanks."

Wanda looked down her nose. "Where's Patty?"

"She's going to be late."

"How inconsiderate," Wanda huffed. "She missed the first session, and now she's late to this one. Merry, you should get more reliable friends."

Heat flooded my face, and I sputtered, "She's the best person I know."

"You may as well try on your dress." Wanda looked at her watch. "I need to leave soon."

Sandy said, "We fitted Merry's dress last week."

"Get the dress." I sighed.

April said to Sandy, "I'll do it. You continue with the girls."

Sandy put her head down and began pinning Ann's dress.

I walked into the dressing room and eyed the tufted sofa. *I could hide in here till the store closes.*

April gave a quick rap and opened the door. She came in with the dress carefully draped over her arm. "Scary lady."

"You've only gotten a taste." I shrugged out of my clothes and quickly donned the dress. It was loose. *Strange.* I walked out, stood in front of the mirror, and turned right and left.

Sandy turned as I walked back into the showroom. "Have you lost weight?"

I shrugged. "Sorry about that."

"No problem. I'll finish up here and then look at yours again." Sandy took one last look at Ann. "There. That's better."

Wanda stood and walked closer. "Maybe a little bit more here and here?"

"It's fine." Ann strode away. "You can work on Amy next."

Amy was leaning against the wall in the corner, and Wanda snapped. "Don't slouch. That dress looks like a bean bag on you."

"I told you black would look better."

"Nonsense. Stand up straight." Wanda sighed. "I better call Mac. It looks like this is going to take quite some time."

Amy's face turned bright red. Sandy began to work on her dress and said, "Don't worry, we'll get you looking spectacular."

Wanda pulled out her phone, and I touched my hand to her arm. "Wanda, this is the first fitting. It's far more important for you to be at the final one. Why don't you go ahead and meet Mac? We can handle this. I'd hate to upset your plans."

She gave her watch another glance and sighed. "I guess you're right, though I hate to leave you in the lurch—"

"We'll be fine."

Patty rushed through the door. "I'm so sorry I'm late. You won't believe the day I had."

Wanda lifted her purse, locked eyes with Patty, harrumphed, and left.

Jenny tiptoed to the outer door and peered through the window. "She's getting in her car. And—she's gone."

It seemed like everyone exhaled at once. I turned to Amy. "You can play your tunes again but at a lower volume. And no dancing while getting pinned."

Amy smiled, unzipped her purse, and pulled her phone out. A baggie containing what looked like dried algae tumbled out and fell at her feet. She grabbed it and shoved it into her purse.

I gasped.

"Just a little weed, nothing to get excited about. It's legal in a bunch of states," she mumbled.

"Not that many. And certainly not here."

"It's better for you than the champagne we're drinking. One day it will be legal here too."

"That day is not today." I gritted my teeth. "Jenny, since it looks like you're done, why don't you go on home? I'll be back in a bit."

Jenny slipped out the door without saying a word. Ann followed her, and as she walked past Amy, muttered, "Idiot. I'll wait for you in the car."

Patty took the glass of champagne April offered her. Sandy rushed through pinning Amy's dress, and before too long, Amy left.

Patty slid her dress over her head and asked, "What else did I miss?"

* * *

As Rob finished laying the last sprinkler line to the rose garden, I perched next to him on an overturned bucket. "...so, it hits the floor, and she is as cool as tonight's breeze as she scoops it up. If Wanda had been there, I don't know what would have happened. She was hard enough on the girl about her posture."

"Maybe Mother would have been okay with it." Rob wiped his hands on a towel.

"Your mother? Okay with pot?" I chuckled.

"Success. First laugh I've gotten out of you all night."

I rubbed the back of my neck. "The fun at the lake seems so long ago, and it was just this weekend. How can that be possible?"

He stood, pulled me up, and kissed me. "It's because you take on the world's problems."

"It's pretty hard to ignore when the problem drops at your feet. Literally. Jenny was standing there. How did I let these people into my life? I'm a terrible mother."

"You didn't let them in. My mother did. And I guess, by extension, I did. Maybe I'm a bad future stepfather."

I rubbed his arm. "You're going to be the best stepfather ever." I started to giggle and then couldn't stop.

"What?"

"The look on Amy's face. It was priceless. It was like a kid who gets caught red-handed with the last cookie her mother told her not to eat."

"Hopefully, it's just grass and not grass mixed with something else."

My eyes widened, and I stopped laughing.

CHAPTER 14

The following day, I woke early and decided to be virtuous and make oatmeal. After dressing for work, I retrieved the paper from the front stoop, wandered into the kitchen, and put water on to boil, almost tripping over the cats in the process. "If you kill me, no one will feed you." They appeared unaffected by my statement, so I shook kibble into their bowls, and they set upon it like they hadn't been fed for days.

I stirred oatmeal into the boiling water, poured coffee into a mug, and opened the paper. Thank heavens there wasn't another death reported. The most exciting thing was an ad for the upcoming festival at the Greek Orthodox Church. My mouth watered, thinking about baklava. I added a reminder to my phone, gave a final stir to my breakfast, added raisins, and poured the results into a bowl.

As I ate, I flipped through the rest of the paper. There wasn't much else that caught my eye. I pulled up the city news on my tablet and scrolled through. There was an investigative article on the opioid crisis. *I wonder if Rob knows this woman. Maybe she has more information about what's happening.* I pulled over a pad of paper and began to doodle. *What am I missing?* I started a new checklist: Has Matt's fiancé Trudy Jones remembered anything else? Status update from Beth on Tammi's condition. And ask Rob about the reporter.

I checked my phone. Still kind of early, but not too early for Rob. I pressed his number.

"Hello, beautiful. Did you call to hear my voice?"

I laughed. "I love your baritone, and had I thought of it, I would have." I paused. "Did you see the article on opioids in the city paper?"

"Hold on. Let me pull it up." He paused. "Uh-huh, got it right here."

"Do you know the woman who wrote it?"

"I used to play poker with her husband and some other people. Why?"

"Let's put our heads together at lunch today. I want you to reach out to her and see if she's been following what's been happening here."

"Noon? Tempting Treasures and Tasty Treats?"

"It's a date. Love you."

"Love you too. I'll be counting the hours."

I laughed and hung up. I still had time before I needed to leave for work, so I opened the door, and the cats darted out before I could stop them. I sighed. I'd give them a few minutes and then bring them in. The roses were in full bloom again as the summer heat had left. I fetched my clippers, cut a few, and deposited them in a pail with a few inches of water in the bottom. As I turned to take my prizes in, I spied oak leaf hydrangea that would make a nice addition to the bouquet.

Jada called, "You're out early."

I held up my bucket. "Cutting a few blooms."

"Very pretty."

"Have time for a cup of coffee?"

"Love one." She opened the back gate and followed me into the kitchen. I handed her a mug and the pot, and she poured herself a cup while I retrieved a vase.

"I'm embarrassed we haven't firmed up a date for dinner. It's been so crazy." I gave one of the roses a fresh cut and placed it in the container. "I know it's short notice, but how's Friday night at six?"

She pulled out her phone and checked. "Looks like we could make it. Strange to think the kids will be back in school the end of next week."

"That's when the craziness will start. Is Imani signing up for any extracurriculars?"

"She's thinking about basketball, which is fine with me. That starts later in the fall, so it gives her a chance to focus on the new school first." She blew on her cup and sipped.

"Jenny's on the team. I'll let her know, and maybe she can help."

"I'd appreciate it." Her phone buzzed. "And apologies; I need to run."

I finished the flower arrangement and put it on the kitchen table. Then, I called the cats. Nothing. I sighed as I reached for the treats. I shook the bag, and they came running. Three on the floor for each, and I shut the bag. Courvoisier looked at the meager offering and then stared at me. Drambuie took advantage of her inattention and swiped one from her pile. I chuckled. "Snooze, you lose. And now it's time for me to go to work."

✳ ✳ ✳

The morning dragged, and finally, it was time for my lunch with Rob. I hurried out the door and up the street to the restaurant. Rob was surveying the menu board when I arrived, and Andy was pointing out his recommendations. I hugged Andy, kissed Rob, and asked, "What's good?"

"Ed's special today is crepe-wrapped scallops—white wine, mushrooms, swiss cheese topping. Comes with a side salad."

"Sign me up."

Rob studied the board. "Cheddar cheeseburger, side salad instead of the fries."

"You know we have people who take orders at the table."

I laughed. "When have you ever stood on protocol?"

"Outside or in?"

"Outside." I started walking.

Rob said, "If it's in the shade," and followed me.

We sat at a table under an umbrella, and a waiter brought us two iced teas. After he left, I said, "Before I forget, we're going to have dinner with Jada and DeShawn on Friday."

Rob placed the napkin in his lap. "Sounds like fun. We haven't had a chance to get to know them. Now, what did you want me to call my reporter friend about?"

"Jumping right into business. No how wonderful I look—"

"You look lovely. Every moment apart is misery, and I can't wait till we're married and spending every waking moment together." He kissed my hand.

I smiled. "Good. I want to know who's involved in investigating the drug trafficking and if she's heard anything about the three people we know."

His mouth dropped. "I'll do it, but only if you say something nice back."

"I love everything about you. Your smell, your sense of humor, and, at this moment, your contacts."

"My smell?"

"Mm-hmm. So good. Makes my toes curl. Bay leaves, argan oil, and buttered rum."

The back door to C'est Magnifique opened, and Amy, in her habitual black garb, darted out, scurried down the alley, and turned left onto the street. I touched Rob's hand. "What was Amy doing in April's store?"

"Maybe she was shopping?"

"Amy? They don't have much in black there, plus, she wasn't carrying a bag."

He shrugged.

"That reminds me. I told Jim I'd try to do a girls' day with Amy to see how she's feeling. I should probably do that soon, especially after what happened last night. I have a feeling she needs guidance."

The rest of lunch was uneventful, and Rob had to run, so I stopped at the Tempting Treasures part of the store to talk to Andy. He was with a customer, so I wandered, looking at what he had gotten in since I'd last been there. A brass desk lamp caught my eye. It was a Tiffany that looked almost like the design of an old school bell, and the glass had a wavy green pattern to it. I lifted the tag and gasped at the price. The other customer left, and Andy joined me. "It's beautiful, isn't it? Just got it in."

I nodded. "Rob would love it. I think it would make a perfect wedding gift. If I buy it now, can you keep it for me?"

"Of course."

"You know, lunches here are quite expensive."

He laughed. "But you end up with things that have character and are one of a kind."

I handed him my credit card. "Is there any chance you're both free Friday night? I'm having DeShawn and Jada over and would love to have you and Ed join us."

"Let me check." He pulled out his phone. "No invite from Queen Elizabeth, so I guess we're free." He handed me my credit card. "Rob will love this."

When I returned to my office, I made a few calls and then set my shoulders. I needed to call Beth. I chewed my lip as I pressed the number. She answered the phone, "Yes?"

"Hi, Beth. It's Merry March. I called to get an update on Tammi."

There was a pause, and she replied, "I'm sorry I didn't call you. Tammi made it through but has been temporarily committed." There was another, longer pause. "I don't want to talk about this on the phone. Can you meet me for coffee? Maybe tomorrow around two when the kids are still at school?"

"Is Hopeful okay? Delightful Bites is a nice place. I'll treat."

"I could use a drive. I'll see you tomorrow."

✳ ✳ ✳

I put the last number into the spreadsheet, saved it, grabbed my purse, and headed out the door. "I'll try not to be too long."

Cheryl said, "Kind of slow, don't think it matters."

I gulped. It had been slow. I needed to drum up more business. I made a mental note—maybe it was time for another sales contest. A few minutes later, I walked into Delightful Bites, where the wonderful scent of vanilla permeated. The owner, Gary, was piping some type of white something onto small pastries. I asked, "What smells wonderful?"

"New cream puff recipe. Try it?"

"You bet."

He handed me a bite-sized one. The pastry looked delicate and flaky, with a white drizzle instead of chocolate. I popped it in my mouth and closed my eyes. After a moment, I said, "It tastes like there's vanilla everywhere."

"There is. It's in the dough, the cream, and the icing."

"Let me know when it hits the menu."

Beth dashed into the store. "I'm sorry I'm late."

"No problem. What would you like? Iced coffee, hot, or tea?"

She stepped to the counter. "I haven't had a latte in ages."

I said, "We'll take two, Gary."

"Have a seat. I'll bring them over to you."

"Do you mind if we sit inside? I went for a walk earlier, and the air conditioning feels great." Beth gestured to an inside table.

I led the way, and we sat. I asked, "You said Tammi had been committed?"

"The doctors recommended it. They were worried that, without treatment, she'd try again. Her sister traveled from Peoria, and she made the decision."

Gary deposited two large ceramic mugs on the table. I took a sugar packet and shook it, getting ready to open it. Beth said, "Sugar's bad for you. I have something better."

I put the packet down, and she reached into her purse and pulled out a tiny jar of honey. "I get it from a farm stand near me."

I drizzled it into the coffee, stirred, and sipped. "This is a treat. Gives a faint taste of clover." I paused. "I feel so bad for Tammi—and you."

"You know how everyone always asks how many kids you have?"

I nodded.

"I used to know how to answer. Four. Now, what do I say? People don't expect it to be a difficult question. It's small talk, kind of like about the weather or how you're feeling. Now I have to pause, catch my breath, and try not to break down." She gripped the table like it was a type of lifeline.

"Losing a child is like part of your soul being torn off, and I've had two chunks taken from mine." She lifted her latte, and the liquid sloshed because her hand shook. She took a long sip, straightened her shoulders, and said, "Enough of that conversation."

"If you need to talk—"

She shook her head. "Not now. Someday, maybe."

"I wanted to know more about the girl Kevin dated, the one you said gave off a strange vibe."

"That was six years ago. What possible bearing could that have on what happened?"

"Jane said Kevin might have gotten speed from a person he used to date."

Beth sat back in her chair and stared out the window. She was so still that I began to worry. Finally, I said, "I'm sorry to ask about such a painful subject."

"That's not it. I can't remember her name. Isn't that odd? It's right there, and yet it's not. She was a pretty ordinary kid. Brown hair, brown eyes, average height. Normal. Except for the vibe." She shivered. "There was something not quite right."

"That's the second time you've said that. I'm not sure I understand what you mean."

144

She leaned toward me. "Someone who stares a moment or two longer than they should, or laughs a second after everyone else, or makes the hairs on the back of your neck prickle. I don't know how to explain it any other way. It may have been she was at that awkward age. The only thing I knew was I didn't like her and was glad when Kevin came to his senses." She stood. "I'm sorry I couldn't give you more information, but I'll keep thinking about it."

I shook her hand. "Thanks for driving in, and if you think of anything—"

"I'll call you."

As I walked out the door, the same tattooed man drove into the parking lot and backed into the spot near the service entrance. He hurried to the door and opened it. I paused, open-mouthed. *What is going on?*

After a few minutes, Gary and the man loaded several boxes into the back of the man's SUV. I stepped behind one of the large planters. The man palmed Gary an envelope, slipped into his car, and drove from the parking lot.

I walked back to the office like a zombie. I hated loose ends. First, Beth couldn't remember that girl's name, and second, what was Gary doing? I almost walked past my door. I stopped short and pulled it open.

Cheryl was on the phone and gave me a finger wave. I strode in, threw my purse in the drawer, and opened another spreadsheet.

My phone rang, it was Rob, and before I could say 'Hello,' he said, "I hope you love me a lot."

"Why? What did you do?"

"Nothing I did. Mother is having a family dinner on Sunday. Attendance is mandatory."

I sighed.

* * *

Andy and Ed arrived a few minutes early on Friday, bearing wine and an apple pie with intricate lattice work on top. Jada and DeShawn walked in a few minutes later with a large bowl of salad. I loved casual gatherings like this. Everyone relaxed, wearing shorts and sandals—no pressure to be anyone other than ourselves. The mood was jolly as Rob played bartender, and there was quite a din as everyone greeted one another. I laughed. "You'd think it'd been centuries since we'd seen one another. Dinner is in the oven, the table in the dining room's all set, so why don't we go into the living room for a few minutes." I took a tray with carrots, celery, and cheese from the refrigerator.

Rob put the wine on the coffee table, and I followed with the tray as I urged everyone to sit. Jada, DeShawn, and Ed sat on the sofa, Andy and I the facing chairs, and Rob carried in a chair from the dining room.

I lifted my wine glass. "To new friends."

My toast was echoed, and everyone drank.

"Jada, I know you're a guidance counselor, but with being gone this summer, I missed what you do, DeShawn."

"You'll have to watch yourself, Merry. DeShawn's with the Drug Enforcement Agency." Andy laughed.

"The DEA?" I asked, stunned.

"Anything to hide?" DeShawn took a celery stick, dipped it in ranch dressing, and lifted his eyes to mine.

"Not at all. Unless you count antacids. I seem to be relatively addicted to them." I squirmed.

"Last time I looked, they weren't on the controlled substance list." DeShawn chuckled.

I sat back in my chair. "I saw you twice recently. You were meeting with a man in the alleys near town." I gasped, "Was he your informant?"

"Can't say."

"How did I not know you were with the DEA?" I turned to Andy, "You might have mentioned it when you asked me to help Yvonne. As a matter of fact, why did you ask me instead of DeShawn? Isn't it his job?"

"We're looking for the big fish. We're looking for the suppliers." DeShawn shook his head.

My eyebrow lifted. "Wouldn't you find the supplier if you traced back from the individual cases?"

DeShawn shifted in his seat. "We're working very closely with local law enforcement and sifting through their data to try and identify trends."

"I can't believe Jay's been working with you. Why didn't he say something?" I shook my head. "I'm so out of the loop."

DeShawn leaned toward me. "I don't know if this will make you feel better or not, but we do think there's someone important operating in this area. You need to be very careful. A lot of money's involved, and those kinds of people don't take well to anyone sniffing around their business."

The timer rang, and I stood. "Enough of this depressing discussion. Let's eat."

We moved on to less rigorous subjects through dinner; the conversation was lively and punctuated by laughter. When coffee and dessert were on the table, Rob brought us back to the earlier topic. "DeShawn, you mentioned a kingpin might be operating in this area. Is there more information you can share?"

He sipped his coffee. "I don't know that I said 'Kingpin.'"

"Okay, scratch that. Anything else you can share?"

"Off the record?" He stared hard at Rob.

"If need be."

"It does."

My teeth started to clench from the tension in the room.

"Then, okay. Off the record." Rob sat back.

"Stays in this room?" DeShawn looked at each of us in turn and waited for a nod. We assented, and he continued, "There's someone relatively new operating in this area. The numbers are spiking, and our informants don't know who it is. That means his operation is still relatively small. But it could grow."

Andy asked, "His?"

"Could be 'hers.' Statistically, most people higher up in the drug chain are men."

Jada nodded. "At the schools, sometimes the runners would be women, but the people controlling it were men."

"What do you look for when you're investigating someone?" I cut a piece of pie with the side of my fork.

"Some of what you might consider the 'boring' stuff, the things you don't see in movies or TV. It's the financial investigation, following the money." He bit into a piece of pie and mumbled to Ed, "This is great."

I asked, "How do you do that?"

"One thing is looking at people who buy money counters—you know, the machines banks use to count bills when you make a large withdrawal or deposit. The drug trade is a huge cash business, so people involved buy the machines in bulk. We cross-check those people against FBI data to see if any of them have a criminal record." He sipped coffee. "It's a lot of leg work."

"What about travel?" Rob asked.

"We also profile travelers on planes and trains and interview them if we find something suspicious. We look for one-way tickets. Tickets bought with cash. That kind of thing. Think of it like a spider web. The strands form a circle that is more spread out at the edges but then, toward the middle, become tighter and tighter. More leg work and data will expose who sits at the center."

CHAPTER 15

Rob and I relaxed on the couch after cleaning up. He said, "I'm so full I could burst. That chicken was delicious."

"Are you sure it was the chicken and not the second piece of Ed's apple pie?"

He put his arm around my shoulder. "Might have been the pie. Or the ice cream."

I lifted my face to him for a quick kiss. "Fun evening."

"Though it ended on a serious note." Rob kicked off his shoes. "Speaking of which, I was able to chat with that reporter."

"The one doing the series on drug trafficking? The cute one?"

He kissed the top of my head. "The married one. And don't forget, I'm engaged now. Can't be looking at other women."

I pulled away. "You were before?"

"Not since I met you."

"Good answer." I settled back against him. "What did she have to say?"

"There's been an uptick in this area, but they're not sure who's involved. She's been working on the supply in the city, and her informants have been good at giving her inside information, but it dries up when it gets near here. She's going to keep me informed; we may work together on a story."

"It's frustrating not being able to get answers." I rolled my shoulders. "And, speaking of annoying things, we need to settle on our wedding invitations. I came home today, and Martin, your mother's—" I air quoted, "'—social secretary,' left approved samples leaning against the front door." I stood, slid off my shoes, and padded to the brown envelope I had stuffed next to the TV.

"Do we have to do this now?" Rob groaned.

"His note had a lot of exclamation marks."

"I don't know about you, but this requires Baileys." He stood and walked to the cordial cupboard. I held up two fingers, and he poured, returned, and handed me one as he sat. "Okay. Ready now."

I spread the samples on the coffee table. One was on light blue paper with very elaborate type. Rob lifted it. "I can't even read this. Nope." He tossed that one to the side.

We whittled the selections down to two. Both were formal enough and had heavy black leading. I caressed the paper stock on the ecru one. It seemed richer to me. "I like this one."

Rob pointed to a sample that was stark white. "That's a good contrast to the black."

I put the two side by side, took a picture, and sent it to Patty. After a moment, my phone binged: "One on the left."

I lifted the white linen. "You're right. Let's go with this."

"The designer liked my choice better." He laughed.

I snapped a photo and texted it to Martin. "Hopefully, that will be all he needs for a few weeks."

Ding. "Next: linens for the tables."

* * *

When I woke the following day, the scent of bacon tantalized my nose. I rubbed my eyes as the downstairs clock chimed nine and leaped from bed. *How on earth had I slept so long?* I washed my face, moisturized, put on my robe, and trotted down to the kitchen. Jenny was turning bacon.

"Yum."

She smiled. "I thought you were never going to get up."

"What's even more surprising is you being awake and cooking. Isn't it the middle of the night for you?"

"Ha, ha. I wanted to talk to you." She handed me a cup of coffee as I sat at the counter.

"Sounds serious."

She put the cooked bacon onto paper towels. "I've decided I want to go to State. I was impressed with them, it's not far, and I liked the campus. The best part for you is that the tuition's cheaper, since it's in our state, and after talking to Amy and seeing what she got, I should be able to get some money too."

I squirmed. "So, you want to cancel the other tours? Are you sure? Maybe you should go anyway, just to be certain. What if they don't take you?"

"My grades are good. I've volunteered at lots of things and have good recommendations. I'm pretty sure I'll get in. I love the school. They have a good intramural basketball team and a pretty campus." She crossed her arms. "I've decided."

I opened my mouth and closed it. *So young to be making these kinds of decisions. Should I make her go to the other schools? State's a good one. It checks a bunch of boxes, including the money one. I can't believe she's old enough to be going to college. Two days ago, we took the training wheels off her bicycle...*

Jenny waved her hand in front of my face. "Earth to Mom, did you hear anything I said?"

"I trust you. If this is the school, we don't need to visit the others." I sipped my coffee and felt my eyes moisten. Luckily, she was busy stirring pancake batter.

"Too bad Mr. Jenson's not here. He makes the best pancakes."

"That he does." I stood and gathered plates and silverware. "Why'd you decide so early? Applications aren't due for months."

She peeked under a pancake. "I talked to Jacob, and then I called Ann. She had me go through my checklist and describe my priorities.

By the time we finished the call, I knew. She also said Amy loves it there."

I poured juice. "You know I'd be happy to be your sounding board."

"You've been kind of preoccupied with the wedding, work, and those kids dying. I thought it'd help if I took the trip off your plate." She flipped the pancake, and it began to puff.

I came around the counter and hugged her. "Jenny, I'm never too busy for you. You are my number one priority. And I love having time together, just you and me."

Jenny shrugged, put the pancakes on a plate, and carried them and the bacon to the table.

❋ ❋ ❋

After breakfast, I put on my girl bands playlist and began to vacuum. Courvoisier jumped off the couch when I neared and went running for the laundry room. I was happy Jenny had decided, but it bothered me she thought I had priorities higher than her. I liked Ann. She had a solid head on her shoulders and her advice to Jenny, so far, was on target. I sighed. *I don't want to be supplanted, especially not by a girl in her twenties.*

I dusted the bookshelves and then decided the house was clean enough for now. I called up the stairs. "What's on tap for today?"

She looked over the railing. "Going to the pool with Jacob, Cindy, and Imani."

"Want me to come?"

"To the pool? With us?" She laughed as she walked back to her room.

I guess that's a no.

❋ ❋ ❋

"This is so good." A strand of mozzarella bungee jumped from the chicken parmigiana on its way to Jenny's mouth.

"Careful." I pointed.

She scooped it with her fingers and deposited it in her mouth. "Thanks for making my favorite."

"Anytime." I squeezed Italian dressing onto my salad.

"By the way, Ann said we could go riding after dinner at Wanda's. She'll bring me home, so you don't have to wait."

"Those horses are so tall. Are you sure you want to try riding? It's pretty dangerous." My stomach clenched as I envisioned her in the saddle trying to corral a thousand-pound bucking bronco. It was a long way to the ground.

"Ann said she'd taught a few people to ride."

"You'll be a natural." I pushed the rest of the chicken around my plate, visualizing my daughter's crumpled body after being thrown by the horse.

"Not hungry?"

"I'll save it for lunch tomorrow. I made chocolate chip cookies for dessert." I stood. "Do you want ice cream?"

"All my favs. Yes, please."

I retrieved a bowl, placed it on the counter, scooped a large portion, and then brought it and the jar of cookies to the table.

"Aren't you having any?" She pointed at the bowl.

"I'll nibble on a cookie." I poured milk into two glasses and handed her one. "How long do you think you'll ride?"

"Ann said the actual ride wouldn't be long. She wants to make sure I'm comfortable around the horse first." Jenny took a cookie from the jar. "Don't worry. She said she wouldn't have me jumping the first time out."

"Jumping," I gasped, and my heart rate accelerated. I dropped my cookie, shook two antacids into my hand, and chewed them instead. "Promise me we'll have a long discussion before you get to that point."

* * *

Rob picked us up at one. I wore a creamy yellow sundress and low-slung sandals. Jenny looked cute in beige shorts and a deep blue, crew-neck shirt. She carried a bag with her jeans for riding. Rob started the car, and I turned in my seat. "Are you sure you don't need boots?"

"Ann said Amy's my size, and she doesn't ride anymore."

I muttered, "Smart girl."

"Huh?"

"Nothing. I'm sure you'll have a good time."

Rob gave me a sharp look, and I shook my head. He turned back to the road. I said, "It's a shame Elizabeth couldn't join us."

"Mother's not happy with her, but Elizabeth promised she'd come to the next one."

I sighed. "The next one?"

Rob cleared his throat. "In two weeks."

"Is this going to be a regular thing?" I rubbed the back of my neck.

"Apparently." He darted me a glance. "But after the wedding, they'll be traveling through the New Year, so we'll have a break."

"Uh-huh." I pressed recline on my seat, and Jenny yelped.

"Hey! Long legs back here."

"Sorry." I put my seat up.

I leaned my head against the window as Jenny and Rob prattled about her newfound passion, feeling the muscles in my shoulders tense into even bigger knots. We finally made the turn onto Mac and Wanda's long tree-lined drive. Rob parked the car in the back, and we got out.

Martin came to my side. "Good, you're here. I have a few things we need to go over."

154

"Isn't it Sunday?"

He nodded.

"Aren't you off?"

"Off?" He chuckled. "Not when Wanda has need of me. Now, please follow." He marched toward the house.

Rob asked, "Should I come?"

I shook my head and trailed after Martin.

Martin opened the door to a back entrance, and we wound past a wine cellar with a massive oak door. Windows graced either side, and I stopped to peer in one. It seemed to be a room made of stone with built-in arches supporting dark wooden shelves filled with bottles upon bottles of wine. There was a large wooden bar at one end and several metal bistro tables with matching chairs scattered on the multi-colored slate floor.

Martin tapped his ever-present clipboard. "They have parties in there all the time. Now, time's wasting."

We finally ended up in a minuscule office with a tiny turret window and dominated by a large wooden desk. He opened the coat closet, pulled out several linen samples draped over coat hangers, and laid them out. "Here are the ones Wanda chose. If you can't find something you like, you could come with me to the warehouse."

I shook my head. *Not doing that.* "I'm sure I can find something here." I stretched my arm to stroke the material. "Can we layer these?"

"Of course." Martin pulled his glasses down his nose. "Was there something that appealed?"

I lifted an azure sample and placed it over butter-colored raw silk. "I like this combination. It reminds me of the colors in my dress."

"Wanda thought so too." He put the remaining linens back into the closet. "Next, we'll have to tackle chargers and china."

"Chargers?"

He sighed. "The large plates that go under the china."

"Is that necessary?"

Martin's eyes widened, and I shook my head. "Never mind."

His phone alarm peeled. "Dinner is in the small dining room." He began to sit.

"Aren't you coming?"

"Family dinner." He made a show of checking something on his clipboard. I shifted from foot to foot. "Erm. I don't know where that is. I've only been to parties in the barn."

He huffed as he stood, "I'll direct you."

We wandered through a few non-descript corridors, then past a cavernous great room complete with two stone fireplaces, a formal dining room with a table that looked like it could fit thirty, and finally arrived at a cozier room with a rectangular rustic barnwood table, muted floral wallpaper, and lower ceilings.

Wanda glanced my way. "Oh good, you're here. Please sit next to Mac."

Mac sat at one head of the table, Wanda the other. I was next to Mac, on the right-hand side, Mac's brother Jim was next to me, and his daughter Amy sat between him and Wanda. Rob was next, followed by Jenny and then Ann on the other side of Mac.

I made my way around the table, nodding to Amy and then being bear-hugged by Jim, who said, "So good to see you again, Merry." I gave Mac a peck on the cheek and sat.

Wanda rang a bell, and salads were promptly delivered along with two bread baskets, one of which was placed in front of me. It held breadsticks as well as pumpernickel and pretzel rolls. The latter studded with what looked like salt and onions. I put one on my plate and passed the basket. Wanda cleared her throat and stared down her nose at me but didn't say anything.

A server poured rosé into Mac's glass. He swirled, tasted, and nodded. The remaining glasses were filled with wine, and soda was brought to Jenny.

Mac stood and toasted, "To the first of what I hope will be many family dinners. Wanda and I were reminiscing the other day about the Sunday dinners of our childhood at our grandparents' houses and how that made us closer as a family. So, now that we have a grandchild," he beamed at Jenny, "we want to start our own traditions. To us." He lifted his glass.

Jim said, "Here, here," and lifted his own. We followed suit and then drank.

The wine was light and crisp, with a hint of something floral. I broke a piece from my roll, buttered it, and turned to Jim. "Have you stayed put since we had lunch, or have you been traveling again?"

Mac laughed. "Jim's the original rolling stone. He never stays put for long."

"Let's see... Since then, I've done the northern leg. Toronto, Winnepeg, and Alaska."

Jenny said, "I'd love to go to Alaska."

Jim smiled. "Beautiful, rugged country with hardy people who know how to live off the land. But it's nice to be home with Ann. Always thought she'd be a scientist with all the courses she took. But I guess the call of the book was too much." He beamed at her. "Strange to imagine twins being so different."

"Twins? Fraternal?" I asked, looking between Ann and Amy.

"Identical." He shook his head.

"But you look so different. I thought Ann was older."

Ann pulled her hair back from her face. "It's the hair. It's naturally brown, but Amy dyes hers black, and I dye mine blonde. We used to take each other's place and try and fool people."

"That was a long time ago." Amy took a roll and put it on her plate. Wanda moved the plate away from her.

As the discussion veered from Ann and Amy, I couldn't help but notice Wanda. Amy put her elbows on the table, and Wanda tapped her and shook her head. When Amy slumped over her salad, Wanda pointed to her own erect posture. Amy sighed and sat straighter but shifted her chair closer to her father and farther away from Wanda. Jim seemed focused on Ann and oblivious about what was going on with his other daughter, and I felt sorry for her. "Amy, Jenny's excited to be going to State next year."

Amy looked happy for the chance to comment. "You'll love it, Jenny. In fact, if you want, you could come stay with me overnight to better experience the campus this fall."

I had been mid-sip on the wine and began to cough. *Jenny can't stay with someone who smokes pot!*

Jim patted my back. "Are you okay, Merry?"

I held up my hand as I switched to water. After a moment, I said, "I'm fine. Just went down the wrong way." I turned to Amy. "That's such a sweet offer, but Jenny will be back to school next week, and her schedule is kind of hectic."

They cleared away the salad plates, and dinner arrived. The server intoned, "Chicken Cordon Bleu." A plate etched with a pretty blue and yellow pattern was placed in front of me containing chicken that looked perfectly brown and crisped on the outside nestled against asparagus spears.

Ann used her knife to shift the components of her plate away from each other. She caught me staring and explained, "Tastes better that way."

I cut into the chicken, and the cheese oozed. As I was about to take a bite, Wanda said, "I told Mac that you'd probably prefer plain chicken with a squeeze of lemon like this, but he insisted you'd prefer that. It's not too late to get you one of these."

I glanced down the table at her pallid chicken breast and shook my head. "This will be fine."

I put the bite in my mouth and chewed. Tangy cheese, salty ham, and that sauce—it had to have butter in it.

Jenny turned to Ann, "I can't wait to go riding. I hope I do well."

It now felt like I was chewing sawdust, and my appetite fled. I focused on the water in front of me as my head began to pound.

After dinner, Ann and Jenny ran to get changed. Rob said, "Maybe you'd feel better if we went to the stables. You'll see how calm the horses are." He turned to his mother. "You don't mind if we wander over to the stables, do you?"

"That's fine. Stop back before you leave." She stood.

Amy jumped from her seat. "I'll go with Merry and Rob."

"We'd love to have you come with us." I hooked my elbow through hers, and we left the room.

She whispered. "Thanks. I'd scream if I had to be with that woman for another moment." She clasped her hand over her mouth as she looked at Rob. "I'm sorry. Sometimes I forget she's your mother."

Rob laughed. "She can be a bit trying."

I turned toward Amy. "There's a charity bowling event this upcoming Saturday morning, and Jenny and I are going. If you're free, we'd love to have you join us."

She smiled. "I like bowling. I'll be there."

We strolled to the stables, and as I entered, the horses whinnied. Rob took my hand. "See, it's not that bad. Friendly horses."

"So tall. Such a long way to the ground." I popped two antacids in my mouth and chewed, eyes wide.

Ann and Jenny came into the stable talking and laughing. Amy looked wistful. "Maybe I shouldn't have given up riding. It was the one thing Ann and I had in common. But I had that bad fall."

"Oh, no." I walked toward Jenny as Ann showed her how to put the saddle on. "Maybe you should wait for another day. You did just eat."

"I'm not swimming. I'm riding." Jenny petted the horse. "I'll be fine."

"Have fun," I said through clenched teeth.

Rob and I walked back to the car. As he held my door, he said, "You could have told her not to ride."

"I don't want her to be afraid of trying new things." I rubbed my sweaty hands on my sundress. "No matter how much it kills me." I looked up, "Please God, send her back to me in one piece, arms, legs, and head still working. I don't know how I'm going to stand the wait."

CHAPTER 16

Jenny arrived home late, and when I heard the downstairs door shut, I hurried to the kitchen. She was washing her hands as I came around the corner. Before she turned, I examined her appendages and gave a deep sigh. Everything appeared to be in working order. She opened the refrigerator and asked, "Milk and cookies?"

"How'd you know I was here?"

She turned as she lifted the jug. "No way you'd be sleeping." She put the milk down, retrieved two glasses, and grinned. "It's kind of nice knowing you're waiting up for me."

"You could have texted. I was worried. I had to call Wanda, and she said you were going to Jim and Ann's."

"Sorry, I was so excited about the ride I forgot." Jenny brought the cookie jar to the table and sat down.

"Don't make me pull this out of you a sentence at a time."

"Riding was fun, my butt's a bit sore, and Uncle Jim's house is charming."

"Charming how?" I tipped the jar toward me, pulled out a cookie, and sat.

Jenny broke one in half and dipped it in milk. "Sort of story-book-cottage-ish. It's in the middle of a group of trees at the edge of a cornfield. It almost looks like it doesn't belong. The drive is kind of hidden, and the house has one of those swooped roofs like in 'Hansel and Gretel.'"

"Did it give you that feeling?" I bit into the cookie.

"What, like an evil witch was going to eat me?" She laughed. "The opposite. It wasn't big, like three bedrooms. But lovely rugs, comfy chairs, and a permanent game table. We played cards."

"I'm glad it was fun." I sipped milk and took another bite of my cookie. "Now, more about the riding part."

"Are you sure you can take it?"

"Of course." I stiffened my spine. "I'm not a wimp."

"Ann had me take the horse around the paddock first. Then, when she could see I was comfortable, we went for a short ride into the hills around the—" she air-quoted "—'grandparents" place. We brushed the horses when we returned. And then we stopped by to thank Grand Mac and Miss Wanda."

My eyes widened. "Grand Mac and Miss Wanda?"

"That's what they told me to call them. Miss Wanda said she's way too young to be a grandmother, so she didn't want me to call her that."

"Uh-huh."

"Love you, Mom." She kissed my head, then turned and ran up the stairs.

Miss Wanda?

* * *

I texted Patty: "Meet me for afternoon coffee? Two? DB?"

"Yes. DB?"

"Delightful Bites."

I opened my office door and asked Cheryl, "Have a few moments?"

She walked into my office, pad in hand. "What's up?"

"Sales have been down. I think it's time for another office contest. I'd like to put you in charge of the competition."

Her eyebrow arched.

"Think large tote board, maybe on the wall in the break room—people's names, where they stand against goal, that kind of thing. Plus, anything you can think of that will spur our associates to work those phones. Let's run it for a week or two, bonus for the winner, and maybe dinner out for the winner and a friend."

"What about an email every morning that gives the leader from the previous day, maybe phone calls made, any sales, those kinds of stats?" Cheryl scribbled on her pad.

"Great idea. Keep them coming."

"Let me work on this. Meet tomorrow?"

I nodded. "First thing. I want to get this going."

Cheryl was still writing as she walked out the door.

I lifted my purse and followed her. "Having coffee with Patty, back in an hour." I hurried down the street and met Patty going into the shop.

"Let's sit outside."

"It's a little hot today." She frowned.

"Get an iced coffee." I stepped to the counter.

Gary smiled. "Good afternoon, Merry. What can I get for you?"

"I'll have a large iced tea and that blueberry scone." I pointed. "Patty?"

"Large, iced coffee, and the apricot danish."

Gary gathered our purchases and put them on the counter in front of us. "Enjoy, ladies."

I took my tea and scone and pushed the door open with my hip. "This table back here. You sit there." I gestured with the plate the scone was on.

"So demanding." Patty sat. "Dish. What's going on?"

"We're on a stakeout."

She looked around. "Here? In broad daylight? Exactly what do you expect to see?"

I leaned toward her and whispered, "Drug deals."

"In Hopeful?" Her mouth dropped.

I nodded.

"Can I eat my danish?" Patty poked at it with her fork.

"Of course."

"Who is the drug dealer?"

"Gary."

"Nope. I don't believe it. He gave us cooking lessons. He wouldn't sell drugs."

Just then, the SUV I had seen previously pulled in and backed to the service door. I poked Patty's arm. "There. Watch this."

The same tattooed man climbed out of the driver's seat, scanned the surroundings, and spotted us. He seemed rooted to the macadam but then jumped back into the car and drove away, pulling his baseball cap lower over his face as he passed us.

Patty had paused, bite of pastry halfway to her mouth. "That was strange."

Gary came out the service door, looked up and down the parking lot, shrugged, and ducked back into the store.

"See? When I saw it the last time, I hid behind that planter there." I pointed. "And saw the tattooed guy give Gary some type of envelope, and then they loaded his car with what looked like bakery boxes."

"It's a bakery. Maybe he was hungry. Maybe he's an overeater and doesn't want his wife to know."

"That guy can't weigh more than a hundred and sixty soaking wet. He looks like skin and bones."

She shrugged. "Fast metabolism?"

"Drugs. It's a perfect setup. Who'd think anything else? Bakery deliveries in the middle of the day." I popped the last bit of the scone in my mouth and mumbled, "I may need to get Jay involved and maybe DeShawn."

* * *

Later that night, Rob and I sat outside looking at the stars. He said, "Such a lovely evening."

"Uh-huh. Not too hot, a little wind to keep the bugs away, just right." I sipped wine. "So, what do you think?"

"The ambient light means we can't see the smaller stars. It might be better to be further out of town."

I pushed on his arm. "What do you think about Gary?"

"I don't know. It certainly sounds suspicious. But it's hard to believe they are carrying on in the afternoon."

"Do you think I should talk to Jay?"

"It is odd."

I picked up my phone.

"Now? Let's enjoy the evening."

"What if another kid dies?"

He sighed. "Call him."

I pressed his number. "Jay, I was wondering if you had a few minutes to swing by."

Dead silence.

"Jay?"

"I'll be over."

He disconnected.

Rob stood. "I'll put coffee on."

We walked into the kitchen, and I retrieved the cookie jar. Rob pressed the button on the coffee maker and set three mugs on the table.

A few minutes later, there was a sharp rap at the door, and Jay walked in. "Is this something new, or are you still working on the drug case I told you not to work on?"

I put a few cookies on a plate and handed it to Jay as Rob poured coffee. I sat. "The latter. I think I may have found something." I outlined what I had seen.

Jay's eyebrow rose. "Gary's on the town council—the people who pay my salary. And you want me to accuse him of being a drug dealer with thin-at-best evidence?" Jay took one last bite of a cookie and finished his coffee. "Not going to do it." He leaned forward. "You should stay out of this, Merry. Bigger people than us are working on it." He stood. Just before he reached the door, he turned. "By the way, the dollar bill found near Jane tested positive for cocaine and fentanyl, so it's highly unlikely these cases are related."

"What do you mean?" I asked.

"Methamphetamines and fentanyl, cocaine and fentanyl. If it were murder, they'd use the same drug versus hopscotching. Thanks for the cookies and coffee."

The door shut. I turned to Rob. "I can't believe he's not going to do anything."

"I see his point about his job."

"I do too, but he is a detective. It shouldn't just be when it's convenient."

"You're not going to give this up, are you?" Rob sank onto the seat next to me.

"No. And I wouldn't think you'd want to either."

"I don't. But I'm worried about you. I want you safe and sound for our wedding." He kissed me.

"I will be. What's our next step?"

"Tomorrow afternoon, if the guy shows up, we'll follow him."

* * *

We sat in Rob's car facing Delightful Bites across the street in the municipal lot. I turned toward the store. "Are you sure we're going to be able to see from here?"

Rob reached behind him and pulled out a pair of binoculars. "If we can't, I have these."

"You keep binoculars in your car?"

"Reporter." He shrugged.

Not sure how to respond, I stayed silent. The petunias in the square were looking scraggly. If I had my pruning shears, I'd have given them a bit of a trim.

"There." Rob pointed. "Is that the guy?"

A maroon SUV pulled into the Delightful Bites parking lot, moving slowly. He turned and backed to the service entrance. The tattooed guy exited the car, looked left and right, and approached the door. Gary came out, the man handed him what looked like an envelope, and they again loaded his car. When they were done, he scanned the parking lot, hopped in the car, and took off.

Rob eased from the lot and stayed a few cars back. The guy took a meandering route that seemed to make no sense. Rob asked, "Where is this guy going? He's doubled back a few times."

"He's looking to see if he's being followed. I can't count how many times he's looked in the rearview mirror. Do you think he saw us?"

"I don't think so." Rob shook his head.

The guy made a left, then a quick right, and pulled into Fiorella's parking lot. Rob looked for a place to park where we could watch what happened, but the only available spots were in the empty lot. He drove past, went around the block, and returned. The SUV was deserted, and the tattooed man was nowhere to be seen.

"I guess he went in," I said.

"What now?"

"Let's go back to town."

As Rob drove, I asked, "Did you know that was the way to Fiorella's?"

"Pretty circuitous route."

"I agree. That means something suspicious is going on, and there's another connection."

"What?" Rob flipped his turn signal.

"Jane Creedy was a cook at Fiorella's. And she's dead."

CHAPTER 17

I baked a double batch of brownies with walnuts. Once they were cool, I put half into a container, snapped the lid, and walked next door. I knocked, and DeShawn answered, "Come in, Merry."

I followed him into the kitchen and stopped, my mouth dropping. "When did you do this?"

The kitchen had been transformed from the outdated canary yellow with off-white cabinets to a sleek gourmet showpiece with steel range hood. It looked like an after picture from one of those home shows on television.

He said, "Earlier this summer. Jada and I always like to have a project or two going to de-stress."

I touched a cabinet. "What type of wood is this? It's so warm looking."

"Ipe. Most people use it outside because it's durable, but we liked the way it looked."

"You did all this work yourself?"

He laughed. "We brought in the experts for plumbing and electrical, but the rest was all us."

I handed him the brownies. "I was baking and decided to make enough for your house and ours."

"Thanks, Jada's out right now, but I'm sure she'll appreciate the thought. And Imani and I will appreciate eating them." DeShawn grinned.

I hesitated. "I'm here to talk to you. Do you have a few minutes?"

He motioned to a chair. "Latte?"

"If it's not too much trouble." I sat.

DeShawn walked to a coffee bar on the other side of the room and took his time making two coffees, complete with art that looked like a rose in bloom. He handed me one of the cups, and I exclaimed, "You do this too? You're one talented fellow."

He sat next to me. "So my wife tells me. Now, what's this all about?"

I filled him on what had been happening at Delightful Bites.

"Maybe an innocent explanation." DeShawn shrugged.

I nodded. "But people are dying, and if I didn't tell you, I'd never be able to live with myself."

He lifted a brownie and took a bite. "Good," he mumbled.

I sipped coffee.

"I'll look into it. Anything else?"

"Nope." I finished my coffee and put the cup in the sink.

"You've handed it off. Now stay out of it. These people are merciless."

I gulped as I walked out the door and headed to my house. I ran up the back steps and into the kitchen. Jenny turned, "Mom, is it okay if I go riding with Ann again today?"

My stomach clenched. "Again? You went last weekend. Aren't you still sore?"

"That wore off by Monday."

"Don't you have homework?"

"It's Saturday. I have plenty of time. Plus, it's only the first week, and there isn't much to do."

"Wait. We have bowling at eleven. I told Amy to meet us here."

Jenny rolled her eyes. "You act like I can't do more than one thing a day. That's over at two. I told Ann I'd meet her at three."

I took two antacids and chewed them.

"Mom, you need to stop taking those. They can't be good for you."

"I guess it would be okay," I grumbled as I went into the laundry room and tossed in a load of wash. "Any other darks?"

The wall vibrated as she ran upstairs. After a moment, she rounded the corner, handed me a few things, and said, "Thanks."

I caught her arm. "You know I'm happy you're expanding your horizons, right?"

She nodded. "Even though your words don't quite match the expression on your face."

I glanced in the mirror as she walked away. She was right. *Need to work on happy face.* I put soap in the dispenser, twisted the dial, and pressed "on." *How has life gotten so complicated?* The machine whirring, I ran upstairs to get changed for bowling. The doorbell rang, and I yelled, "Would you get that?" I brushed my hair and walked down the stairs. Jenny and Amy were sitting on the sofa, chatting.

"Skip lunch in the cafeteria. It's the worst. Breakfast is great though. And the best hamburgers are at this dive place down the block on Main Street," Amy advised.

I laughed. "Getting the inside perspective?"

Jenny nodded. "Ready? Can I drive?"

I tossed her the keys. "Let's go."

We walked into the bowling alley. Large pink ribbons hung over the lanes, and people were already practicing. Some wore official-looking bowling shirts and had their own vivid, multi-colored balls. CRACK. One rolled down the lane and hit just to the right side of the lead pin, and all ten went down in a strike. Amy bit her lip. "I'm not that good."

I pointed to a trio wearing pink tutus. "Not everyone is as serious. We're here to have a good time and support breast cancer research."

We signed in and changed our footwear to the red and tan bowling shoes provided. Patty and Cindy arrived, and Patty plopped down in the scorer's chair. "What should we call ourselves?"

"Pink Marauders," said Jenny.

"Pink Pythons," Amy suggested.

"Pink Roses," Cindy proposed.

Patty reviewed the other team's names. "Marauders already taken. Let's go with the Pink Pythons. Has a nice ring to it."

Amy smiled.

I said, "Why don't you start us off, Amy?"

Her face turned bright red. "Uh—"

Jenny jumped up. "I'll start. Cindy next, and then Amy. Mom and Mrs. Twilliger can fight for last."

There were a few gutter balls, Amy managed to get a spare, and then Patty rolled a strike, which everyone applauded. We broke for lunch, and Amy and I returned to the table behind the lane first. She slid onto a seat, and I sat next to her. I said, "I thought I saw you coming out of C'est Magnifique the other day."

"Wasn't me. I haven't been there since our last fitting." She popped a chicken nugget into her mouth.

"I could have sworn—"

She shook her head. "Thanks for inviting me. It's been years since I bowled. Mom and Dad used to take our friends and us on our birthday." Her shoulders drooped. "Back before they got divorced."

I nodded.

"Everything was more fun then. We had a puppy—a dalmatian whose name was Bo. When Mom moved to California, she said she couldn't take him. Dad never liked pets, so they sent him to a shelter. I cried for days. Ann didn't. She was upset that he chewed her precious shoes. He didn't mean to do it. I told them I'd take him to obedience classes. They didn't care. He was too much work. Just like me."

"I doubt that you're a lot of work. And it's sad that they needed to get rid of your dog. Now that you're getting out of school next year, maybe you can get another one."

Cindy and Jenny plopped down at the table with a full bag of popcorn.

"That's not all you're eating." I gave Jenny a "Mom" stare.

"Appetizer." Jenny smiled and held the bag toward Amy. "Want some?"

Amy shook a few onto her napkin. "Thanks."

Patty joined us with her plate piled high with popcorn and a hot dog in a bun with a thin line of mustard running its length.

I stared. "You're as bad as the kids."

"Guilty." She tossed a few kernels in her mouth. "They're starting back up again. Shall we play and eat?"

* * *

I wandered into the living room, lifted my book, and sank onto the sofa. My phone buzzed with a text from Martin: "Gold, silver, or bronze chargers?"

I groaned and tapped in: "Bronze."

The back door shut, and Andy called. "Anyone home?"

"Hammered or plain?" dinged Martin's text message.

I yelled at my phone, "Stop with the questions."

He walked in and plopped next to me. "So rude."

"I wasn't talking to you."

Andy made a point of looking under the sofa. "Not seeing anyone else here. But there is a rather large dust bunny."

"Really? I vacuumed." I bent and glanced at the gap between the sofa and floor.

"Made you look."

"Very funny. Wanda's assistant is driving me up a wall with questions about the wedding, and I'm beginning to regret the fact that I told Wanda she could plan it." I sighed. "But you didn't stop by to hear about my problems. What's up?"

"Yvonne called. She tired of you avoiding her and wants an update."

"I don't have one. Maybe we'll know something later this week."

He eyed me. "Spill."

"Can't. May be nothing."

"I am the soul of discretion. You can trust me." He gave me a Cheshire cat smile. I shook my head. He huffed and got to his feet. "What am I supposed to tell Yvonne?"

"People are working on it."

Jenny ran down the stairs and out the door. "See you later!"

"Where's she off to?" Andy asked.

"Horseback riding." I rubbed the back of my neck.

"Isn't that dangerous? Christopher Reeve. Just saying."

* * *

I was putting the finishing touches on a spreadsheet at work when Martin phoned. Before I had a chance to say hello, he said, "Merry, I need your guest list. We have to send the save-the-dates. People travel for Thanksgiving, and I'm afraid if we don't get them mailed, people will have already made their plans."

I doodled on the pad in front of me. "When do you need it?"

"Yesterday." Martin hung up.

I walked to Cheryl's desk. "I need to finalize the wedding list. Martin's badgering me."

She grabbed her laptop and came into my office. "It's in a database, so all we have to do is put checkmarks next to the ones you want to invite."

I sat next to Cheryl on the other side of my desk. "No. Yes, Yes, Maybe—what do you think?"

"Yes."

"Okay, Yes, No, this is stupid. I don't want to waste your time. Why don't you send me the file, and I'll go through it? If there's someone I have a question on, I'll make a note."

"Are you sure?"

"Positive."

She stood. "What are you going to do about the other people?"

"Huh?"

"Friends? Relatives?"

"Most of them are in your database. But Rob will have a lot of people who aren't, I guess." I walked around to the other side of my desk. "I'll give him a call, and he and I can work on it tonight."

I picked up my phone and pressed Rob's number as Cheryl left.

"Hello, beautiful."

"Homemade dinner tonight? Grilled salmon?" I asked.

"Sounds wonderful."

"If you have time today, it would be great if you could compile a list of people you want to invite to the wedding. That way, we could talk about it over dinner."

Silence.

"Martin's looking for the list. He says he needs to send the save-the-date cards."

"The wedding's not till November," Rob protested, "we have time."

"It's the beginning of September. He's right. We need to get them out."

"I'll be there," he grumbled. "Love you."

"Back at you." I pressed end. *I don't want to do this either, but one of us has to be the adult. Just wait till seating chart time.*

I checked my email, and Cheryl had sent the list. I turned off my laptop, put it in my bag, and stood.

Why on earth did I agree to a big wedding? It brought back memories of my first. Teased hair, lacy gown, the dreamy smile on Drew's face when I walked down the aisle. I kicked a stone on the sidewalk. *Too bad that fairy tale didn't last. Rob will. He has rough edges, where Drew is smooth. Beyond smooth.* I shuddered. *A nightmare I'm happy is behind me.* I opened the back door to my house, slid my bag in, shut the door, and walked to the car. *Salmon, new potatoes with herbs, and corn on the cob. Maybe grilled peaches for dessert.* My mouth started to water, just thinking about it.

I grabbed a cart at the store and began my meandering journey, chatting with clients as I passed. The corn display looked sparse since it was the end of the season. I picked up three ears that looked larger, tossed them in the cart, and turned toward the seafood counter. As I was giving my order, Gary came up behind me. "Hi, Merry."

I jumped.

"Sorry, didn't mean to scare you. Just wanted to say hello."

"How are you?" My heart raced.

"Picking up a few things while it's slow."

"How's business?"

He laughed. "Better than ever because I always jump on expansion opportunities. In fact, I'm going to start my cooking classes again. What would you think about that?"

"The ones this spring were fun." I squirmed.

"I'll let you know." He walked away with his full cart.

My hand wobbled as I took the salmon from the clerk. *He won't be able to do classes from jail.* I put the package in my cart and shook my head. *He seems so nice. No way could he be dealing drugs. What would he say if he knew I reported him to the DEA?* I shivered.

✳ ✳ ✳

Rob and I sat in my living room with classical music playing softly. "If this is our list, we're at close to one hundred and fifty guests." Rob chewed the eraser at the end of the pencil.

"That many?" My eyes widened.

"You have close to ninety clients you want to invite, and then between us, we have another sixty close friends and relatives. And that doesn't even count the people my mother and Mac want to invite."

"I'll ask Martin what their count is." I picked up my phone and tapped out a text. My phone pinged. "A hundred," I gasped.

Rob sat back on the sofa. "Two hundred and fifty guests."

"That's a lot of people. Should we pare the list?" I rubbed my eyes.

"We've been over it a few times, and I'm not sure we want to question Mother on hers."

"I don't. That's for sure."

"Then we have our list. Bulging as it is." Rob saved the spreadsheet and closed his laptop. "I'll send it to Martin in the morning."

"Won't be able to back out after the note is mailed."

Rob pulled me toward him. "Would you want to?"

"Not a chance." I kissed him, then chuckled. "But now I'm glad Mac and your mother talked us into letting them pay for the reception."

* * *

I doodled on my to-do list as oatmeal bubbled on the stove: check on status of sales contest, follow-up with DeShawn, Trudy Jones. My pencil hovered over her name. I still hadn't tried to reach her, but I doubted she'd have anything to tell me. I crossed off DeShawn's name. *Too soon.* He'd be mad enough to think I still wanted to know what was going on, let alone if I had only given him a few days to investigate Gary. I picked up my phone, scrolled to Trudy's name, and pressed call.

"Hello?"

"Hi, Trudy. This is Merry March. I know we haven't talked in a while, but I was wondering how you were doing."

"I'm keeping busy. Trying not to overthink."

"I hate to bother you, but I wanted to touch base to see if you had found out if Matt had been looking into Kevin's death."

"It's a coincidence that you called. I was just about to reach out to you. Yvonne said you might have discovered something."

I gulped. "I didn't tell her that."

"The antiques guy she buys from told her."

"Andy?"

"That's him. He said you might have a lead."

I doodled and cursed the day Andy was born.

"Merry, are you still there?"

"It may be nothing. Just something strange going on in town."

There was silence. And then Trudy said, "I have a right to know what's happening. My fiancé is dead. Yvonne and I will meet you at the antique store at five."

"That's not going to work—" She had already hung up. *What on earth am I going to tell them?*

I called Andy. The phone rang four times and went to voicemail. "I can't believe you told Yvonne I knew something! Yvonne and Trudy are meeting me at your shop at five. You better be there."

The oatmeal had bubbled over, and now the top of my stove was a mess. I took out my frustration with Andy while cleaning it.

As I scrubbed the cooktop, Drambuie hopped onto the window seat and swiped at a bird sitting on a branch outside. I said, "Not going to get anything that way." DeShawn walked out his back door and into the yard. *I'm going to need to tell Yvonne and Trudy something.* I rushed out and asked, "Do you have a moment?"

"Just. What's up, Merry?"

I strode to the gate and opened it. "I was wondering if you knew anything more about the lead I gave you on Gary."

His eyebrow arched. "The one you gave me a few days ago? I told you, I work on the long game, gathering lots of data to see what patterns emerge. So, to answer your question, I have no update to give." He turned to get into his car.

"Wait. The dead boy's mother and fiancé are meeting with me tonight, and they want to know where the investigation stands."

"If they want to know what's happening with the case, they should be talking to Detective Ziebold, not you. I told you to stay out of this, Merry. End of story." He sank into his car, turned it on, and drove forward to the alley.

I sat on my top step. *What the heck am I going to do?*

CHAPTER 18

R ob held my hand as we walked to Tempting Treasures and Tasty Treats. I stopped. "I'm not looking forward to this. All we have are suppositions, and I don't think we should share them yet. You know how Yvonne went off on Jay when I told her about Jane Creedy's death."

"Let's play it by ear." He held the door for me, and I slipped past.

Yvonne was sitting in a gilded bergére chair, and Trudy stood next to her. Yvonne's lips formed a strict line. "Finally."

I glanced at the ornate kitchen clock that rested on a faux mantle. I was only two minutes late. "You haven't met my fiancé, Rob, yet."

He shook their hands, and Yvonne stood. Andy came out of the café. "Good, you're here. Let's sit on the patio. Ed's prepared hors d'oeuvres, and I thought we might have wine."

Andy led the way, Trudy and Yvonne next, and we followed. I whispered, "Going to be fun," to Rob. He gave me a grim look.

We sat at the table, and Andy poured a crisp rosé. Ed joined us with a small tray of cheddar cheese puffs. "They're better when they're warm, so eat them now."

I bit into one. It was a comforting mix of cheese with a hint of Italian seasoning.

"I want to know what you've been doing to find out what happened to my son. The police have been no help. It's like they're trying to sweep it under the rug. I bet they'd feel different if he was one of their sons." She lifted her wine glass.

"Or their fiancé." Trudy chimed in.

Rob leaned forward. "They are trying to find out what happened. There are so many who have died. I've been speaking with a friend of mine who's a reporter in the city. This is a widespread problem. Detective Ziebold told me there had been two more deaths in the outlying counties in the last week alone."

Yvonne's hand trembled as she lowered the wine glass to the table. "I know my son. He did not take drugs. But he's dead anyway." Yvonne turned toward me. "What have you been doing?"

"I've been talking to people and trying to figure out what happened. I've spoken with Kevin Percher's mother several times. The only thing she can think of is he dated someone who was a bit off; she's trying to remember the girl's name. I've also reached out to the police on several occasions. And I spoke with Jane Creedy before she died and Jane's mother, Tammi. Jane told me Kevin might have gotten speed from an ex-girlfriend. That's why we're trying to figure out who she was."

"That's it? You think the culprit is an 'off' young girl Kevin knew years ago?"

Andy crossed his legs. "Merry's also engaged our local drug enforcement agent."

"Who's he? Maybe I should speak with him." Yvonne struggled with her purse and pulled out a pad and pen. "Name?"

I rubbed the back of my neck. "I'm not sure what he'd have to say. He's concerned about drug trafficking in this area but doesn't seem to know who is behind it."

"I want to meet with him anyway." Yvonne folded her arms across her chest.

"Me too," Trudy said.

"Have another cheese puff, and I'll call him." Andy scrolled on his phone, pressed a button, and walked into the other room.

"I am sorry I'm not further along," I said. "I know how painful this must be."

Yvonne sighed. "I know you're trying. It's not like I'm paying you. I'm so frustrated not knowing anything."

Andy walked back into the room. "He'll meet with us next Tuesday at ten in the city. I'll drive."

Rob checked his calendar. "Can't do it."

I looked up. "I can."

"I'll open the shop," Ed offered.

"So, it'll be Yvonne, Trudy, Merry, and me," Andy said.

* * *

Rob picked his sister Elizabeth up from the airport on Friday and delivered her to my house in time for dinner. I hugged her. "I'm dreading another family occasion, but I'm so happy to have you close."

She chuckled. "It can't be that bad."

I gave her a look. "I've got Sandy and April all set with several things for you to look at tomorrow for the wedding."

"Is Mom coming?"

"She couldn't make it, so it'll be us and Jenny, if she wants to come."

"Sounds like fun." Elizabeth took the wine glass Rob held out to her.

"The bad news is it'll be an early morning because I wanted to do it before they opened for the day. So, we'll need to get there by eight. But Rob promised us breakfast afterward."

"I'm an early bird, so that's no problem. And I'm glad we decided against a tux for me."

"We can only go so far with your mother."

Jenny walked in the back door. "You're here." She hugged Elizabeth.

"Are you coming with us tomorrow?" Elizabeth stood back.

"It's too early for me, Doc. But I am going horseback riding with Ann in the afternoon. Do you ride? You could come with us."

"Sounds like fun."

* * *

The next morning, Elizabeth and I grabbed to-go cups of tea and took the long way to the shop. Approaching from the other side, we wandered through the duck pond right before town. Mallards quacked as they glided for a landing, and weeping willows edged the oval. I sipped from my travel mug. "I don't normally come this way. I almost forgot this place is here."

"What kind of duck is that?" Elizabeth pointed.

"The one with the brown head and white stripe going up by its ear?"

She nodded.

"Don't hold me to it, but I think it's a Northern Pintail."

"Pretty."

We sat on one of the benches, enjoying watching a mama duck leading her young ones to the water, and as they began to swim away, a couple walking the path on the other side of the pond started to argue. I leaned forward as I realized the woman was Sandy Poole, one of the owners of C'est Magnifique, our eight o'clock appointment. She looked summery in peach slacks and a crisp white blouse. I didn't recognize the man with her, but it looked like he hadn't seen the cleansing waters of a shower in recent times, and his clothes were not what you might call fresh.

Sandy jerked her arm away from him and said, "I don't care what you say. I'm not going any further with this. People are getting hurt."

He yanked her back, and spittle flew as he berated her. Unfortunately, his voice was low and didn't carry. I started to stand, feeling I should intervene, but they resumed walking, and the scene was less intense.

"They don't look like they belong together," Elizabeth said.

"That's a fact." The church bell rung eight. "Oops. We're going to be a few minutes late. We should hustle."

We hurried around the pond and down the street to the shop. I knocked on the door and waved when April looked out the sidelight. She unlocked it and let us in. I said, "Sorry, we're late. We got caught up watching the ducks cavort."

Sandy blanched. April held out her hand. "April. You must be Elizabeth. Merry's said such nice things about you."

"She's going to be a great sister-in-law."

Sandy stood there, not moving.

April gestured. "And this is my sister Sandy. We own the shop."

Elizabeth moved forward to shake her hand. "Pleased to meet you. I'm looking forward to seeing the things you've selected."

Sandy shook her head as if waking up. "Great to meet you too. I can't wait to show you what we have. Follow me." She led the way into the back room to a rack brimming with different types of outfits. "Feel free to browse. We'll be back in a moment." She grabbed April's arm, and they went back into the main shop.

Elizabeth and I looked through the rack and selected a few things for her to try on, and I showed her the larger dressing room.

April's whisper carried, "What do you mean you were at the pond with him?"

Sandy's voice was a low murmur.

"I don't like it, but I guess there's nothing we can do now." April walked into the room. "Did you find anything that appealed to you?"

I sat in one of the comfy armchairs and pointed to the dressing room. "She'll be out in a moment."

Elizabeth tried several dresses that, while pretty, weren't quite right. Then, she waltzed out wearing wide-legged, eggplant-colored chiffon slacks, a spaghetti-strapped top of the same material with a long-sleeve sheer overlay. It came with a tailored jacket she had draped over her arm. "What do you think?"

"Love it. Looks great with your coloring. But more important, what do you think? How does it feel?" I touched the fabric. "So soft."

"It feels so good if I don't get it for your wedding. I'm buying it anyway. I get invited to charity fundraisers for the hospital all the time, and this would be perfect."

Sandy circled Elizabeth. "We may need to take it in here and here, but other than that, it fits you pretty well."

I stood. "I think you should get it. That aubergine will be a perfect foil for what I'm wearing."

"Show me."

I glanced at April. "Could you grab my dress?"

"No problem." She went through one of the doors and came back carrying the white garment bag. She unzipped it, lifted the dress, and held it against Elizabeth. "You're right, Merry. It will work beautifully."

Elizabeth smiled. "It's a sale. And since we did that quickly, we still have time before we have to meet Rob. Why don't you show off your dress for me?"

"Now?"

"Yep. While Sandy pins me, you can put it on."

April took the dress into the fitting room and shut the door. I donned the dress and walked out into the room.

Elizabeth clapped. "You look beautiful, but it seems a little big at the waist."

"We noticed that the last time I was here, I guess it hasn't been taken in yet." I glanced at Sandy.

"I did it the other day. If you keep losing weight, you're going to disappear by the time the wedding happens."

Elizabeth looked me up and down. "I'm going to have to talk to my brother. He's not feeding you enough."

I frowned. "I haven't been hungry lately. It could be the stress of everything that's happening."

"Maybe you should get your doctor to check you out."

* * *

Rob and I were unloading the dishwasher while Jenny and Elizabeth were out riding. "It was the strangest thing. Who was that guy, and how did he know Sandy?" I frowned.

Rob said, "Might be a family problem."

"He didn't look like he could've been part of their family." I took a wine glass from Rob and set it on the table.

Elizabeth walked in the back door. "That was fun."

Jenny followed her. "You should see the Doc ride, Mom. She's a natural."

"I'm sure she is." I put another glass on the table. "We'll eat in about twenty minutes if you want to get cleaned up. Feel free to use my shower."

"Thanks." Elizabeth ran up the stairs with Jenny right behind.

Rob placed cutlery, and I put the salad bowl in the middle of the table.

"Did you ride?" I asked Rob.

"Wasn't my thing. I was a baseball fanatic. Played second."

"Ooh." I hugged him. "I didn't know my future husband was a baseball star."

He laughed. "Didn't last longer than high school."

Rob took the ziti, sausage, and black olive casserole from the oven, grated some parmesan, and placed the dish on the table. Elizabeth came downstairs and into the kitchen. "Something smells wonderful." She peered over my shoulder. "And looks great too."

Jenny ran down the stairs. "Starving."

I dished out portions. Elizabeth dipped a piece of bread into the olive oil and spice mixture and popped it into her mouth. "Ann seems level-headed, very driven but wound a little tight. I wouldn't think being a librarian was stressful. I mean, it isn't exactly life or death." She chuckled.

I lifted my wine glass. "I'm sure any profession can be high-pressure. Especially if you want to do a good job, and it's public-facing. People can be quite challenging."

"Riding was fun. I hadn't been on a horse in ages." Elizabeth put down her fork. "Merry, you should try."

"Not happening." I shook my head.

"I'm almost ready to start jumping. Ann said she's never seen anyone progress as fast as me." Jenny preened.

I popped two antacids in my mouth and began to chew.

"Mom! You should eat instead of chewing those things." She took the bottle and stuck it in her pocket.

"Jenny—" Rob protested.

"No, she's right. It's getting to be a bad habit. I need to learn other ways of coping." I gave him a strained smile. "Jenny, no jumping yet. We need to have a conversation about that first. And now, let's talk about something else, shall we? Elizabeth, where are you planning on for vacation this year?"

"I thought I might go to Ireland. I've always wanted to see the Aran Islands off the coast of Galway. They have a prehistoric hill fort from the Iron Age that sounds fascinating."

"I'd love to go to Ireland." Jenny took another piece of bread.

"Maybe we should go together and get aunt-niece bonding time. Now, who's up for a board game?"

* * *

"I still don't understand how Jenny beat me last night. I used to own Rob at that game." Elizabeth pulled her seat belt across her lap and snapped it into place.

Jenny said. "Some people are just that good."

"A little respect, please," I admonished.

"Some people are just that good, Doc."

187

"Jenny."

"Sorry." She smirked.

"Just wait till you see what I say when I win." Elizabeth chuckled.

"Like that's going to happen," Jenny bantered.

Rob drove down the long drive to Wanda and Mac's. I sighed. "Hopefully, Martin won't be here. I'm sure there's an answer I owe him."

Rob lifted my hand and kissed it. "If he is, I'll protect you."

I turned to Elizabeth, "He's usually lying in wait."

I opened my door and almost hit Martin. He held up his clipboard. "Elizabeth, did you find an outfit?"

"Done."

He made a checkmark. "Good." He walked away.

"That's it?" My mouth dropped.

Elizabeth laughed. "I must be your good luck charm."

"If that's true, I'm taking you everywhere. The dining room's this way." I took a deep breath. "Are you ready?"

"Yep."

Rob led the way and opened the door. No one was there.

Wanda called from a room down the hall. "We're in here. I thought we'd chat before dinner."

We joined Wanda and entered a light and airy atrium. The walls were black-framed glass, the floor was slate, and several comfortable over-stuffed floral sofas surrounded a well-worn coffee table. Similar to the last family dinner, Jim, Ann, Amy, and Mac were in attendance. Wanda motioned to one of the sofas. "Elizabeth, sit by me. I still don't understand why you don't stay here when you're in town. People would think we aren't close."

Elizabeth kissed her mother's cheek. "Maybe next time; right now, I'm getting to know Merry and Jenny better." She nodded at Jim. "Nice to see you again," and then said to Amy, "I missed you yesterday. Do you ride?"

I sat next to Ann, and Rob sat on the other side.

Amy reddened. "I stopped riding, but maybe I should take it up again. Actually, I think I'll take a walk down to the stables now. When is dinner?"

"A half-hour. Don't be late," Wanda said.

Jenny jumped up. "I'll join you." Jenny and Amy walked out the door.

Wanda motioned for Mac to give her more wine as he was pouring us some. "Ann, I've meant to talk to you about this library job you have. You're a smart girl with an advanced degree. You could be doing so much better."

Ann's color rose. "I love my job."

"All those children." Wanda shuddered. "It's fine for now, but there's no money in it—kind of a waste of your master's. Trust me. You should go back to school and get something you can actually use." She tapped her finger on her chin. "Maybe an MBA. Look how well your uncle did in the stock market." She beamed at Mac.

"Now dear," Mac said, "It's not for everybody. Look at me. I left."

"But you made your money first. It set you up to chase your passions." Wanda turned to Elizabeth. "Or take a page from her book. She's a successful surgeon. I'm sure that pays well too."

Ann's hand slid into her purse, and she opened a bottle of antacid tablets, took two, and dry swallowed them.

I sat forward. "Wanda, you don't have to have money to be happy. There are many different paths to success in this world."

"Uh-huh. Believe what you want." Wanda draped her arm on the back of the sofa and began a conversation with Jim.

My stomach churned. *This woman is too much.* I touched Ann's shoulder and whispered, "Can I have some of those?"

She handed me two, then scrounged around in her purse and gave me a bottle. "You can have those now, and here's an extra bottle I opened by mistake. It looks like it's going to be a long afternoon. You might need more."

"Thanks." I stuffed the container in my bag and used wine to wash down the other two.

Rob glanced at me. "I don't think you should take those with wine."

I shrugged.

Mac sat next to me on the arm of the sofa. "So, how's my favorite-soon-to-be-daughter-in-law?"

"The wedding can't get here soon enough."

* * *

After dinner, Rob left to drop Elizabeth off at the airport, Jenny had homework, and I headed for my bath. Lavender was calling to me, so I tipped the bottle into the stream of water, and a lovely scent filled the room. My shoulders relaxed as I climbed into the bubble-filled tub, sunk to neck depth, and stretched my legs. *Ann has a good and meaningful job, is a good kid, and all Wanda can see is the dollars attached to it. She probably doesn't think too much of my career or Rob's either. Her loss.*

I opened my book and began to read. After a moment or two, I put it down on the tub caddy, picked up a pad and pencil, and wrote "Gary" on my to-do list. I still needed to get to the bottom of what was going on there. Was he dealing drugs from his shop? We'd be seeing DeShawn on Tuesday, so he might have an update. I doodled. And how about Sandy? *Who was the guy by the duck pond?* I tapped my pencil on the caddy. I needed to find out what she was up to.

CHAPTER 19

Andy honked from across the alley. I swung my purse over my shoulder and walked out the door. He called, "Hurry up, slowpoke."

I unlatched the gate and strode to his garage. "Maybe if someone were on time, I wouldn't need to hurry."

"Tomato-tomahto."

I hopped in the car. "It seems silly we have to go all the way into the city to see DeShawn when he lives right next door."

Andy put his hand on my seat back and turned his body toward the alley as he backed up. "If you were a DEA agent, would you want everyone coming to your house?"

"I guess not. Especially not the bad guys. Not with my family there." I shivered.

"Rest my case." He put the car in drive, and we left. "Trudy will be at Yvonne's house, so we only have to make one stop."

I fiddled with the radio stations. "Don't you have anything preset?"

"I usually listen to what's on my phone."

Static dissipated as I landed on a station and country music played. "Really?" His eyebrow rose. "Do we have to?"

"Since you're making me do this, yes." I reclined my seat a bit.

"What do you think DeShawn's going to tell us? Do you think he has a lead?"

"Doubtful." My foot tapped in time with the song. "I spoke to him last week, and he didn't tell me anything."

"But he wouldn't make Yvonne and Trudy come all the way into the city if he had nothing to say." His eyes widened. "Would he?"

"Shh. I like this song." It was Carrie Underwood's "Drinking Alone," and Andy started to sing along. I stared.

"What? I love me some Carrie."

We pulled up to Yvonne's house, and she and Trudy came out and climbed into the back seats. I pulled mine forward as Trudy snapped her seatbelt in place.

Yvonne tapped my chair with her pen. "Merry, what are the names of the other women whose children died. I remember you said Beth. Who was the other one?"

"Tammi."

"Give me their phone numbers. I think it's time for us mothers to meet. The authorities may take us more seriously if we approach them as a group."

I took her pen and pad and wrote the numbers. "Tammi may not be home yet. She had a tough time after her daughter's death."

My stomach began to churn. All of these women had lost so much. I pulled out antacids and started to open the jar. *No. I promised I'd cut back.* I slid the container into my purse and focused on breathing exercises.

The songs continued as the mileposts rushed past. When Andy activated his turn signal for the exit, Yvonne said, "I hope this DEA person has leads. My husband wants to put this behind us. He wants me to accept the fact Matt took drugs and died. That it was an accident. I can't do it. I just can't."

We came around the back of a tall glass building ringed by strategically placed cement posts and into the parking garage. Andy found a spot, and we got out and walked to the elevator. He scanned the listing and pressed the button for the 12th floor.

Andy told the receptionist who our appointment was with and our names. She nodded, told us to have a seat, and lifted the handset.

After a moment or two, the door opened, and a man said, "Come with me, please." We walked past a large open area filled with metal desks and people working the phones. At the end of the area was a conference room. The man opened the door to it and said, "Wait in here. Supervising Special Agent Jenkins will be with you shortly." He shut the door.

We sat at the table, and Andy surveyed the room. "Why do I always feel guilty when I enter a government building?"

"You don't want me to answer that, do you?" I started to laugh but noticed Yvonne's stern face.

DeShawn opened the door, strode in, and extended his hand to Yvonne. "You must be Ms. Logan. I was so sorry to hear of your son's death." He turned to Trudy. "And that of your fiancé." He shook his head. "Such a sad business."

"I wanted to find out what you are doing to find my son's killer." Yvonne shook his hand.

DeShawn flipped the blinds, so we looked out on the sea of desks we had passed. "Those are the data analysts. They synthesize information from our investigations, documents we've seized, confidential informants, social media, etc. It's tough work, but we have our best doing it. This is more than a job for these people. It's a calling. Those people out there are working twelve-hour days to make sure no one else who does drugs dies needlessly."

I stood and walked to the window. Agents peered intently at their computer screens, and one who was closest to the conference room waved a tall guy over to look at her monitor. I squinted. *Was that Amy on the screen? It sure looked like her.* I moved closer, and DeShawn shut the blind.

"Matt did not do drugs." Yvonne's shoulders sagged.

"I checked the coroner's report. He had drugs in his system." DeShawn sat at the end of the table.

Yvonne rose, walked to the window, and parted the blinds with her forefinger and thumb. "Someone gave him those drugs on purpose. They must have put something in his drink. You hear about those drugs they give girls—"

"Rohypnol, or roofies as they're called on the street," DeShawn said.

"Maybe someone slipped him one of those." She nodded. "Maybe someone murdered him on purpose. It may not have been tied up in this thing you're working on."

Andy stood and guided Yvonne back to the table. She sat, and Trudy covered her hand with hers.

"There weren't any marks on his body that would be consistent with someone forcing him to do something he didn't want to." DeShawn stood and opened the door. "I'm sorry I couldn't give you better news. We are working round the clock, and we will find out who is at the bottom of this."

✳ ✳ ✳

The ride home was somber. Yvonne seemed in a trance, Trudy wasn't doing much better, and I was still trying to figure out if I could trust my eyes. *Why would the DEA be looking at Amy? Surely they didn't care about a little bit of pot.* Andy tried to turn on the radio, but I shook my head. It didn't seem appropriate. After we parked in Yvonne's driveway, she didn't get out of the car. She said, "No one believes me."

"I do." Andy helped her from the car. "We're not going to stop looking into this."

I put my head in my hands. *What on earth can I do?*

Yvonne leaned on Trudy as they went into the house. Andy got back in the car, turned it around, and headed down the driveway. I glared at him. "DeShawn was trying to get her to accept the truth. Kids have ways of fooling their parents. They're the experts; how am I going to do anything?"

"I know you have somebody you suspect."

I huddled against my side of the car. *What kind of person am I? Suspecting Gary, and now April and Sandy. Pretty soon, I'd be suspecting everyone. That isn't the kind of life I want to lead.* "Music, please."

He turned on a station.

"Want me to drop you at work? Or home?"

"Work, please." I pulled down the visor to open the mirror, ran a comb through my hair, and applied tinted lip gloss. Andy pulled toward the curb. I got out and turned toward him. "Thanks for driving. Talk soon."

As I walked into the office, I examined the tote board to see who was leading the office sales contest and was pleased to see three people running neck and neck. When I got to my desk, I sent them a note thanking them for their efforts and reminding them there were only a few days left in the contest.

I was working through the call list when my cell phone dinged with a text from Jenny: "Ann wants to know if we're free for dinner tomorrow night. Uncle Jim asked her to call."

"Grand Mac and Miss Wanda?"

"Busy."

"Okay. But tell her early night because of school."

I sighed as I put my phone down. *All these new relatives.*

My phone dinged with a text from Patty: "Late lunch? One thirty?"

"Look forward to it."

Patty and I had been so busy lately we hadn't had a chance to connect. Even though I had a lot to do, I was looking forward to seeing her. I finished my calls and began working on expenses. My phone alarm chimed, and I stood and stretched.

I meandered down the block, examining the changing storefront displays. Extreme Indulgence had a sale on chocolate-covered pretzels, so I made a mental note to stop on my way back to get more for Rob.

When I opened the door to Delightful Bites, Patty was already at the counter ordering. I walked up behind her and waited my turn. After she paid, I ordered a Reuben with french fries, retrieved an iced tea, and joined her on the deck.

Patty chattered about a new client whose kitchen she was remodeling. The woman was having difficulty choosing between light gray and dark gray cabinets. Patty displayed the samples. "What do you think?"

"She should go with wood and a natural stain. A year ago, it was white, then it was two-toned cabinets, and now gray. Wood is classic, always in style."

"You have no design sense whatsoever."

When my lunch was delivered, her eyes widened. "All those calories. That's not like you. Are you are having a bad day?"

I told her about the meeting with DeShawn. "I'm making myself crazy about something I have no control over." I chewed a piece of the sandwich and swallowed. Although it was tasty, it wasn't going to help. I put it back down. "What do you think I should do?"

She laid her fork on the table. "I think you may want to lay it to rest. Tough as it is to believe, those kids could just have gotten in over their heads."

The mysterious SUV I'd seen before pulled into the parking lot, and the same twitchy guy darted to the side entrance of the café. I pointed to Patty's mostly eaten lunch. "Are you done?"

She speared one last shrimp. "I could be."

"Follow that car." I grabbed a french fry and ran to Patty's minivan. "Hurry."

"I didn't know lunch would be so exciting." She pressed start and backed out of the space. "Or that you would eat so little of yours."

I shrugged. "Instead of tailing him, head for Fiorella's. That way, we'll be there before him."

"What are we going to do when we get there?"

"We're going to park. They're open for lunch today, so there will be other cars in the lot. Then, we're going to find out what's going on."

Patty pulled into the half-full parking lot and found a spot behind a big black Hummer. "I don't think he'll notice us behind this behemoth."

I slid out. The space by the back door was empty. She moved next to me. "What do we do now?"

"Wait."

"We'll look suspicious if we're standing here. People may think we're trying to rob their cars."

I looked her up and down. Pink pedal pushers and a white organza blouse with a camisole. "Doubtful."

The maroon SUV pulled up to the loading area. The tattooed man took two of the boxes and carried them into the shop. I edged closer, and Patty held my arm. "What are you going to do?"

"Stay here. I'll be right back."

"This guy looks like bad business. Rob will never forgive me if you get hurt."

I darted toward the SUV, grabbed a box, and ran back toward Patty. My heart was racing and felt like it had lurched into my throat. I yelled, "Get in the car."

She started the car, and I jumped in. "Let's go." My hands were sweating, and it was hard to breathe.

Patty peeled out of the parking lot and drove down the road. "Where to?"

I pointed and croaked, "The park on Tremont."

"Aren't you going to open it?"

I shook my head. "Let's get away from here first."

She turned onto the tree-lined drive and parked the minivan, so it was partially hidden behind a sizeable forest-green dumpster. My hands shook.

"I can't believe you took the box. What if it is drugs? That guy could come after you. Or me." She gulped. "You don't think he noticed my plate number?"

I raised my right eyebrow. "And when would he have done that?"

"Open it."

"Not in here. If there are traces of fentanyl, it could get on us and in the car. Let's go to that picnic table under the tree over there. It'll be better to open it outside." I slid from the car, making sure the box remained closed, walked to the table, and put it down.

Patty stood next to me, shifting from foot to foot. "Should we be ready to run?"

"Maybe. I don't know. Ready?"

She nodded but looked like she was going to bolt. Then, she said, "Wait! I have gloves. Let's use those." She ran to the car, got them, and handed them to me. "Now I'm ready."

I donned the gloves and then edged the box open, stretching my arm and turning my face so when I opened it, it would be as far away from my nose and mouth as possible. As I flipped the box lid, Patty ran pell-mell toward the car.

Ten decadent-looking cannoli were nestled in bakery tissue paper. My mouth dropped.

Patty called, "Are you okay? What was in there?"

I started laughing and couldn't stop.

She crept toward me. "Does fentanyl cause euphoria?"

"I don't know. But these might." I lifted one and bit into it.

Patty and I drove back to Fiorella's and parked. She said, "This is on you and your overactive imagination."

"You're not going in with me?"

She shook her head. "I'll wait here."

I groaned, got out of the car, and walked to the server's entrance.

CHAPTER 20

Rob picked Jenny up after basketball practice, and when they walked in, they talked a mile a minute about free-throw strategies. Jenny's eyes lit on the bag from Fiorella's, and she said, "What did you get?"

"Dinner."

Rob kissed my cheek. "Wanted take-out?"

"Long story. Dinner will be ready in five."

Rob lifted a bottle of Chianti. "This good?"

I nodded as I put a salad on the table. When Jenny came back, I took the aluminum tray of stuffed shells and garlic bread from the oven. Everyone helped themselves, and Rob said, "If I had known you were in the mood for Fiorella's, I could have saved you a trip and stopped by on my way here."

"I was already there," I explained what had happened.

"But why were they getting their cannoli from Delightful Bites?" Jenny asked.

"And how did the chef react when she found out you stole a box?" Rob jumped in.

"She was quite gracious. She laughed about me thinking her nephew was a drug dealer. He's a sous chef and doing well in culinary school. Their pastry guy quit a month ago, and instead of hiring another, they formed a pact with Gary to supply the cannoli. He's basically wholesaling. The deal is he'll supply them with what they need and not offer a similar product in his shop. They save salary money, and he gets a new revenue stream. Win-win."

"But why was the guy so nervous?"

"She threatened him because she wants this kept quiet. They're known for baking everything in-house and are using this as a test to see if quality or access suffers. If it's a success, they'll eventually reveal some of the food is made outside. She swore me to secrecy, except for you two."

Jenny lifted another cannoli. "Tastes as good to me."

* * *

I leaned against Rob on the sofa. "Poor Gary, I was suspecting him of being a drug kingpin. The only thing he's guilty of pushing is flour. I'm going to have to fess up tomorrow. Hopefully, the people at Fiorella's have been too busy to call him."

Rob kissed the top of my head. "You were trying to do the right thing."

"I'll have to let DeShawn know. Can't have them chasing their tails."

"I thought you were sworn to secrecy."

I sat forward. "I have to tell him something. I didn't mention the DEA to the chef because I was too embarrassed. Plus, I don't think she would have thought it was funny if she knew I reported her nephew to the DEA and the police. In fact, I should probably take care of that right now."

I lifted my phone and pressed DeShawn's number. It rang once. "DeShawn? It's Merry. I was wondering if you had a few minutes. I have something I need to tell you."

"Jada had a headache, so she went up early. I'm outside in the back."

"Thanks." I hung up and stood. "He's outside."

I then called Jay. "Could you meet us at DeShawn's? I have something to tell you both."

"Okay."

Rob got up, and we walked out the back door. The cats tried to gain freedom with a burst of speed, but I uttered a sharp "No," and blocked the door with my leg. They whined and slunk back to their perch on the window seat.

We strolled the three stairs to DeShawn's back patio. They had strung poles with fairy lights and had large ceramic planters overflowing with flowers on the bluestone. DeShawn was lying on a lounge chair, staring at the stars.

He shifted the chair into an upright position. "Have a seat."

Rob and I sat on the picnic bench. I crossed my legs. "Jay's coming too. Do you mind if we wait for him?"

"No problem." DeShawn got to his feet. "I have your brownie container. I may as well get that." He disappeared into the kitchen.

I nudged Rob with my shoulder. "This is awkward."

"Yep."

Jay trotted up the steps and sank onto one of the chairs. "What's up?"

DeShawn came out of the kitchen door and handed me the container. "Here you go." He sat on the recliner again.

"Um. You know how I told you I suspected Gary of being involved in the drug trade?"

"Yes," Jay said.

"He isn't."

"I told you he wasn't involved." Jay sat back and smiled. "Just goes to show you should leave the detecting to professionals."

I rubbed the back of my neck. "You're right."

Rob came to my aid. "She was just trying to help."

"So, what were they doing?" DeShawn asked.

"I can't say, specifically. It's a new business venture that has nothing to do with drugs."

"Thanks for letting me know." Jay stood. "And now, Merry, will you lay off on the investigating?"

"You have my word." I did the three-fingered Girl Scout salute.

He trotted down the stairs muttering, "When have I heard that before?"

Rob and I walked to his car. He lifted my chin. "Don't be so down. You're doing the right thing."

* * *

Early the following day, I was in line at Delicious Bites. Since I had to see Gary, I figured I might as well pick up a few treats for the office. He was working the register, and the minute his eyes met mine, he started to laugh. When I reached the counter, I ordered two danish rings and coffee. He slid them into boxes and handed me a cup. "Too busy now, but I can't wait to hear this story."

"I wanted to apologize."

"Not needed. Just come by later today or tomorrow to fill me in." He moved to the next customer, and I went to the coffee station to fill my cup.

As I left the shop, I nearly walked into Beth Percher. I asked, "What are you doing here?"

"I brought one of the kids to the orthodontist's, and I thought I'd enjoy myself for a few minutes. I've been craving a latte since I was here with you the other day."

I turned around. "I'll join you."

She got in line, and I sat at one of the tables. After a few moments, she sat. "I was going to call, so I'm glad we ran into each other. Yvonne reached out to me yesterday. She's so frustrated with the police and the DEA and how they are dragging their heels. She wanted to get together with Tammi and me." She sipped coffee. "Tammi's still in the facility. Her sister says she's getting better, but she's worried about what she'll do when she's released." Beth rubbed her forehead. "Anyway, there was a free room open at Yvonne's library, so I met her there. And the strangest thing happened."

I nodded for her to continue.

"You know the girl my son dated? The one who was a little off?"

I leaned forward. "Yes?"

"Yvonne went to check out a book as we were leaving, and I saw her. Older, of course. And her hair was a different color. When Kevin dated her, everything was black, so dour, but she was wearing very bright clothes that day."

"Are you sure it was her?" I gasped.

She leaned back. "I have a good head for faces. I'm positive."

"Thanks for letting me know." I stood and bumped the table, making Beth's coffee slosh from her cup, so I grabbed a napkin and handed it to her. "Sorry."

"Are you okay?" She looked at me with concern.

"Fine. Just late." I started toward the door.

"Merry, your danish." She pointed at the boxes still on the table.

"I'll be in touch." I picked up the danish and walked out the door. *Was Ann or Amy Kevin's girlfriend? I told them about people dying... did I say his name?*

I wandered to the office on autopilot, handed the boxes to Cheryl, entered my office, and shut the door. I sat, picked up a pencil, pulled a pad toward me, and wrote: Ann or Amy? *Had one of them driven to the Bishop's Retreat Conference Center and dropped off the fentanyl-laced methamphetamine that killed Kevin? Ann was a librarian. Librarians help people. Maybe it wasn't Ann at all. It could've been Amy. More likely to have been Amy. She has dark hair, wears black, and smokes pot. She'd probably know where to get other drugs. But she seemed so nice. It was unbelievable to think it was either one of them.*

I put the pencil down. We were having dinner with them tonight.

Eileen Curley Hammond

There was a rap on the door, and Cheryl walked in. "Your clients are here. Are you ready?"

I plastered a smile on my face and went to greet them.

* * *

Rob walked in the back door as Jenny was getting ready upstairs. I pointed to the laundry room. "In there."

His eyebrow rose, but he followed me.

I shut the door.

He leaned against the washing machine. "Something with Jenny?"

I shook my head. "Your new step-cousins. There's a problem." I filled him in.

"You think they're involved in this?" Rob rubbed his face. "I can't see it. They're so young."

"Kevin was young. And whoever it was dated him. And Beth said she recognized Ann."

"From what you said, she thought she recognized her. She also said she only saw her for a few moments."

The dryer buzzed, and I took towels out and started folding them. "That's what worries me. It could have been Ann or Amy."

"Or neither of them." He lifted a towel and folded it.

I put the one I had been working on in the laundry basket. "What are we going to do?"

Rob dropped the final towel into the basket, and Jenny opened the door and said, "Are we ready to leave? I told them we'd be there by six."

Rob extended his arm. "After you."

I lifted my purse from the stool by the door. "Can't wait."

He locked the door, followed us, and we got into the car. As he was backing up, he said to Jenny, "What are we going to do about this Mr. Jenson stuff? Have you given it any more thought?"

"Of course."

204

"And?"

"I think I'm going with 'Rad.'"

I turned. "Rad?"

"She's saying I'm radical. That's cool. I don't mind being 'Rad.'"

Jenny laughed. "That wasn't what I meant. 'R' because your name is Rob, and 'ad' because you're going to be my new dad."

"I love it. I can't wait to be your Rad." His eyes welled, and he covered it by playing with the radio dials.

I touched his hand, he looked at me, and I blew him a kiss. He smiled.

A country song came on. Jenny said, "Nope. I had to listen to that the last time I drove Mom."

I chuckled and turned toward the window. As farmland rushed past and we approached Jim's house, I grew more nervous. *Could one, or both, of the twins have had something to do with this? If they did, could it have been an accident? Maybe they didn't know about the fentanyl.* I opened my purse and played with the jar of antacids. *Just one.* I took a quick look over my shoulder. Jenny was staring at me. *Better not.*

We turned down the heavy tree-lined drive. Jenny was right. It was like going into an enchanted forest that was so dark, so heavy. After a few minutes, we entered a clearing, and the house sat directly in front of us. It was a charming cottage that looked warm and welcoming. Too bad it was hot. It would have been picture perfect with white smoke puffing from the ornate chimney.

Jim must have been waiting for us because he walked out the front door as soon as we parked. "Welcome. I'm glad you were able to come on such short notice."

I got out of the car and was enveloped in a bear hug. After a beat, he stepped back, and Jenny was next. She giggled, and then it was Rob's turn.

"Come in, come in," he said. We followed him through the stout wooden door and into the living room. The floors were polished hickory, and the sofas a deep mahogany leather. The room was saved from being overly masculine by artfully draped bright-colored afghans. Jim pointed to a couch, "Please have a seat. The girls will be out in a minute. They're putting last-minute touches on dinner."

Jenny said, "I'll help," and went through a door near the dining room I assumed went to the kitchen.

My stomach clenched, and I started to follow. I wasn't sure I wanted her alone with them.

Jim handed me a wine glass. "They've got it under control. Have a seat. White okay?"

I nodded, and he poured. I took a sip and placed the glass on the coffee table. "Maybe I should—"

"Don't be silly. Sit." He poured Rob's wine, and we sat on the sofa.

Rob said, "I'm surprised you're not traveling."

"Next week. I have to confess the thrill of the hunt is getting a bit old." He chuckled. "Or maybe I'm just aging. I've begun to appreciate the comfort of one's bed."

"Do you focus on a specific type of antique? I don't know a lot about it, but my friends specialize in eighteenth-century French furniture. Though they do vary when they come upon something they love." I sat back on the sofa, but my nerves were jangling, and my hands felt like ice. *I'll feel much better when Jenny is back in view.*

"I dabble in just about everything. Pre-Columbian art, this and that, you know."

Rob looked at his watch and started to rise. "Maybe I should see if they need help."

As if they had heard us talking about them, the kitchen door swung open with Jenny in the lead, carrying two dishes. I exhaled. Amy and Ann followed, each with their hands full, and Ann chirped, "Dinner's ready."

We gathered around the table, and Rob said, "Something smells great." The air was redolent with charred onions and peppers.

Amy smiled. "We have fajitas, refried beans, and rice. Ann taught Jenny and me how to make tortillas with a press she got in Mexico."

Jenny passed tortillas, which had been individually wrapped in aluminum foil. I held one in my hands, relishing the warmth. Then the rest of the dishes were passed.

Rob gave me a platter of thinly sliced skirt steak, followed by onions and peppers. I laid them on top of the tortilla, rolled it, and took a bite. "This is wonderful. Where did you learn to cook like this?"

"Dad made the steak, Amy and I worked on the rest. You should taste the street food in Mexico." Ann sighed. "Heaven."

I took a small portion of rice and an even smaller dollop of refried beans. "Have you spent a lot of time south of the border?"

Amy laughed. "We all have. Dad jokes it's our second home."

"Do you speak Spanish?" Rob asked.

"Si," Ann responded. "Actually, we know a little bit more than that."

Amy snorted. "A lot more. Ann speaks like a native. Dad's next best, and then there's me."

"You'd be better if you practiced." Jim encouraged, "Why don't you come with me on my next trip?"

"School."

Jim's face reddened as if he was embarrassed to have forgotten.

The rest of the dinner was pleasant. At the end, Jim stood. "It's still early. How about a game of cards?"

I glanced at my watch. "It's a school night for Jenny."

"A quick one."

Jenny gave me a pleading look, and I said, "No more than an hour, and then we have to go."

Ann began to clear the table. "I can help." I stood, grabbed a few plates, and walked into the kitchen. It was painted bright lemon, with a farmhouse sink centered under a large window that looked onto a kitchen garden. A large metal rack held copper pots and saucepans carefully arranged according to size. "This is pretty." I placed the dishes on the island. "Can I ask you something?"

"Shoot." Ann squirted dishwashing liquid onto one of the platters.

"Did you date someone named Kevin Percher when you were in high school?"

"Nope." Ann scrubbed the platter.

"Are you sure?"

She rinsed the platter and then looked at me. "I haven't dated so many people that I've forgotten who they were." She put the dish on the drying rack. "Why do you ask?"

"His mother was meeting people at the library and thought she recognized you."

Ann shrugged. "Maybe I have one of those faces."

I wandered to a bookshelf behind a built-in bench. Cookbooks by subject and then in alphabetical order lined the shelves. I ran my hand over the spines. "Someone likes to cook."

"Me. And Dad, but most of what he does is outside." She swept her hand in a circle. "This is my domain."

A book was open on the well-used wooden kitchen table. I thumbed the pages. "And chemistry?"

She laughed and pointed to the name on the inside front cover. "It's Amy's. I just borrowed it because so much of baking is chemical changes. Knowing science helps you bake better cakes."

I followed Ann to a small sitting room complete with game table. The others were already seated, so Ann and I sank into the two remaining chairs.

Jim looked up from shuffling the cards. "Poker okay? We'll play for bragging rights."

I nodded, and Rob doled out chips.

CHAPTER 21

The lights were low, and soothing sounds of a babbling brook intermixed with soft chimes came from the speakers. I slid onto one of the padded, high back, black chairs as Patty stuck her toes into the footbath. "Ouch. A little too hot." The attendant adjusted the spray, and Patty leaned back in the chair and shut her eyes. "Perfect."

I played with the chair remote, moving the seat forward so I didn't have to stretch my legs as far. "You have the best ideas."

"I know. What polish are you using?"

I held out the tab. "Tempestuous Tulip."

"Nice." She flipped through the selections and held up a lilac swatch. "I'm going with Poetry in Pansies."

"I'll let you soak while I get your wine," the nail technician said, and then she and the other tech left the room.

I studied the colors. Maybe the one I'd chosen was too bold. I put the selections to the side. "I'm having issues with Ann."

"Still afraid she'll steal Jenny's affection away?"

"That's silly. It's just she's wound so tight. Everything has to be in its place. You should see her pots and pans. And the way her cookbooks are arranged."

"She's a librarian. It would be more surprising if she weren't organized."

"Amy is much more laid back."

"Likely the weed she smokes."

"Not funny." I rubbed my feet together. "We had dinner there last night. Ann had a chemistry book in her kitchen, and when I asked her about it, she told me knowing the science helps her with baking."

Patty tilted her head. "It is pretty exact. I mixed buttermilk pancakes once and had already put in the baking soda. Then one of my usual household disasters happened. I think an entire jug of milk went on the floor, anyway, because I didn't get the batter on the heat right away—let's say I found the true meaning of 'flat as a pancake.'" Patty reclined her seat further.

The two technicians walked back into the room and handed us glasses of wine.

Patty sniffed, "Would be better if these weren't plastic."

"Until you dropped it." I pointed to our bare feet.

"I still don't know why you think someone wanting to improve their baking is weird." She tapped on her phone and then stiff-armed it to me. "See, there's even a Facebook group about chemistry and baking."

"There's a group for everything. I wasn't being critical. I just thought it was strange. Of course, the book did have Amy's name on it, so maybe Ann was telling the truth when she said she borrowed it from her."

The technician began to scrub Patty's feet, and the scent of mandarin oranges arose.

"Maybe you should be more worried about the other twin. That and being glad she isn't using her chemistry knowledge to cook up something worse." Patty reclined her seat and closed her eyes.

✳ ✳ ✳

"How do you like my toes?" I lifted my feet for Rob to admire.

"Very pretty. A hundred years ago, it would have been scandalous for me to see your feet before we were married." He put his arm around me.

"I don't know about that. People have been pretty frisky throughout the ages."

"Don't get me started." Rob kissed me. "I almost forgot. Elizabeth's wondering if she should stay with Mother this time. She's worried she's wearing out her welcome."

"Not at all. She's welcome to stay here anytime."

"I'll let her know. Oh, change in plans."

"What now?"

"Family dinner is at Jim's this week."

I nodded and then put my hand to my mouth. "We're not going to have to have it here, are we? We're not taking turns?"

"You entertain all the time. Would it be so bad if we did?"

"For normal people, no. For your mother..."

"We haven't gotten that far yet. Jim wanted to host the dinner because he's adding a few more beehives in the back by their pond. He wants Mac to take a look."

I crossed my feet on the coffee table. "What would Mac know about beehives? He's not an entomologist."

"Bees are animals in the broader scheme of things. You know how antibiotics have been over-prescribed, and a lot of bacteria is resistant to it?"

I nodded.

"Beekeepers used to be able to get antibiotics over the counter. They can't now because of that problem, so they need a vet to prescribe it for them. Mac thinks it could be a lucrative new side business for him."

"How do they give it to them? They don't take a pill, do they?" I laughed.

"They dust the hive with the antibiotic mixed with sugar."

"How on earth do you know so much about bees?"

"While you were in the kitchen with Ann, Jim told Jenny and me all about it. I'm surprised Jenny hasn't brought up the idea of a colony in your backyard."

"Too small. We'd get stung all the time."

Rob smiled. "That's what I told her."

✳ ✳ ✳

"They said your outfit was ready. I figured we could pick it up, and then you could leave it in the guest closet until the wedding." I pulled in front of the store and turned toward Elizabeth. "Do you want to try it on again?"

"I probably better. The next time I put it on will be at your wedding, and I'd prefer not to have any surprises."

We got out of the car and walked to the door. Someone was yelling. I peered in the window. Sandy and April were talking to the guy we saw Sandy with the last time Elizabeth had been in town.

"I don't care. We've started a new life, and you're not part of it."

Elizabeth had her hand on the door. "Do we go in? Or wait?"

"In." I motioned to open it.

We entered the store, and April jumped. "Merry." She glanced at the antique clock on the wall. "I had no idea it was so late."

Sandy grabbed the guy by the arm. "We'll continue this later. You need to leave." She escorted him out the front door.

April's face flushed, and she seemed unsteady on her feet. I looked at her with concern. "Is this a bad time? We could come back later."

She took a breath and straightened her shoulders. "Not at all. Elizabeth, I put your outfit in the first stall, in case you wanted to try it on."

Elizabeth walked into the dressing room and shut the door.

"So, who is he?" I asked.

"My brother." She paled. "If you don't mind, I'd rather not talk about it."

Sandy came back, and April gave her a long look.

Elizabeth modeled her outfit, which was tailored perfectly. After she took it off, Sandy carefully draped it with a long plastic covering. "Should I wrap this for the plane?"

"I'm leaving it at Merry's." Elizabeth lifted the hanger and followed me out the door. As she placed it on the hook in the back of the car, April and Sandy's brother came back to the store and slipped through the entrance.

"I wonder what that's all about."

"We all have people in our family who drive us nuts." Elizabeth sat in the passenger seat.

"Are you saying Rob isn't an angel?"

"Oh no, he is. At least, that's my story until the ring is on your finger. Only then will secrets be revealed."

I laughed. "Now you have me worried. Lunch?"

"I promised Jenny I'd go riding with her and Ann this afternoon. You should join us. The horses are quite docile. I think you'd enjoy it."

"Hard pass. I'll take you home, and we can make sandwiches there."

After lunch, Jenny and Elizabeth left, and Rob had errands to run, so I was by my lonesome. I put in a load of wash, walked to my office, and started shredding papers. I had let the pile get too large, and now was as good a time as any to check that task off my to-do list.

As I fed paper into the shredder, I began to feel guilty. Jenny had been riding for a month, and I hadn't watched her once. I fed one last piece in, turned off the shredder, and walked out the door.

There wasn't much traffic on the road, so I got to Wanda and Mac's quickly. I parked by the barn, hoping Martin wouldn't see my car. When I got out, the large barn door was open, and Elizabeth watched something in the paddock. I strode through to where she was standing. A dark-gray horse circled and then jumped over a low rail. Jenny was jumping. It felt like my heart lifted to my throat. I wanted to scream but was afraid I'd scare the horse.

"Looks like a natural, and this is her first day," Elizabeth said.

The muscular horse trotted, and Jenny said, "Let's try the crossrail."

I squeezed my eyes shut.

"Not yet," Ann cautioned, "You're still landing on his neck. Circle again."

My eyes opened. Jenny's horse cantered toward the obstacle, gathered its haunches, and leaped. She was still on the horse. I breathed again.

"Are you okay?" Elizabeth eyed me with concern. "You're awfully pale."

"Mom, did you see?" Jenny yelled.

"Yep, I saw."

* * *

By two on Sunday, we were loaded into the car. Elizabeth had made a carrot and broccoli salad, and my offering was a cherry-topped cheesecake.

"I don't know why you're still upset," Jenny said. "I was fine."

"We've had this discussion. We don't need to have it again in front of Rob and Elizabeth. You know you should have asked me." I yanked my seatbelt and slammed it into the buckle. "You're not old enough to be making these decisions on your own."

"Fine," she huffed. "I'll let you know the next time I'm jumping."

"Which is not going to be for a while. Enough now, we have a guest."

Jenny's lip jutted as she stared out the window. I looked over my shoulder at Elizabeth. "Tell us a fun story about growing up with Rob."

"Do you know Rob used to interview squirrels?" She asked.

"Did not," Rob retorted.

"Do tell," I said.

"I was about twelve, and Rob was eight. He had this microphone he made from a stick and a ball of tinfoil. He used it to interview everyone. A squirrel was perched in the tree, and Rob asked him about his life, how it felt to be able to scurry up a vertical surface, if he liked acorns, and if he was one of those squirrels that could fly."

Jenny laughed. "Did the squirrel answer?"

"There was chittering, but to be honest, the squirrel wasn't much of a conversationalist," Rob deadpanned. "Now, let me tell an Elizabeth story."

"No fair. I had to live with you badgering my boyfriends. This is payback."

"Oh no," I chuckled.

"You wouldn't believe the questions he came up with. I was always surprised when I was asked on a second date. It's probably why I'm still single today."

We pulled into Jim's long drive. As the house came into view, Elizabeth gasped. "You weren't kidding. It is out of a fairy tale."

Jenny said, "I can't wait to see the new hives."

After we parked, Jenny jumped from the car and ran to the door. Ann greeted her, "The new bees just got here. C'mon, we're introducing them to the hive."

We followed through the house to the back terrace. Jenny hesitated. "It's fine, go ahead," I said.

"Thanks." Jenny flashed me a smile as she and Ann donned suits.

They ran toward the crowd at the back of the property, and Ann called over her shoulder, "You may want to wait there. Miss Wanda should be out in a minute."

As we sat on the rattan furniture, I said, "I'm kind of glad they didn't have enough suits. I don't want to get stung."

Rob elbowed me. "That's the point of the suits."

"All this fuss over bees. I don't understand it." Wanda walked out the back door, glass in hand. "I found lemonade in the kitchen if anyone wants it." She sat.

"What are they doing with those boxes?" Elizabeth asked.

"They'll put the queen in, and then her soldiers will follow," Rob stood. "Anyone else for lemonade?"

Elizabeth and I raised our hands. Rob went through the back door.

Wanda groaned. "Now Mac will want bees."

"Your property's big enough and think about all that lovely honey." Elizabeth smiled.

"You know I don't eat honey. Too fattening."

"But oh so good for you. Honey was significant in early medicine."

"Give me a good old-fashioned pill any day." Wanda sipped lemonade.

Jim strode to the patio, removing his hood and then smoothing his hair. "The new bees look good. Very active."

"Mom, they're so cool. We should get some." Jenny ran up behind Jim, holding her hood.

I shook my head. "Maybe if we move out into the country but not in our current house. We'd get stung, and our neighbors would too."

She plopped down onto a chair, and Ann perched next to her. "Don't worry, Jenny, I'll let you know when we're harvesting the honey, and you can help."

Rob rushed out of the kitchen. "Jim, it smells like something is burning in the basement, but the door is locked."

Ann and Jim rushed into the house.

A few minutes later, they returned. Ann said, "The dryer vent got a little hot. I guess I was too lax about cleaning it."

"That can start a fire. You need to be careful," I cautioned.

"Why do you lock your basement door?" Jenny asked. "Afraid of the bogeyman?"

"Dad travels a lot, and the basement has an outside door over there." She pointed.

"Safety first," Rob said.

Jim walked out of the house carrying a tray full of patties. "I guess I better get the hamburgers on the grill."

Wanda's eyebrow rose.

"Don't worry. I have plain salmon for you," he said.

She settled back into her chair with a smile.

"I guess that's my cue to get moving." Ann stood.

"I'll help." Jenny jumped to her feet.

Elizabeth started to stand, and I touched her elbow as I rose. "Sit. I'll go. You visit with your family."

Amy strolled out of the house, nose in a book, and almost walked right into me. I said, "Whoa. What's so interesting?"

She showed me the cover, *Marine Life Medicines and Dosing*, and said, "Getting a head start on my books for next semester."

"Sounds fascinating." I followed Jenny into the kitchen.

Ann turned from the refrigerator. "Oh, Merry. I have something for you." She went to the pantry, lifted a small honey jar, and handed it to me. "This is from our bees. I thought you might enjoy it."

"Thank you. I will." I wrapped a paper towel around the glass jar and carefully placed it in my purse. "What can I do?"

"Please fill the water glasses. Jenny, can you put the salads on the table?"

I walked past the cellar door and frowned. No wonder Rob wasn't able to get in the basement. It was a keyed lock. *That's weird. Why not a deadbolt?*

Mac and Jim walked in the back door carrying trays covered in tinfoil. Jim said, "Let's eat."

CHAPTER 22

I twirled the wine in my glass. "I'm getting the strangest feeling about Ann." The sun slid lower in the sky, casting pink and purple hues behind the garages and creating an increasing shadow from Andy and Ed's house.

"How so?"

"You'll think I'm silly."

"Never." Rob kissed my nose.

"First, the fact that Beth thought Ann looked like the strange girl Kevin used to date."

"We talked about that. She only got a glance at her. And didn't she say she had black hair? Ann's is blonde."

"The chemistry book. Why would someone have that in their kitchen? And then, the locked cellar door." I leaned forward. "Something is going on."

"I thought she said it was Amy's, and she used it for baking." He rubbed my back. "And she explained the door. Made sense to me. That house is in the middle of nowhere."

I frowned. "She has an explanation for everything. The door is weird. If you have a keyed lock, and there aren't any sidelights on the door, wouldn't you get a deadbolt? And if you weren't going to get a normal deadbolt, why wouldn't you leave the key in it? It's an inside door to the basement."

"Maybe they don't like people sifting through their dirty laundry." Rob chuckled.

I elbowed him. "Not funny. What if she's the drug kingpin DeShawn can't find?"

"Ann? A librarian?" His mouth dropped. "I think you're still miffed about Jenny jumping without asking you."

"I am," I sniffed. "And I have every right to be."

Rob put his arm around me and squeezed. "I think you're way off base on this."

"Maybe we should tell Jay."

"That my step-cousins might be involved? Based on what? A chemistry book in the kitchen? A too-quick denial of knowing someone? Merry, you seem to be jumping at shadows in the interest of solving this thing."

"I don't think that's fair," I grumbled.

"First, you thought it was Gary, then Sandy, and now Amy and or Ann."

"I'm whittling down my list."

"And accusing innocent people." Rob lifted my hand and kissed it. "I love you, but you need to learn when to stop."

"People died. I want to find out who killed them. You said you would help."

He sighed. "What do you want me to do?"

"Talk to your reporter friend. See if she's heard anything new."

"Okay." He turned my head toward his. "But you need to promise me you won't talk to Jay or DeShawn about my step-cousins. My mother would go nuts."

"I promise." I kissed him.

"Getting late. I should be going." He stood and then leaned over for one last kiss. "I'll see you tomorrow."

Rob walked through the gate, and I picked up the empty glasses and wandered back into the house. *Could Ann be mixed up in this? Am I unfair?*

✳ ✳ ✳

The following day, I woke to the faint sound of a lawnmower that grew louder and then quieter. I leaned toward the window and parted the drapes. DeShawn was cutting swaths of his lawn from side to side. I checked my phone. *Pretty early to be doing yard work.* I wandered into the bathroom and got in the shower. *Is Rob right? Am I seeing things that aren't there?* I turned off the water, toweled, and dressed.

When I rounded the corner to the kitchen, both cats' heads swiveled in my direction. "Yes, I know it's early. But if you're not hungry yet..." I walked into the laundry room and grabbed their bag of kibble. Two thuds sounded as the cats bounded from their perches. I filled their bowls, went to the kitchen, and pressed start on the coffee maker.

Gary didn't turn out to be a bad guy, but what's up with Sandy and April's brother? I sighed. *What if Amy or Ann is involved? What would that mean for Rob's family?* Absently, I reached for my purse and pulled the antacid bottle toward me. I stared at it and turned it left and right. Ann gave it to me. But she took two of the tablets. I saw her. And she had given me two, which I took. It had to be safe.

I placed it on the counter, poured a cup of java, and sat staring at it. *Could Ann have thought I was getting too close?* Rob was right. I was jumping at shadows. I tossed the jar back into my purse.

Chemistry. Why Chemistry? I pulled the jar back out, grabbed a baggie from the drawer, dropped the container into it, pressed the seal, and shivered.

DeShawn's lawnmower droned. Before I could second guess myself, I took the bag, walked out the door, across the driveway, and up the steps to his backyard.

As he neared, he turned off the mower. "I know it's early, but Jada, Imani, and I are going to the lake on Thursday, and I wanted to get it done before we left."

"Not why I'm here." I held out the baggie.

He lifted it. "Antacids?"

"I'm worried they're laced with fentanyl."

"And why would you think that?"

"Can't say. I'm probably being silly, but I'd appreciate it if you could test them for me."

He glanced at his watch. "I have a meeting soon out of the office, so I won't be able to get this to the lab until later. Is that okay? If you need it sooner, you can get free test strips at the county board of health and do it yourself."

My eyes widened. "Do it myself?"

"It's easy. You put one in a baggie, smash it, add water, and put the dipstick in."

"In my house? With my daughter there? What if I get it on her or me?" I shook my head. "I'll leave it with you."

"I'll give you a call when I get the results." He put the baggie in his pocket and gave me a stern look. "If they are fentanyl, I'm going to need to know where they came from."

"It's probably nothing. But thanks, it'll set my mind at ease." I started down the stairs and then turned. "I appreciate this."

He waved and started the mower.

I walked back into the house and sank onto the stool. *What have I done?*

* * *

As I made my way to work, I stopped by the pharmacy and picked up another jar of antacids. *Just in case.*

Cheryl met me at the door to the office. "Great news, we have a winner of the sales contest."

"That's the kind of news I needed to hear. Come to my office. When I left last night, it was neck-and-neck."

She followed me, and we both sat. "Who won?"

"Doro. She pulled ahead under the wire."

"Good for her. I'll run over to the bakery for goodies, and we'll announce it at the all associate meeting this morning."

"I made a certificate for her to display." Cheryl handed me the award notice, which she had slipped into a clear plastic stand.

"Very nice. Thanks for thinking about this and running the contest."

She blushed. "I'm glad sales rebounded."

"Me too. You'll see a nice surprise in your next paycheck." I stood. "I'll run to Delightful Bites. Back in ten."

The day had turned cooler, almost crisp, the kind that makes you think hot apple cider and cinnamon donuts wouldn't be too far away. The baskets of hanging flowers lining the streets were past their prime and would soon be replaced by mums. Time was moving too fast.

I headed into the shop and approached the counter. The morning rush had subsided, and Gary leaned against a back table, reading the paper. He looked up when the door buzzed. "Merry, what can I help you with?"

"Need sweet treats for the staff."

He moved to the bakery racks. "I have crumb cake I just pulled out of the oven, blueberry danish, and apricot danish."

"The crumb cake and blueberry danish, please."

He rang it up. "Did you hear you suspected the wrong person all along?"

"What?"

"All I was guilty of was private labeling cannoli. The police arrested April and Sandy's brother this morning. They caught him selling drugs."

"That's terrible."

"I saw April coming from the Police Station. She looked stricken like she hadn't slept in a month, and you know how put together she always looks."

"I'll have to drop by the shop later."

I walked back to my office in a daze. It was April and Sandy's brother all along. How sad for them.

* * *

Finally, at two, I had time for a break. I strode up the street to C'est Magnifique. The blinds were shut, and a closed sign hung from the door. I knocked, and April's pale face peered from the sidelight. I mouthed, "Let me in."

She grimaced, turned the lock, and opened the door. "I'm not feeling well, Merry. Now is not a good time."

I walked past her. "I'm sorry about your brother."

"You know?" She sagged onto a chair. "Of course, you do. Probably everyone in town knows by now."

Sandy came from the back, eyes red and swollen. "Who was—oh, hi, Merry."

"We moved towns because of him. He was selling drugs there too. I didn't know he was here, so I thought it was someone else when people began to die. It had to be. In the past, he sold pot, never the hard stuff..." April's voice trailed off.

"When we found out he was here, I told him we were going to the police." Sandy's jaw jutted. "But they caught him first. It would have been better if he had turned himself in."

"That was never going to happen. He's always only been concerned for himself. Never others." April stood. "Now we'll have to move again."

"Why?" I asked.

"Small town. Everyone will know." April moved a dress from one rack to another.

"You weren't the ones selling drugs."

"But he wouldn't have come if we weren't here." Sandy shuddered.

"This town is forgiving. I should know, after everything my husband did. It might take time but stick it out. You won't regret it."

There was a knock. April sighed. "Who now?"

She opened the door. Andy stood there with two bouquets. "I saw Merry come in, so I took a chance." He handed April flowers, then Sandy. "I'm so sorry about your brother, and I wanted you both to know Ed and I support you."

* * *

"It seems so anticlimactic somehow." I petted Drambuie. "A random bad guy who ends up in our town because his sisters moved here."

Courvoisier leaped onto Patty's lap. "Do you feel neglected?" She nuzzled the cat's neck. "I'm glad they found out who was selling the stuff. One less thing to worry about."

"Until someone else takes his place."

"Aren't you Miss Gloom and Doom."

"You're right. I'm happy they figured out who was involved, and we can get back to our real lives." I continued to stroke Drambuie's fur.

My phone dinged. I glanced down and groaned.

"What's up?"

"When I agreed to marry Rob, I didn't think I was adding so many additional family members. Wanda wants to give Rob a surprise for the wedding, and I have to meet her at Jim's house tonight."

Patty looked at her watch. "Tonight?"

I stood. "Hate to run off. I'll call you tomorrow."

"Can't wait to hear what the surprise is."

I put treats in a bowl, jiggled them, and opened the door for the cats. They danced around my feet, waiting for me to relinquish the bowl. When I put it down, they vied like gladiators in an arena. Drambuie won, and Courvoisier looked at me with sad eyes. I retrieved another bowl, shook a few treats into it, and placed it on the floor. Drambuie looked up with interest, but Courvoisier was already chowing down.

I left a note for Jenny, picked up my purse, and got in the car. The radio station had an episode on "Cooking Italian," so I spent the time learning how to make a sausage and fennel ragù with homemade pasta. After I parked at Jim's, I took a moment to make a note of the show on my phone to look at the recipe later.

Wanda pulled her car in behind me, and we walked to the door together. She said, "Merry, you know I'm a busy person. I didn't appreciate you insisting on meeting tonight."

The door opened, and Ann said, "Come in."

I stopped in the doorway. "What are you talking about? You texted for me to come here because of a wedding surprise for Rob."

"I certainly did no such thing. You texted me." Wanda brushed past into the house and gave Ann a long look. "Ann, you need to tone down the colors. That pink is too garish for your complexion."

I scrolled on my phone as I walked toward Wanda and handed it to her, saying, "See, here's the text."

She examined it. "I didn't send it."

"But it says it's from you."

Ann shut the door. "I've read about stuff like this. It's called SMS Spoofing, where someone can send you a text or email and have it appear to be from someone else."

"Why would anyone do that?" Wanda sat on the sofa.

"Usually, it's a type of scam, like when people are trying to obtain personal information from you by disguising themselves as a representative from your bank."

"That's awful." I shook my head. "But how would someone benefit by having Wanda and I come here."

"No idea." Ann shrugged. "But I'm glad you came. Dad and I are thinking about remodeling the basement to add square footage, and I'd love to get your perspectives."

Wanda glanced at her watch. "I guess I have a few minutes."

"Me too."

Ann unlocked the basement door, and we followed her down the rough-hewn stairs. "We're thinking about removing that door and carpeting the stairs. Then maybe if we remove the drywall on either side of the staircase, it wouldn't be so closed off."

The door behind us slammed shut, and I jumped. "How did that happen?"

"Old house, another reason to get rid of the door." Ann turned to the left, and there was a definite click from above as if someone had turned the key.

"Did someone lock us in?" I asked.

"Dad. He's always worried I'll forget to lock the door and didn't realize we were down here. No problem, we can always go out the cellar door, or I'll call him when we're done."

The hair on the back of my neck began to rise. I didn't like the idea Jim had locked the door, but before I could open my mouth, Wanda said, "Call him at once. I have no intention of being down here for any period of time, and I have no desire to be creeping around in the dark in your yard."

Boxes surrounded us, although the pathway between looked like it had been swept. The high windows facing the back were way too small to crawl through. "You'll have to put in egress windows," I told Ann as I studied the room. "This can't be the whole basement. The house is much bigger than this." I walked to a sturdy-looking steel door a few feet away. "What's in here?"

Ann said, "Open it and see."

I pulled on the door. It led to what looked like a state-of-the-art lab. White tile, Bunsen burners, flasks, pill presses, the works. "This is some lab."

Wanda grabbed my hand. "I don't like this."

"I don't either." I pulled her closer to me.

At the far end of the space was the door leading to the outside. Unfortunately, it too had a keyed lock, but the key was missing.

CHAPTER 23

Ann trailed her hand across the stainless-steel countertop. "Impressive, isn't it? It took a while to set up, but it's been worth it. My suppliers were overcharging, so I figured profits would skyrocket once I started to produce my own fentanyl. And they did."

Wanda flinched and turned her head from side to side. "Here? But it's dangerous. Am I breathing it?"

"It's been moved. And besides which, I know how to store things safely." Ann looked offended and pointed to two large vents. "State of the art circulation as well."

I backed away, pulling Wanda with me until we ran into another counter behind us. "Why are you showing us all this?" I gasped. "You were the one who sent the texts."

"Not as slow as you look." She sighed. "One of my runners was arrested this morning."

"April's brother worked for you?"

"I had to smile every time I walked into that shop. It was so delicious, no one knowing and yet, all connected."

Wanda looked quite pale. I asked, "Do you have a place for her to sit? And water?"

"No, no water. Nothing to drink," Wanda murmured.

"Here." Ann shoved a stool toward me. I pulled it the rest of the way, and Wanda perched on it.

"How did this start? You have a good career. You're a librarian," I sputtered.

"Do you know what librarians make? Not near what they're worth. Plus, I had a mountain of student loan debt. They're paid off now, and I have an extremely healthy off-shore bank account. Wanda, you should be happy to hear that, since you thought I was wasting my talents." She preened. "Plus, being a librarian is a perfect cover. It's a great way for me to assess new clientele."

Wanda said, "Those parents trust you with their kids."

"I'm not the one who approaches them. I have runners for that. But I can see who's having difficulty fitting in. The ones who might need help dealing with day-to-day life."

"Why are you telling us all this?" I asked, not wanting to know the answer.

"I saw you checking out the lock to the basement the other day, and don't think I didn't notice your sly questions—who I dated, why I had a chemistry book—it was only a matter of time before you figured out what was going on." She sat. "We'll need to leave now. Abandon my lab. The authorities thought Kevin was just a drug overdose—you made them focus on him. You, and your questions."

"You did know Kevin," I exclaimed.

"Of course. I loved Kevin. We dated when I was in high school until he realized who his 'true love' was." She air quoted. "When he called me that night for a little pick-me-up, I couldn't believe it. It was like a slap in the face; he's at Pre-Cana with her when he should have been there with me. It was too tempting. I mixed a little fentanyl with the methamphetamine, and goodbye, Kevin." Ann shined the countertop with a white cloth.

Wanda moaned, "Amy, was Amy involved?"

"Of course not. All the brains came to this twin." She smirked. "Although I dressed as her when I was meeting with runners. Can't be too careful."

Wanda's hand felt like ice. I patted it and continued, "What about Matt? And Jane."

"Matt got my name from someone and started sniffing around at the library. My place of work! I needed to get rid of him fast. I felt bad about that because he may have been a nice guy. I enjoyed killing Jane though. What a fool. She met me in the woods where we used to smoke pot in high school. She was so sure I had nothing to do with Kevin's death."

My mouth dropped. "Those are people you killed."

"I know. And you and Wanda are next."

"Why Wanda?"

"Pick, pick, pick, ever since she married Uncle Mac. The world's going to be far better without her in it."

Wanda slumped on the stool. I bent over her. "Wanda, Wanda, are you okay?" I turned to look at Ann. "There's something wrong. We need to call an ambulance."

Ann laughed. "Saves me the trouble. Actually, it isn't all that much trouble because, you see, this lab is going to explode without a trace." She kicked a box with wires running from it. "Just need to set up the detonators, and you won't need to worry about Wanda anymore."

"Jim, Jim!" I yelled.

Boom, boom, boom. It felt like a wrecking ball was hitting the house.

Ann jumped. "What the heck?"

Boom, boom, boom. Boom boom boom. BOOM. The metal cellar door imploded. "Drug Enforcement Agents, don't move, don't move."

The next moment, a sea of people wearing navy-colored jackets emblazoned with yellow DEA letters swarmed the room, yelling for us to get on the floor. It looked like Ann was going to argue, but she seemed to reconsider and got down on the ground to be handcuffed. Wanda was in no shape to comply, and, since I was keeping her from falling off the stool, I couldn't move. Bile rose in my throat as agents approached us with guns drawn. Luckily one saw that Wanda was in bad shape and helped me lower her to the floor as another called for medical assistance. Then I was cuffed, and an agent read me my rights.

Wanda's stretcher was carried out first. She looked as pale as new-fallen snow, and I pleaded with the agent holding my arm, "I need to go with her. She's my fiancé's mother."

His face was impassive as he shook his head. "Not happening."

CHAPTER 24

As Ann and I were ushered through the cellar door and around the house to the front, an ambulance peeled out of the driveway, sirens blaring. I closed my eyes and prayed for Wanda's safe recovery. When I opened them, DeShawn stood in front of me. "Why can't you leave things to the proper authorities?"

"What are you talking about?"

"I told you we were getting close. We busted one of her—" he gave Ann a disgusted look, "vermin this morning, which gave us the confirmation we'd been looking for—that this was the place. After we mobilized, we raided the house and found you. You could have died." He pointed toward me and told one of the agents, "You can take the cuffs off this one."

She removed them, and as I rubbed my wrists, I couldn't stop shaking. DeShawn opened his car door and gestured for me to sit in the passenger seat. I did, and he put a mylar blanket over my shoulders as someone pressed hot coffee into my hands. As my shivering subsided, I stared into his dark brown eyes. "I thought you said the kingpin was a guy."

"He was." DeShawn pointed toward Jim as he and Ann were led to waiting police cars. "He was the money guy with the contacts. Ann was his 'pharmacist' and recruiter. They were in it together. At first, we thought it was the other one, Amy, from the surveillance photos. But then we realized it couldn't have been her because she was at school."

"All those trips south." I shook my head, then grabbed DeShawn's hand. "You have to know. It wasn't an accident. Those kids were killed. It was murder. Ann murdered them."

He shook his head. "And she tried to murder you earlier. You were right. The antacids were laced with fentanyl."

CHAPTER 25

Rob sat in a chair by his mother's bed at the hospital. The stress of the night before had brought on a stroke. Luckily, she had treatment in time, and the doctors felt her long-term prognosis was good. Her right hand touched the slackened left side of her face. "I must look awful."

"Temporary, mother. It will pass."

"Elizabeth?"

"On her way."

"Merry, be a dear, and get me a mirror."

I gave Rob a nervous glance. He nodded, so I handed Wanda my compact. She gasped. "Worse than I thought."

"Wanda, the doctors say with therapy and care, you should be looking good as new by the wedding. No stress, so let's put away the mirror." I took it from her. "You have to let Mac in. He's been waiting for hours."

She paled. "I can't let him see me like this."

"He loves you. He won't care."

"Get me my lipstick and try to do something with my hair."

I handed her the lipstick and brushed her hair, so at least the front looked somewhat normal.

She gestured for Rob to open the door and squared her shoulders. "No time like the present to be rejected."

Mac rushed in. "Oh, my darling, I'm so sorry." He embraced her. "My brother and my niece. How can I ever apologize? No wonder you didn't want to see me. I promise I'll make it up to you."

"Don't be silly. I didn't want to see you because of this." She circled her face with her hand.

"Beautiful as the day you married me. I've been on the phone with a group in Switzerland that does amazing things with stroke therapy. They'll have you looking good as new in no time. I have a jet on standby, and we'll leave as soon as they clear you." He hugged her.

Wanda's smile, though droopy on one side, was bright. She said, "I'll agree, with one condition."

"What's that?"

"We take Amy with us. We can't leave her to the press vultures. She didn't have anything to do with what Jim and Ann were doing."

"Mother, your son is a member of the press. And your late husband," Rob protested.

She shooed him with her hand. "You know what I mean."

"C'mon, Merry, let's leave these two lovebirds alone. Mother, I'll be back in a few hours when Elizabeth gets here." He kissed her on the cheek.

I turned toward the door.

"No kiss, Merry?" Wanda waved me toward her.

I stopped, leaned over the bed, and kissed her cheek.

She grabbed my hand. "Thank you. I wouldn't have made it through this without you."

CHAPTER 26

I put my feet on the footrest. "On your way back, would you bring me a blanket? Getting a little chilly out here." I smiled. "It's good to be able to relax on a Saturday night and not worry about going anywhere except for church tomorrow."

"You said it." Rob walked back into the house, retrieved the bottle of wine and an afghan. He draped it over me. "Good?"

"Perfect."

He topped off our wine glasses, carefully set the bottle on the grass, and kissed the top of my head. "No more investigating. I want us to live to be a ripe old age."

I shivered. "Not going to get an argument from me."

"Mother, Mac, and Amy arrived in Switzerland. Mother loves the place, says it's very spa-like."

"Jenny said Amy texted her, apparently Wanda's become very laid back."

"Doesn't sound like my mother." Rob sipped wine.

"People can change."

Jenny came out of the house and sat on the back steps. "I just realized something."

"What's that?" I asked.

"Today's exactly two months till your wedding."

Rob lifted his glass. "I'll toast to that."

ABOUT THE AUTHOR

Eileen Curley Hammond is an author who retired from a successful marketing career in the insurance industry. She and her husband share the house with two cats that are having a hard time training them.

For those of you who have been keeping up on this page, you know that Eileen and her husband restocked the fish pond last year with koi, shubunkins, and minnows. They are still happily swimming in peace with screens and motion sensors guarding their kingdom.

It's been such a blessing to be able to physically see people again. I hope that the world and all of you continue to recover from this terrible pandemic.

www.ingramcontent.com/pod-product-compliance
Lightning Source LLC
Chambersburg PA
CBHW022109240626
47153CB00007B/2296

* 9 7 8 1 9 5 6 3 5 6 0 1 4 *